Cooper B.

& THE SCAVENGER HUNT

BY

MICHAEL SHANE LEIGHTON

ILLUSTRATIONS BY LUANA *de* SOUZA SINCLAIR

vii
PUBLISHING

www.michaelshaneleighton.com
Follow us on Twitter @viipublishing
Follow us on Instagram @Cooper.B.Book.Series
Like us on Facebook: @CooperBBookSeries

First Edition 2020
Paperback ISBN 13: 978-1-7354559-0-7
Hardback ISBN 13: 978-1-7354559-1-4

Vii Publishing
Box 144
Morrison, IL 61270
www.viipublishing.com

Printed in the United States of America

To my loving wife and amazing children
~ may your dreams take you beyond your
wildest imaginations.

Contents

Cooper B.

& THE SCAVENGER HUNT

PROLOGUE

Nearly ten years ago, a young child, not more than eighteen months old, was found alone on the edge of a desolate and gravel roadway just outside a sleepy town known as Cooper, Maine. On that same day, this tiny, chestnut hair boy with eyes like a cloudless sky would be handed over to a peculiar looking Child Protective Services caseworker, Ms. Pedigree. She was a tall, red-headed woman, dressed from another era long ago, with glasses, shaped like cat eyes, perched on the tip of her long narrow beak. Some had believed their first encounter seemed familiar.

For years to come, newspapers would run articles about that mysterious boy who had been abandoned and forgotten by his parents. Journalists created rumors that thrived with grand tales of his origins. But the print would soon fade as did the interest in his story.

Moved from one orphanage to another, the young child was always in search of his place in this world. His true identity. But the truth would never be known—not yet anyway. His life forever changed before it had even begun. A life wrapped in secrecy. A life thus far—full of sadness.

Given a name by those who discovered him in that small town of *Cooper, Maine*. A name that contained a single letter for his last, to compliment his first, simply because he was indeed a *boy*. A name that would follow him his entire life. That boy would become be known as, *Cooper B.*

I should know—this is my story.

CHAPTER ONE

ST. MARY'S ACADEMY FOR EXCEPTIONAL YOUTH

When foster families tired of me and were ready to move on, Ms. Pedigree would always return. Placing me back into the system that I had come to know quite well. I never minded seeing her and her never changing attire of a yellow dress with a matching belt and shoes, and a glittering pewter brooch decorated with three entwined branches pinned to her chest. Ms. Pedigree was always kind to me. Sharing a sincere smile that I believed she saved just for me.

Gazing upon me through her outdated glasses, she outstretched her white gloved hand and gently took hold of mine. It was time again to follow her to my next home.

"No matter my dear boy, for this time, I do believe I have the perfect place for you," she said with a loving grin. "I trust it will be splendid—splendid indeed."

Soon afterward, we arrived at my twelfth and final orphanage, known as St. Mary's Academy for Exceptional Youth. The name sounded spectacular, even inviting, but the school was most certainly far from it. Maybe long ago, when it was built for children who were orphaned during the Civil War, it had its moment of grandeur, but it had lost its intended charm throughout the years.

Splendid, it was not.

What was once a place sprawling with well-mannered children who had lost their parents to the tragedies of war, was now a place for relocated and troubled youth. Deep inside the peeling plastered walls that were fitted with electrical fixtures that would fail any inspection, should the state have ever actually come to inspect, were ill-mannered, mean spirited, nasty children of all ages.

The white and gray decaying massive structure was an old four corner farmhouse, surrounded by failing and weathered wooden planks. The decrepit front porch dared anyone to try their luck and step foot onto the wooden boards. Boards that let out a gawdawful scream when under the weight of any size—signaling those unfortunate guests they were moments away from collapsing into a bottomless pit within the earth.

The orphanage had two large bedrooms on the second floor. One for boys and another for girls. Most of the time, I could be found lying on my rusty cast iron bed bunk, staring up at the brown water stains on the ceiling tiles above.

It was unlike my bedroom in the home before, where the Martins had placed glow-in-the-dark stars on my popcorn riddled ceiling. When the lights were out, I would be immersed in a galaxy of tiny bright dots, allowing my mind to wander to faraway lands, dreaming of someplace better.

That felt like a lifetime ago. Now, more often than not, I sat patiently waiting to use the bathroom we all shared. Whoever said girls were cleaner than boys, never met this group of six young ladies.

The attic above our rooms had been transformed into a bedroom for Sister Elsa, who transferred in just two days after my arrival, replacing Sister Jude, who apparently had suffered some sort of mental breakdown. Who could blame her? If you had asked me, I would say this was the first time Sister Elsa had ever met such a group of misfit boys and girls. In fact, she didn't seem prepared at all to tolerate their behavior. And tolerate them, she did not. Within the first few days, she had earned their respect, and no one misbehaved—at least not in front of her.

In the early morning hours, the sun would beam through my bedroom window, waking me from my sleep. It never failed—by the time I wiped the sleep from eyes, the room was already empty. I was always the last up and the last downstairs for breakfast. While enduring the line of adolescent cranks, I often imagined a mother's caring voice calling to me for breakfast. The food would be hot, plentiful, and have an abundant aroma of love. However, in an orphanage such as this, you had one chance to get breakfast. If you were late, you waited for the noon hour to try again.

Even if I managed to beat the rush and line up in time to get a cold bowl of some shredded fiber soaked in lukewarm milk, Theodore Barron would take it all away. He wouldn't stand for me eating before him or his degenerate disciples—always shoving me to the back of the line.

Theodore must have watched one too many films starring the rebel James Dean. He even wore a leather jacket that he had more than likely stolen from a second hand store. I heard a rumor that the greasy haired boy told Sister Jude he had collected cans and used the money he earned to buy the jacket. Only a woman suffering from a mental breakdown would believe such a tale. A reform school would have been more fitting for the likes of this adolescent boy.

Theodore fancied himself as the head of the forgotten children, considering he was the oldest. In fact, he was just a few months away from being sent to the Transitional House for Young Adults at the stroke of midnight—on his eighteenth birthday. If I knew how to bet, I would wager he would have ended up in prison shortly afterward.

The younger orphans who didn't know any better thought Theodore was a mentor of sorts, but not a chance. Theodore was mean to the core, and no one should look up to him.

"Get in the back of the line, you motherless punk," Theodore growled at me, shoving my left shoulder backwards. "You eat last."

Theodore was the epitome of a bully. Every chance he got, he would remind me I was orphaned, as though he was sent to St. Mary's Academy for Exceptional Youth by choice. Oftentimes it would go unnoticed, but every once in a while, when Theodore would step in to ruin my morning, a voice cried out.

"That is enough, Mr. Barron," Sister Elsa would bark out. "You, young man, have not only earned your place in the back of the line, but dish duty as well. I expect they will be spotless."

Sister Elsa would scorn him and simply walk out of the dining room. My pleasure was short lived. The look on Theodore's face said it all. *You'll pay for that.* It was destined to be the bleakest period of my entire youth. It felt as though I was the one trapped in the prison Theodore belonged in, but all of that would soon change.

One early afternoon, during a scorching summer day, the doorbell rang. It was a very distinctive, low, forbidding chime that sounded the arrival of a guest. The old wooden front door swung open, and standing over the threshold was Ms. Pedigree, holding a small suitcase decorated in pink flowers. I couldn't believe my eyes. I felt a rush of excitement spread from my head to my toes. I was finally leaving this dreadful home of displaced energy. I thought to myself, *see you later, Theodore Barron, you monster*, but before I could race up the stairs to pack my things, Ms. Pedigree stepped aside. She wasn't there for me.

Her eyes shifted back and forth nervously, at the group of kids that had quickly assembled into the foyer to observe the new arrival. Ms. Pedigree wasn't what you would call a kid-friendly caseworker, and she never seemed to like any of them, except for me, of course. She made an odd twitching gesture if any young boy or girl got too close to her personal space.

"Now, now, children. Give this poor woman and her guest some room," Sister Elsa told all of us in a stern voice, rescuing Ms. Pedigree. "Who do we have here?" she asked politely.

Her name was Aria Santiago. She was my height and seemingly my age, with long dark curly hair, piercing emerald green eyes, and lightly bronzed skin. But I didn't see color or gender. Through the eyes of an eleven-year-old boy, I only saw another orphan. Another child discarded by those who should have loved her. Protected her from the apparently cruel world we shared. She was dressed in a pair of ragged jeans and an unbuttoned red and black, long sleeved flannel that revealed an old rock concert T-shirt. This girl was too warmly dressed for these blistering summer temperatures.

More interestingly, Aria didn't appear to be like the other newcomers that had come before her. She didn't seem afraid. Her head didn't hang heavy, and her eyes weren't focused on the wooden planked floor below her feet. No, not her. Aria looked angry, scowling at each of the nosey onlookers, ready for a fight. I immediately knew this wasn't her first home. I am positive I would have been deathly afraid of this new girl had it not been for a little voice in the back of my head telling me she would soon become my best friend and an ally in this prison of mine.

"Please make the acquaintance of Aria Santiago, all the way from Silver Springs, Colorado," Ms. Pedigree told the group, in a similar fashion as if she were introducing her at a grand ball. No one cared. In fact, everyone turned and walked out of the room—mumbling vulgarities under their breath. Not me. I stuck around.

Ms. Pedigree didn't seem bothered by the disrespectful greeting the other children had shown. She turned her attention toward me and smiled. "And how is Mr. Cooper B.?" she asked.

"He is doing well, now that he has proper supervision," answered Sister Elsa.

Ms. Pedigree paid her no mind and placed her hand on my shoulder. "So good to see you, young man. I think you will get along marvelously with this one," said Ms. Pedigree, motioning toward Aria.

"May I have a moment with you, Ms. Pedigree?" asked Sister Elsa in a shallow voice.

"Why, of course, madam, I'm always available to take a moment with the help," snickered Ms. Pedigree, continuing to gaze upon me with a warm smile.

Sister Elsa and Ms. Pedigree walked off, down a hallway of peeling paint and out of our sight. I slowly made my way to Aria and extended my hand in friendship. Instead of reaching out and accepting my olive branch, she stared at it, as though I held a poisonous snake—that was preparing to strike.

"Cooper B.," I said. "Pleasure to make your acquaintance."

Aria looked away from my hand—refusing to accept my courteous gesture.

"Why?" she asked, with a snarky tone.

"Why what?" I responded, with a nervous smile.

"You don't know me. So why would it be a *pleasure* to meet me?"

I began fidgeting with my shirt collar and asked her, "Well, why not?"

There was an uncomfortable silence for a moment, and I slowly began to lower my hand. This girl was not ready to be my friend, let alone my best friend, and I would have to accept that for what it was.

Suddenly, Aria's shoulders relaxed, and if I didn't know any better, I would say she even smiled. Not a gleaming smile, more of a twitch in the corner of her mouth kind of smile, but it was good enough for me.

She reached out and shook my hand. "Aria, nice to meet you, I guess," she said and let go of my hand just as quickly as she had taken it.

We stared at each other for what felt like an eternity. I had so much to say, so many questions to ask. However, I realized it was easier to think of the conversations I would have with someone one day then it was to actually have that conversation.

"What's that?" asked Aria, pointing to the thin silver chain draped around my neck with a medallion dangling from it.

Engraved in the center of the small, button-like pendant that gently came to rest on my chest was a curious symbol. Reminding me of a water circling inside a drain. It was quite unique.

I reached up and held it in my hand, almost forgetting that I had it. "Oh, this is something I got… well… I don't remember where I got it actually," I said, fumbling over my own words. The answer suddenly came back to me. "That's right! Ms. Pedigree said she gave it to me when we first met. I always felt it would bring me luck or something. Stupid I guess, considering."

Aria just stared at me blankly. She had to think I was a mindless idiot. "It's nice," she said, looking away and giving the foyer a once over.

Thankfully, the enthralling conversation between the two of us was interrupted when a voice called out from the hallway.

"Oh, just splendid, splendid indeed. You two little specimens have made nice," Ms. Pedigree said excitedly—clasping her hands together. "I was so hoping you would get along marvelously. Well, got to skedaddle, places to go and people to find you know," she said, running her hand across my cheek. It almost felt like a mother's touch. "I will be back soon, Cooper B.," she said softly.

With that, Ms. Pedigree passed over the threshold she entered through and back outside.

Sister Elsa firmly clapped her hands together, as though she was slapping two dingy chalk erasers against one another.

"Alright you two—run along and play. I will take your things upstairs and you can unpack before bed," Sister Elsa told Aria.

I didn't need to hear another word. "Come on, follow me," I told Aria excitedly, and with that, we rushed off. We ran outside through the tall browning grass and toward the woods.

I had found a spot overlooking an old flooded rock quarry. It was just past the wooded area that surrounded the orphanage and had been forgotten by those who had created it. Sitting atop a log that had fallen during a wicked thunderstorm, overlooking the clear arctic blue water, we visited with one another. We mostly talked about Sister Elsa and Ms. Pedigree. We both found them to be utmost peculiar. At times, we even laughed. I don't remember the last time I heard myself laugh like that.

I didn't want to sour the moment, but I had become interested in how she ended up at St. Mary's Academy for Exceptional Youth. "Where were you before you came here?" I asked her.

"My foster parents' home in Silver Springs, Colorado."

"How long were you there for?" I asked, wondering if every

child moved from one home to the next like I had over the last ten years.

"I moved in with them a year or so ago, after my mom died," she said, lowering her head. It was obvious this was still a painful subject, but I was eleven years old and knew no better.

"How did she die?"

"I'm not sure. They really never talked to me about it."

I felt it troubled Aria to even think about the death of her mother, let alone discuss it, so I quickly changed the subject. "Well, they found me alongside a highway when I was a baby— buck naked."

This bit of personal information had made Aria smile. Then, she burst out laughing. I am not sure I expected her to laugh so hysterically, at least not for as long as she did. Either way, she was wearing an infectious smile.

"So how come you left your foster home? Did you get in trouble?" I asked—still trying to learn more about this new girl.

"Honestly, no reason at all. One day I was sitting on the couch watching a movie, and the next thing I knew, I was being taken away by that crazy redhead Ms. Pedigree. Then bam, I was here," said Aria with a look of confusion.

"Did you drive here or fly?" I asked curiously. After all, it would be quite the drive from Colorado to St. Mary's.

"That's the kicker, Coop," Aria said, apparently giving me a nickname. I never had a nickname and honestly, I liked it. "I don't remember how I got here. We got in her car. Then we were here. I must've been exhausted and slept the entire way."

Before I could think about what she had just said, the sound of Sister Elsa's voice reverberated through the woods and over the tranquil body of water.

"Lunch!"

"We gotta go… you don't want to be late for the lunch line at this place," I said, forgetting about all the questions I had. I grabbed her hand and pulled her from the log. The two of us ran for our lives, laughing all the way through the woods, back to the house.

As the summer days passed, Aria and I became inseparable. To the displeasure of Sister Elsa, we would sometimes skip breakfast so we could run outside and play first thing in the morning. Our favorite game to play was hide-and-go-seek. Sometimes, I even forgot about those loathsome few that roamed the halls of the orphanage. It was the best time of my short life.

But Sister Elsa did seem pleased however, with our blossoming friendship. She often assigned us projects to do together. Busy work mostly. It didn't matter. Our minds were occupied and at times forgot we were forgotten.

One early evening, Aria and I sat in the stairwell discussing the upcoming school year. The two of us were hoping beyond all hope that we would share the same classroom. The summer months were coming to an end when fate had one more surprise in store for me.

Everyone hurried from their respective places throughout the house, when the gloomy doorbell let out a warning of a new guest. Everyone but me. Immediately, my heart sank into the pit of my stomach. My head filled with thoughts of Ms. Pedigree returning as she had promised. Returning to swoop me away from St. Mary's Academy for Exceptional Youth, and place me in a new home. A longing I had once begged for, but not anymore. I had finally found happiness. Happiness because of one person.

I no longer wished to leave. Instead, I would rather stay—even if it meant putting up with Theodore and his band of misfits. For the first time in all of my childhood, I found someone, and Ms. Pedigree wanted to take me away. Far away from the companion I had come to call a friend—away from Aria.

CHAPTER TWO

THE RETURN OF MS. PEDIGREE

Once again, standing in the doorway was Ms. Pedigree wearing her outdated wardrobe and thick lensed glasses. I sucked in a deep breath of relief through my tiny nostrils. She wasn't alone—and she wasn't there to remove me from a place I no longer wanted to leave. This time she was accompanied by a young, red headed, freckled face boy. A boy who wore second hand clothes, just like I did.

He was dressed in the finest tan, corduroy pants with an untucked black T-shirt that was covered up by a short sleeved, green, and yellow flannel shirt. He adjusted his outfit, trying not to be noticed. Unlike Aria, who had a sense of strength about her when she arrived just a few weeks earlier, he appeared depressed and unsure of his new surroundings.

"Greetings my young friends," shouted Ms. Pedigree in Aria's and my direction. There was so much enthusiasm in her voice. "May I introduce you to this fine young gentleman, Miles O'Mallory?"

Ms. Pedigree stepped aside, as if to show off her prized ruby colored calf to a group of judges.

"O'Malley," said the red headed boy with freckles.

"Excuse me, my dear?" asked Ms. Pedigree, shaking her head as though she was shocked by the calf speaking.

"My name is O'Malley, not *O'Mallory*."

"Oh, my goodness," gasped Ms. Pedigree. "Please do accept my humble apologies…" She turned her attention from the now blushing Miles, back to the onlookers with her arms outstretched. "May I introduce you to Mr. *O'Malley*," she said—correcting herself.

Sister Elsa stepped in and stood behind the timid boy. "Welcome Miles, please find your way inside," she said, hurrying him away from Ms. Pedigree.

"Oh splendid," Ms. Pedigree began. "Maybe Cooper B. and his new friend Aria would show Mr. *O'Malley* around the property?" she continued with a wink, emphasizing his name as not to make the same mistake twice.

"Yes ma'am," I responded and stepped forward to introduce myself. But Aria stood motionless, leaving me alone. I reached back and took her by the arm—pulling her beside me. Aria shuffled her feet and just stared at Miles—coldly.

"Names Cooper B., nice to make your acquaintance," I said with a cheerful expression.

Aria remained silent.

"Hello," Miles said quickly, never taking his eyes off the floor.

"This is Aria. Please forgive her—she's a mute."

"Am not you idiot!" Aria shouted while punching me.

I stood there a bit shocked, rubbing the soreness out of my arm. She hit harder than I would have imagined she could.

"Well, well, it can speak after all," I said slowly, minding my words this time.

This seemed to make Miles happy because he was no longer studying the floor under his feet and looking as though he was about to hurl his morning breakfast. Instead, he was watching the two of us as though he expected we would begin wrestling one another. It didn't matter. Miles was smiling. It was all I needed to see. It was all I wanted to see.

"A word please, Ms. Pedigree," said Sister Elsa in a firm voice.

"Of course, my dear, but first *Mr. Barron*," Ms. Pedigree began to say in a somewhat unpleasant tone, "would you be so kind as to get the bags for Mr. O'Malley and take them up to his room?"

Theodore stared in agony at Ms. Pedigree.

"Why should I—"

"—Do as you are asked, Theodore… now," said Sister Elsa, interrupting his ill-mannered response.

Theodore lifted up the small suitcase from the doorway— and as they had when Aria arrived, Sister Elsa and Ms. Pedigree walked off together down the long hall to speak privately. The second the two were out of sight, Theodore dropped the bags at the newcomer's feet.

"Get them yourself Orphan, if you know what's good for ya," Theodore huffed. He turned away and headed back to the couch to join his friends—sharing in the misery they brought one another.

I grabbed Miles' suitcase for him and headed for the stairs. The excitement must have been obvious. I had a roommate I could finally tolerate, and I wanted to get him to his new living quarters as quickly as possible.

"Follow me," I told Miles, nearly tripping over the worn and musty carpet that lined the stairs. There was a little pep in the step of Miles as he trailed behind me up the stairs.

Inside our bedroom, I took his suitcase to the empty, metal framed bed that was next to mine. With this new addition, my bed would no longer appear quarantined from the rest of the cast iron bunks that were forced against the walls.

"You can sleep in this one, next to me," I told him—pointing to the thin rolled up mattress tucked against the railing of the headboard.

Aria followed a short moment later. She either hated Miles, or she was a bit jealous at the fact I had a new friend to share my space with. Since she despised her roommates as much as I did mine, I would guess it was the latter.

"I'll get him some clean linens from the hallway," said Aria in a soft voice. I do believe that was the exact moment she decided to accept the new member of our orphaned gang.

Moments later, we were all together in my room once again. Aria neatly made his bed as I unpacked his suitcase. I removed his neatly folded jeans and shirts, tossing them down to the foot of his bed onto the cold, dank floor. Afterall, the older kids didn't really allow us to use the only dresser in the room. I gently scooted his belongings under his bed with the tip of my shoe, trying not to get them soiled.

"There ya go, all unpacked now," I told Miles energetically.

Miles wasn't quite as enthusiastic as I was. He just stared at the dark void under his bed that now concealed his wardrobe.

"Thanks."

To my delight, Miles snapped out of his dreary mood and plopped himself onto his newly made bed. Before I could take a seat on my own bed, Aria sat down and threw her legs up onto my mattress, making herself at home. I became slightly annoyed, as the only option left for me was a small space at the foot of Miles' bed.

"So, tell us something about yourself, Miles," I asked, trying to make myself comfortable.

"What would you like to know?"

"Where's your parents?" Aria asked bluntly, staring up at the stained ceiling tiles above. By the scowl on her face, I had to wonder if the tiles above her bed were in better condition than mine.

Miles picked at a piece of lint stuck on his pants. "Not sure… not sure if they're dead or just didn't have time for a kid," he said. It was plain to see that he had never known the feeling of a parent's touch. *Something the two of us had in common.*

Aria turned her attention away from the growing dark spots high above my bed and looked over at the red headed boy with sadness. "I'm sorry," she told Miles.

Miles perked up a bit. It appeared as though he wasn't quite ready to talk about his life and wanted to avoid a pity party—

thrown by his two new friends.

"No worries, I've gotten past it," said Miles with a forced grin.

Funny thing about orphaned kids, we understood life and the pain it could bring more so than the adults we were surrounded by. We were experts in hiding our feelings when we wanted to.

"Where were you before you came here?" I asked, changing the subject.

"I was in Jupiter, Florida, living with the Campbells and their twins," Miles told us. "Not a bad place to live if you ask me. Nice house, big yard with a swing set... oh, and the twins... Samantha and Isabell, they were really nice, but they sure were loud when they cried," continued Miles—letting out a nervous laugh.

"So why did you leave then?" Aria asked, turning her head back toward the filthy scenery above. "It sounds perfect."

"Dunno," said Miles a bit confused. "Everything seemed good, until that wacky Ms. Pedigree showed up. She told Mr. and Mrs. Campbell I had to move somewhere else. So, I was sent to my room to pack my things, and the next thing I remember—I was here." Miles paused and looked lost in the thoughts that were trapped in his mind. "I really thought they liked me. At least more than the other foster parents did, but they didn't say anything when she came. Didn't even ask why I had to go."

Finally, another kid who had been to different foster homes like me. A child who never knew if they were going to stay at a home long enough to unpack their suitcase, or if they were just staying for a night before heading to the next. Granted, I never actually went from one place to the next that quickly—but in our situation, it often felt that way.

"How many homes did you live in before the Campbells?" I asked, a little too eagerly.

"That was the sixth."

His eyes were sorrowful. I quickly realized my enthusiasm was showing during a time that it wasn't supposed to. I wish I could have taken it back. Taking back the way I asked him. It was like I hadn't spoken to another orphan before him—especially one my own age. Someone to share my pain with. Like I could with Aria and now Miles. I could feel the warmth of my blood filling my cheeks.

Luckily for me, my embarrassment was interrupted as Aria sat up in my bed—which she had rudely taken over. "Am I the only one that thinks Ms. Pedigree is from another planet?" she asked unexpectedly. Miles and I laughed at her remarks that came out of nowhere. "I'm serious! Why would she be in Colorado, or Jupiter, Florida for that matter?"

"Maybe it's her job to place kids into foster homes," I said to Aria.

"Different states? When have you heard of a social worker for Child Protective Services going from one state to another?" she demanded to know—but it was a rhetorical question. "You haven't, so don't say you have. There's a jurisdiction thing or something like that. And I happen to know for a fact that each state has their own laws and you can't just go wherever you want to—snatching up kids and delivering them here to this place. It's kidnapping!"

Miles and I stared blankly at one another. Neither of us were experts in this field, and I knew better than to question her. Miles on the other hand, hadn't quite learned this important fact about Aria.

"Never worked for them, so I really wouldn't know," Miles told Aria. "Have you?"

"What difference does that make, Red?" asked Aria—officially dubbing him with his very own nickname. This meant she was starting to like Miles.

"We haven't been kidnapped, Aria."

"Whatever, Coop! It doesn't make any sense, and you two are completely and undeniably two of the biggest buffoons I have ever met if you can't see that for yourselves," said Aria bitterly, as she let out a heavy sigh in defeat at the fact we just couldn't see her point. "Trust me on this one—that's all I have to say about that."

But she wasn't quite done yet.

"And how about her choice in fashion?" She looks like some sort of advertisement for housewives of the fifties—and those shoes—who would wear shoes like that? They're just disturbing."

"I think she looks good, in a motherly sort of way," I said hesitantly. I had to admit, at this point, she had a good case against Ms. Pedigree. After all, she was a bit out of place and was dressed from a different time.

Miles began rubbing his chin, studying Aria like a chess board. "Maybe she's right," he added. Aria had either started to make sense to the red headed orphan, or he was trying to get on her good side by agreeing with her.

"Don't encourage her," I said—already being on her good side.

We sat quietly together for the next several minutes. It was peaceful. I didn't care if Ms. Pedigree was an alien, which, of course, was impossible. I felt wonderful, and I couldn't put together a single negative thought in my mind. I was happy now—more so than I had ever been in my short existence.

The silence was broken by a voice that echoed from downstairs.

"Oh, children?" shouted Ms. Pedigree.

We all leapt down from the cold steel beds—heading for the doorway. It must've sounded like a herd of cattle moving across the solid wood floors as we raced out through the doorway of our room. We stopped at the top of the stairs, looking down at Ms. Pedigree through the battered spindles that lined the upper floor.

"Ahh, there you fine children are—looking so content as can be. I regrettably must inform you that I shall be departing now," Ms. Pedigree told the three of us—slightly frowning and smiling at the same time. "I trust you all will get along splendidly."

"Yes ma'am," I responded, looking over to my two new friends. "I do believe we will."

Aria leaned over to her side, pressing up against my shoulder. "I'm warning you two… under that pale skin is a green scaled alien, waiting to put us in the oven," said Aria under her breath—as her eyes narrowed, never taking them off of Ms. Pedigree.

"You mark my words, Coop—"

"—Quit it, Aria," I whispered out of the corner of my mouth—compelling myself not to break out into laughter.

The three of us stood tall at the top of the staircase and waved goodbye to Ms. Pedigree. Watching together, as the woman dressed from another time period, or planet according to Aria, made her way to the large wooden entry door. Then, as she slipped into the darkness outside, I felt a sense of calm.

This time was different than Ms. Pedigree's last visits—for this time, she did not warn me of her return.

CHAPTER THREE

SUMMERS END

The next two weeks were spent playing and working side by side with Aria and Miles. When we weren't playing, we fixed up the deteriorating orphanage and did a little yard work. Sister Elsa put us in charge of painting the front porch too. In our minds, it looked like the Taj Mahal when we were done. In reality, it was splotchy, and we had splattered paint over just about everything that was nearby. But the best part of those days was when we completed our chores. Before the sun set behind the orphanage, Aria, Miles, and I would play loads of games together.

Not board games, or video games—but things we could do together like hide and go seek, red light green light, and freeze tag. My favorite, however, was when the three of us would just let our imaginations run free and head out on adventures in search of a grand treasure. Since none of us knew what true riches would actually look like, we just searched and searched, dodging dragons and other unworldly creatures our minds could create. Never finding what it was we were looking for. I will have to humbly admit, my creatures were far better than what Aria and Miles dreamt up. When it came to magical beasts, I could describe their colors, their smells, if they were good or bad, and whether they were furry, or full of scales. It was as if I had met them before.

The older kids, mostly Theodore and his gang, mocked and made fun of us every chance they had. Those hoodlums never tired of the same old insults. What stood out the most, and often sent chills down my spine, was the look Theodore gave me. I really thought he wanted me dead and was just waiting for the perfect moment to get me alone to fulfill that yearning. It didn't matter. We were free and were writing our own story.

Sadly, it wasn't always fun and games. As hard as we tried, we weren't always together to watch one another's back. Any chance he had; Theodore sought out his victims. If we were unfortunate enough to be caught alone—he'd remind us that he was the oldest and the meanest. Theodore was such a coward. I often felt as though I got the brunt of his tormenting, as was the day Sister Elsa sent me to the basement, to retrieve a scraper to remove flaking paint.

Our basement felt more like a cellar straight from a scene out of a horror film. I really hadn't seen my share of scary movies throughout my life. Maybe one or two horrifying films, back when I lived with the Delbridge's.

Making my way through the basement, I left behind a trail of footprints in the dirt floor. Quickly walking past the web infested storage shelves that kept jarred goods from the turn of the century. Wanting to get in and out of that terrifying chamber of fright, as soon as possible.

I swiftly made my way to the toolbox that was perched against the cinder block wall at the far end of the room. Without haste, I searched the dust covered trunk, gently pushing aside cobwebs that had formed over the tools. I was certain that a large and menacing black spider would engulf my arm. To my surprise, I found the tool I was sent to recover, while keeping my limbs intact.

I turned around to make my way back to the others, but to my displeasure, I was face to face with Theodore. Like a stealth ninja, he had slipped down silently—and unseen.

"Well, well, well… what have we got here?" he said in a low and almost malicious voice.

"Get out of my way, Theodore," I said in my big boy voice that crackled when his name left my lips.

Using his full name didn't sit well with him. Theodore preferred Theo. The look on his face told the whole story. Curled lips, squinty eyes, and a balled fist made me realize doing so just angered him even more.

"It's *Theo*—not Theodore," he said in a looming voice.

Quickly, I tried to navigate around him, meaning what I said but not willing to see if he'd actually move out of the way for me or not.

It wasn't going to be that easy.

He grabbed me by my arm and pulled me back to my place. "Not so fast, orphan boy," he told me with an evil grin.

Oh God, was this his moment? Were my fears about to

become a reality? Is this the moment he was going to kill me? Bury me deep within the dirt floor below my trembling feet?

"I don't want to die…" I thought to myself, but it wasn't a thought—I actually said it aloud.

"I'm not going to kill you freak," he said laughing. "But you're gonna wish you were dead—after I'm done with ya."

He bumped me up against an old chest—tucked in the corner of the cellar. Then, Theodore reached around, causing me to flinch, as though he was about to bring the pain. But he didn't hit me. He simply opened the trunk.

"Get in."

"No! Get out of my way, or I'll tell Sister Elsa," I demanded, standing my ground.

"You so much as make a peep, and I will make you wish you were never born, orphan boy."

Too late, I had often wished that. A wish I had before I met Aria and Miles. In any case, I knew he meant it. I didn't want to feel his fist planted squarely against my jaw, so I obliged. I slowly put one foot inside the open trunk—then the other. Hesitating and hoping someone would come down to check on me before I fully submerged myself into the dark abyss.

But no one came.

"Let's go, maggot!" shouted Theodore, as if I weren't moving quickly enough for him.

I was overwhelmed by the musty smell that permeated from within. This trunk hadn't been opened in years, and the stench festered in the air. I bent down and curled up into a fetal position. Lying down with my knees squeezed to my chest, afraid this was the end—Theodore shut the lid.

The sound of metal against metal within the chamber of horrors pounded against my eardrums. Theodore had locked me in. I could feel a weight settle above me, compressing the top of the lid. It had to be Theodore sitting atop the chest.

"You think you're special don't ya?" said Theodore, as he began his taunting. "Always getting what you want. Never getting in trouble. Well, things are about to change around here." His voice calmed. "I got a few more months left in this dump. Before I go, you all are going to learn who's really in charge."

There was no need for all those theatrics—he had won. I had submitted to his will and did as he told me, encapsulating myself in this tiny box. Couldn't he just enjoy that and go back up the wretched stairs? Not likely.

"You and your little friends get to do whatever you want around here, and I am sick of it. It's about time you all pay your dues if you want to live in this puke hole," said Theodore, as I sat in the pitch blackness of my nightmare.

What else did I have to do in order to have settled my dues with Theodore? The dues we all owed for being younger than he was.

Theodore and his followers did everything they could to make me feel unwelcome from the first day I arrived at St. Mary's Academy for Exceptional Youth. His gang would pour water on my bed sheets just before bedtime, duct tape my hands together, shove me to the back of the line during any meal time, or my least favorite… remove my towel and clothes out of the bathroom while I was taking a shower. I had to sneak back to my bedroom, stark naked before anyone could see.

THUD! THUD! THUD!

Theodore began pounding against the sides of the trunk.

"You hearing me in there, orphan?"

"Yes," I squeaked.

"Now, you're gonna sit there and think about that. I'm sick and tired of *Sister Pain in My Butt* protecting you idiots," barked Theodore, as he continued to rant. "And if you tell anyone who put ya here, you're gonna hurt."

There was a sensation of a weight being lifted off the chest, followed by the creeks of the old steps. Theodore undoubtedly was making his way back up the stairs. The light that peeked through the keyhole, providing me a small sense of security, suddenly went black. Theodore shut off the tiny light bulb that provided me a glimmer of hope. I knew at that moment I was alone, and he had left me for someone to find my lifeless body. No matter what he said, I knew he wanted me dead.

I wanted to shout out for help. I wanted to cry. I wanted to be found—but I was too scared.

I had been trapped in the box for what felt like hours. *Where is everyone?* Does no one notice that I had been gone for so long? Surely my friends would wonder what happened to me and come looking with a large search party. They didn't.

Finally, I heard the door at the end of the worn stairs open. Salvation, or had Theodore returned to finish what he had started and what I knew his heart desired? The desire to pull out my soul and leave my motionless body in this makeshift coffin—

never to be found.

Off in the distance, I could hear the sound of someone walking.

The metal latch began to shake and rattle just before the lid cracked open. This was the end indeed. As the lid slowly lifted, and the rasping of the old hinges let out their cry, I was blinded by the small amount of light emitting from the bulb tucked in between the exposed ceiling rafters.

I felt like a lost sailor at sea, found in a lifeboat that had been drifting for days, or weeks in the vast blue ocean. In my mind, I had been stuck there for so long, I should have grown a beard and my lips were surely peeling and cracking from dehydration.

I squinted at the light shining down on me, as two figures came into focus. It was my two best friends, Aria and Miles.

"Where ya been?" asked Miles nonchalantly, as he chewed on a granola bar he held in one hand.

"Obviously stuck in this box, dummy," snarked Aria.

"What took you so long?" I said, gaining my senses back. What felt like an eternity was more likely to have been less than an hour, if that.

"Figured you were playing hide and go seek," said Miles, lifting his shoulders. "How did ya get in there anyway and lock it behind you?"

"Miles, sometimes I wonder how you ever made it this far," said Aria—reaching in to lend me a hand.

I stood up—stretching my cramping back.

"What do you mean?" Miles responded, looking perplexed as usual.

She slapped her palm against her forehead and dramatically shook her head. "He didn't lock *himself* in that trunk, and *he* isn't playing a game! Did Theodore do this?" asked Aria.

"He said he'd hurt me if I told anyone."

"Well, you must tell Sister Elsa what he did," said Aria with a hint of anger in her voice.

"No, Aria. I really think he meant it. If I tell her, I'm as good as dead," I said, almost begging her to keep it between us.

The likelihood of Theodore committing a crime punishable by death was doubtful. But at my young age, there were far more terrifying things a boy like Theodore could do to me. I wasn't in any hurry to discover just what those things were.

"What now then, Cooper?" asked Miles.

"Let's just go back upstairs and act like nothing happened," I told both of them. "I'll be fine."

Miles brushed some of the dust off my T-Shirt that I had collected while imprisoned in the chest, and we made our way back up the stairs to an awaiting Sister Elsa.

"So good of you to finally join us again, Mr. Cooper B.," said Sister Elsa, with some concern. "Where have you been?"

Aria stepped forward and stood beside me. I could tell she was about to reveal my entire ordeal to Sister Elsa—when out of the corner of my eye, I spotted Theodore and his band of criminals staring at me. I nudged Aria and motioned my head his way. Aria stepped back. Thankfully, his mere presence gave her second thoughts.

"Sorry Sister Elsa, I got a little distracted admiring all the neat stuff in the basement. It won't happen again… promise," I responded, fibbing to Sister Elsa. After all, a lie was less painful than a punch to the eye from Theodore.

Sister Elsa looked over at the other boys, who were still watching us. A look of skepticism washed over her face as she turned back to me. She paused for a minute. At that point, I knew she didn't believe a word I told her.

"Well... let's get back to work then. We have a lot of work to get done around here," said Sister Elsa softly.

A part of me figured she would have scorned me for dilly-dallying around in the basement. She may have, had Sister Elsa actually believed my tardiness was from exploring the old jars and antique furniture in the basement below. Sister Elsa was interesting that way. In the short time I had gotten to know her, I felt she allowed us to experience childhood and the antics that came along with it. She seldom interfered in our affairs, unless it was absolutely necessary.

That night, Sister Elsa gave us permission to make a fort out of our bed sheets and sleep in the gathering room, as she often did on a Saturday evening. It was a chance to eat microwave popcorn and talk amongst ourselves without worrying about the older kids eavesdropping.

"I can't wait until he's gone," said Aria, still upset about the day's events.

"Soon enough. Then, we will never have to speak his name again."

"Hey, not to change the subject and all but what are we going to do about school?" garbled Miles, with a hand full of popcorn shoved into his mouth.

It was the last weekend before heading to school. Public school that is. The summer had flown by and none of us had even given the idea much thought. What if we were separated? Surely, they would put the orphan kids together in the same class. But I truly feared they would place us in different class-rooms—separating us in hopes we would make new friends. I didn't want to make new friends. I liked the ones I had.

"I hate school," said Aria point blankly.

"It's not that bad. I even got all of my grades up to a D and one A last year in fifth grade!" said Miles proudly.

Aria stared through Miles. "What did you get an A in, Miles?"

"P.E.," he said leaning back against the bottom of the fort wall tossing a popped kernel of corn into his mouth. "I'm really good at dodgeball. You'll see."

Deep down inside, I wanted to tell Miles that everyone could get an "A" in P.E. if they simply dressed for class, but I couldn't bring myself to break the news to him. Miles was obviously proud of his accomplishment, so who was I to tell him any different.

"How about you Aria? What kind of grades did you get last year?" I asked.

"I don't remember."

"How can you not remember what grades you got? Did you fail all of them?" asked Miles.

"No! Why would you say that?" barked Aria, with a shocked expression.

"Well then, what kind of grades did you get?" I asked, now curious why she was seemingly embarrassed about the question.

"A's. I've gotten all A's since they started giving real grades to us."

"Holy cow!" Miles said excitedly. "We gotta sit next to each other in class—I'll do terrific!"

"Why do you hate school if you're so smart?" I asked.

Aria sat in silence for a moment. Her eyes started to fill with water, but she never let the tears go. I often forgot how much she was like the rest of us, because she always seemed so confident, never letting anyone get inside her head. On the outside, Aria was the most powerful eleven-year-old girl I had ever met, but deep down inside, she shared the same sorrow as the rest of us.

"It's not because I'm stupid or something—no offense Miles. It's just that I never had any friends at school, and I don't want to go."

I scooted closer to her, pushing my shoulder against hers. "It'll be different this time. We won't be alone this year."

"Speak for yourselves. I had loads of friends. We were always playing football or baseball, and—," Miles began chiming in, before I gave him a look that stopped him in mid-sentence. "—I mean, ya school sucks," said Miles cautiously.

"I almost forgot the best part, guys!" I said, raising my voice in enthusiasm.

The two of them looked at me, waiting for my big reveal. "No Theodore," I said, bringing my voice back down in hopes he couldn't hear me utter his full name.

The three of us all smiled. That would be a bonus if nothing else. We would have eight hours of peace while in school, and since we were all going to be in sixth grade that year together, Theodore and the hoodlums wouldn't even share our building. We would be safe, if only for a few hours a day.

"I'm guessing we will hardly even see him until he's booted out of here," I said, stretching back, putting my hands behind my head. "Yep, it's going to be a good year. I can feel it."

As the three of us nestled into our sleeping bags, I thought to myself, *times were soon going to get better.* No more Theodore issues. No more being stuffed in a box. No more name calling, and no more fearing bodily harm, or even death.

Unfortunately, this was just a dream. He was still living under the same roof. Not only that—but Theodore had set his eyes on a new victim.

CHAPTER *four*

A GIRL NAMED SERRA

Miles, Aria, and I awoke bright and early the following day to the smell of oatmeal and burnt toast. Unlike her predecessor, Sister Elsa couldn't cook, even if her life depended on it. Since we had slept just around the corner from where breakfast was served, we were the first in line. We grabbed our breakfast and sat back down on the couch, surrounded by the fallen fort that had broken apart during the night.

The three of us sat munching on toast with jam—slurping spoonsful of oatmeal and sipping our orange juice. We hurried to consume our meal in order to get outside and make the best out of the last day of summer. It was a Sunday and that meant we didn't have chores. For some, outside the walls of this orphanage the day was spent at church services, but for the three of us, we could roam free. The only rule we had was to make our beds before heading out.

"I made my bed last night," said Aria, as she ran for the front door. "Meet ya outside, slowpokes!"

Why didn't we think of that last night? The answer was simple—Aria was smarter than us boys. She had me and Miles take our bedding downstairs to make the fort, leaving her bed neatly made. With conviction, we bunched the linens together in our arms, and the two of us raced upstairs.

As I finished making my bed, Miles sat on his, tying double knots with his shoelaces. I hardly noticed Theodore had already gone downstairs, and the room was empty. I didn't give him a second thought and Miles and I eagerly ran back down the steps, nearly knocking over one of the older girls who had begun her slow descent down the staircase.

"Pardon us!" I shouted, slightly winded.

Practically ripping the front door off its hinges, we rushed out onto the freshly painted front porch and started scanning the yard for Aria. She was nowhere in sight. Finally, I caught a glimpse of her knee, as she sat back against the large trunk of a moss-covered tree.

We made our way to her. The closer we got—I began to sense that something was wrong. Her head was tucked down between her knees that she held on tightly to with both arms. The faint sound of a sniffle escaped her, and I knew then she had been crying. Something or someone had upset my friend.

"What's wrong?"

"Nothing. You wouldn't understand," she said, still unwilling to look up at me.

"How do you know I wouldn't? I might," I said to her compassionately.

Aria stared up at me, as she wiped the single tear that had

found its way down her rosy cheek. It was just for a moment, but long enough to see her eyes were bloodshot. She rested her chin against her knees and softly spoke, "Theodore called me a terrible name."

It wasn't like Aria to allow someone to hurt her feelings with childish name calling, especially Theodore and his spiteful words. No, this must have been a terrible thing he had said. *Something hurtful and personal* I thought.

"What did he call you?" asked Miles with genuine concern.

Aria had such sadness in her eyes as she looked up at me. "He called me a…" She shook her head and rested it down on her chest again. "It's not important." Aria rubbed the lone tear with the palm of her hand.

"It's important to us if that fart clown is making you cry," Miles responded, looking in the direction of where Theodore was standing with his usual suspects of troublemakers. "I think I'll go punch him in the eye and see how he likes crying."

Aria sniffled and stood up, smiling at Miles. "He'd wipe the floor with you Miles, but thanks."

"Ya, you're probably right," said Miles, relaxing the fists he had made and deflating his pushed-out chest. "But it'd sure feel great to see him cry like a four-year-old lost in a mall."

Aria brushed the dirt off of her pants, and we made our way through the tall grass, heading toward the woods—trying not to get the attention of Theodore and his misfit friends.

"Just a few more months, right?' asked Aria, trying to pull herself together.

"I'm not sure I can take another few months of this. He just keeps getting meaner and meaner and someone has got to stop him," I told them both. "Why don't we just tell Sister Elsa what's going on. She may be able to help—"

"—Same reason we didn't say anything about you getting stuffed in that box, Coop. Guys like that would only come at us harder if we tattled on him. Then he'd kill you for sure," said Miles patting me on the back.

"We could run away. Get as far from here as we can. At least until he is gone," I said.

"Where would three eleven-year-old orphans with no money go?" Aria responded, with a slight chuckle.

It seemed like a great idea at the time. However, Aria was right. We were stuck and there wasn't anything we could do about it.

Aria, Miles, and I just kept walking with nowhere in particular to go. We just wanted to put as much distance between us and that terrible Theodore as possible. Regardless, the further we walked into the woods, it truly felt like we were alone, and no one could ever find us—if that's what we wanted to happen.

"Hello," a startling voice called out from the thick brush surrounding us in the woods.

Standing off to our right was a girl, every bit of our age, wearing all white overalls, a purple long-sleeved shirt, and mittens. She was a bit taller than the rest of us, with bright pink hair, pulled up into pigtails. Holding freshly picked tulips, she waved to us.

"Who are you?" Aria asked in a snippy way.

"My name is Serra," responded the odd, little pink haired girl with some spunk.

Aria and Miles stared at each other and back at me. There was a great deal of confusion in both of their expressions. To be honest, I felt they were being a bit rude to this girl. Who can blame them, since we had just dealt with Theodore and his hateful ways. I didn't want to make her feel unwelcomed, so I took over the introductions.

"Nice to meet you, Serra. My name is Cooper. Cooper B.," I said, starting a conversation for the three of us. "These two are my friends, Aria and Miles."

Aria was slowly stepping back away from me. Miles did the same. "What did you just say?" Aria asked slowly.

"What do you mean?" I responded. Now I was totally lost by her attitude.

"Ya, Coop. I didn't know you spoke Spanish, or was that Chinese? Hmmm, not sure that was either. I've heard people talk in those languages before. What was that?" Miles added.

"It's not Spanish, Miles. I can speak Spanish," said Aria. "So, what did you two just say to each other, Coop?"

I laughed. I was being tricked, but how did this strange girl get in on the prank?

"Okay, you two are funny. Real funny," I said laughing—but they just stared back at me and the pink pigtailed girl smiled at me as well. I let out one more chuckle. This time however—it was a nervous one.

"It's not Spanish or Chinese, Cooper B.," Serra told me. "In order for them to understand me, they will need to wear these."

Serra reached out with her gloved hand and handed me two black bracelets. They didn't tell time or receive text messages. They were just solid, thin, black bracelets made out of some sort of plastic or smooth metal. The bands were nothing like I had ever seen or felt before.

"What are they?" I asked.

"Cooper, you're starting to freak me out here," snapped Aria.

"Ya Coop, you can knock it off now," said Miles, starting to sound a bit irritated.

Serra pointed to the two bracelets. "Have your friends wear these. They are voice translators so they can understand us."

"They understand me perfectly, and I understand you perfectly. Even without these things," I responded with frustration growing in my voice. My mind was beginning to swirl.

"I don't understand that either," Serra added.

I turned to Aria and Miles and grimaced a bit. How do I convince my friends to trust her and put on these bracelets? For all I knew they were mind controlling devices, or worse—an explosive device set to go off the minute they put them on. There was only one way to find out for sure.

"Here, she says to put these on," I told them in a nonchalant sort of way. "It will allow you to understand her—like I apparently already do."

"Coooool," Miles said, as he stepped closer, taking one of the bracelets from my hand. His brown eyes widened, as if he had just found a bar of gold on one of our quests.

"Now hold on a second, Red. For all you know that thing is dangerous and could kill you!"

It was too late. Miles had already slid the bracelet over his wrist. It didn't kill him, not immediately anyway. It appeared safe. "What does it do?" he asked.

"It's a language translator that allows me to talk with others like you," said Serra.

"What do you mean others like us?" asked Miles curiously.

"Are you actually talking to her? I mean, you *understand* what she's saying?" Aria demanded, now holding the bracelet I had tried to give her.

"Ya Aria, put it on—I actually understand her." Miles looked giddy at the gadget on his arm. "So crazy."

"I think if she meant us harm, she wouldn't have said hello— she would just have harmed us," I said, trying to reason with Aria.

Aria studied the bracelet for what seemed like forever. She rolled it around between her fingers, looking for something that may prick her, or a button that would turn it off or on. There was absolutely nothing on the small piece of jewelry. It was perfectly smooth, without an edge.

"Okay, but if this kills me… I'm going to kill you both," said Aria, as she slid the bracelet over her hand and onto her wrist.

Without warning, it tightened, causing Aria to jump.

"Oops, my fault. I should have warned you that it will self-fit itself to the one wearing it," Serra added.

"Now she tells me—Oh my God I understood you!" shouted Aria with wide eyes.

"Duh. It's a voice translator or whatever. Weren't you listening?" Miles added. "Hey, what did you mean by others like us anyway? This some kind of Russian technology?"

"No, Miles. I'm from Alyssum," said Serra.

Miles just stared at his wrist, running his fingertips against the black band around it, oblivious to the others. "Hey Coop, are you Russian? Is that why you understand what she was saying earlier?"

"No Miles, I'm not Russian. And I don't think she is either," I told Miles, getting an uneasy feeling about our new friend.

"What country is Alyssum in?" asked Aria impatiently.

Serra lowered her head and closed her eyes. It was unnerving, but something was telling me this place she was from wasn't from anywhere we knew of or on this planet for that matter. I couldn't explain what I was feeling—but something was churning inside me.

"It's difficult to explain," said Serra lifting her head and looking directly at me. "I'm not from here. Planet Earth that is."

"You're an alien?!" shouted Miles without hesitation.

"I'm not an alien. You're an alien!"

"Am not!"

"Are too!"

Serra squared off with Miles. It seemed as though she was about to let him have it with a punch to the nose.

"That's just nonsense, Miles. She can't be an alien. There's no such thing, right Cooper?" Aria interjected, assuming I would have the answer to the age-old question everyone has ever asked about our Universe—*are we alone?*

"I don't think so?" I said, uncertain.

"Why not?" Miles questioned Aria. "You said Ms. Pedigree

was an alien so why can't she be one too?"

"Ms. Pedigree?" Serra asked mystified. "You know Ms. Pedigree?"

"Ya, why? *You know her?*" asked Aria, eagerly.

"She's one of my Pedagogues," Serra told us all, taking a step back away from Miles before she knocked him down.

"I knew it!" yelled Aria with delight, as she jumped up and down in excitement—feverishly pointing at me and Miles. "I told you! I told you two she was an alien! I knew it—I just knew it!"

"You also said she had green scales, and Serra clearly doesn't have green scales," I pointed out to Aria.

"Ya, that's true. Where's your scales, alien?" asked Miles.

"I don't have green scales, you buffoon."

"Oh, I like her now," said Aria with a big smile.

"Okay, okay. Could you three stop?" I begged. "This is all a bit confusing. Why are you here, and how did you even get here?"

"That's easy, through the *Fold*," said Serra, pointing back from where she apparently came.

"The what?" Miles responded.

"The Fold. It's how we travel from Alyssum to Earth. Well, anywhere really." We all just stared at her, lost. It was obvious we didn't comprehend a word she said. "Okay, imagine if you folded a piece of paper in half, lining up our two planets side by side. The Fold does that with the universe and allows us to step from our world into yours, avoiding the dark matter. Get it?"

No. Now I was really confused. The Fold—dark matter—

Ms. Pedigree. What was going on? Who was this girl? I had to be dreaming. Was I still passed out in the musty trunk, tucked away in the basement? That had to be it! I was oxygen deprived and near death. This was all a hallucination—but I couldn't wake myself up. It must be real.

"The Dark Matter?" asked Aria.

"Yes, you never want to go into the dark matter. Truthfully, I don't know why, but from what I've heard it's a horrible place to get lost in."

"And why are you here?" asked Miles

"For the tulips, but I am really not supposed to be here—since Graysonians aren't supposed to Fold. I can't help it, I just love your flowers," answered Serra, lifting up the tulips she had recently picked.

"Graysonians? I thought you said you were from some place called Asslum?" snarked Miles.

"What did you say?"

Serra looked as though she was becoming a bit irritated at the translation between our languages—or just with Miles in general. Luckily, Aria stepped in between the two.

"How come Cooper understands you?" asked Aria, finally slowing down the back and forth between Miles and Serra. "Without this thingamajig Miles and me are wearing?"

"I don't know? I was wondering that myself. Where are you from Cooper?"

"I—uh—I don't know. I'm… I'm an orphan."

"That's it!" Miles bellowed. "That's why no one knows who you are! You're not from here—*you're an alien too*," gasped Miles.

"I am not."

"Think about it, Coop. You show up from out of nowhere. They can't find your parents anywhere. Then, Ms. Pedigree shows up, the alien she is, and takes you from home to home your entire life."

"Not to mention you speak her language. That's sort of a red flag," added Aria.

"It's impossible. I mean... I couldn't... Could I?"

"Come back with me then," said Serra, as though we were going to head to the local outlet stores together. "We will find out where you belong."

"So cool," whispered Miles.

"Go where? You can't just leave," said Aria.

"Why not? What does he have here? Plus, we'd get out of school tomorrow!" argued Miles with overwhelming enthusiasm.

"What do you mean by *we*?" snapped Aria. "*We* aren't going anywhere with you, Pinky."

"He ain't going to the Asslum alone you know," said Miles.

"Alyssum, it's pronounced *A-lys-sum*," responded Serra in a condescending tone.

I thought about the proposal—but it didn't take long to decide. It was a no brainer. What was there for us anyway? None of us had family. We were all we had. Overall, there was not one good reason to stay. There were however, a million reasons to go. If we went together. And what if—what if my parents were waiting for me? What if I had somehow inadvertently walked through one of those Folds and ended up here, lost. Then again.

What if we stepped through this so-called Fold and were turned to dust?

"Cooper B., if you are from Alyssum then you should come back with me, but we have to hurry. My parents will start looking for me, and if I get caught—well, I don't want to get caught," said Serra.

"Can my friends come?" I asked.

"Of course—but you have to do exactly as I tell you once we get home. Understand?"

"Deal," responded Miles and I in unison, but Aria remained silent.

"Come on, Aria. What do you say?" asked Miles.

"I don't know. This all sounds like crazy talk to me. For all we know, she's some sort of serial killer or something like that. And Sister Elsa will be looking for us, so if we don't get back soon, she'll be worried."

"Don't be silly. She's not a serial killer," I told her.

"Besides, who is really going to notice if we don't go back to the orphanage? No one, that's who. It's not like we're the popular kids that everyone wants to hang out with," added Miles in an attempt to change Aria's mind. "Who knows, it could be fun."

Aria stared at me through her emerald green eyes for a moment and finally relaxed her shoulders.

"Fine. But—"

"—Great! Follow me," said Serra, waving her hands to follow her.

We made our way through the woods—following close behind our new curious friend. Strange though. We had spent so many days in these woods together exploring, chasing dragons, avoiding creatures from deep inside our imagination, and not one time had I ever seen a Fold or anything out of the ordinary for that matter.

Serra stopped. With a look over her shoulder at the three of us, she waved her hand in the air. Suddenly, the leaves began to rustle, and small pebbles littered about the ground began to bounce as a gust of wind surged past us from behind. I couldn't believe what I was witnessing.

A tightly bundled ball of light, no bigger than a softball, hovered four feet above the ground. It burst with sparks that dissipated before they hit the ground. In its center was the purest and brightest white—brighter than anything I had ever seen. It had a soft blue aura, outlining its outermost layers. It was terrifying—but yet familiar and pure at the same time. Every molecule in my body said turn and run away, but I stepped in closer.

"After you," said Serra, inviting me to leave this planet first.

I took two steps forward, slowly reaching out. I should have been scared, but I wasn't. I watched as my fingertips carefully made their way to the center of the light. Sparks bounced off my forearm. I expected to feel a burn as the sparks made contact. Instead, they sent a soothing wave through my body.

As I made contact with the ball of light, I thought for sure the flesh of my fingertips would start to melt to the bone. But I was still whole. Surely, some solid force would prevent me from making contact. *Something, anything preventing me from going any further.* Nothing like that happened. Rather than self-combusting right there on the spot—my hand began to disappear into the void of the bright light.

I could no longer feel my hand as I plunged it further in. Wherever it was, I knew a part of me was not there in the woods with my friends. There was no pain, only comfort. Serra stood alongside me.

"Don't be afraid. Go further," said Serra, encouraging me.

"Are you crazy? Are you some kind of loon? Step away from that this very moment Cooper B.," Aria demanded.

I didn't listen to Aria. Quite the opposite. I was being drawn toward the bright light, like I read about so many times in books. But those people were dead.

"It's okay, you can trust me."

"Trust you? We just met you!" yelled Miles frantically.

"Stop! Please, you're going to kill him!" pleaded Aria, as I stepped in closer. "We've changed our mind. We're just going to stay put."

I couldn't stop. Even as Aria grabbed my arm, pulling me toward her.

"Don't go," said Aria in a soft voice. "Please."

I gently put my hand on hers. "It's okay," I assured her and I turned to my friends and smiled, "I'm not afraid. Aria, let go."

Her hand slowly slipped off my arm, releasing her tiny grip as I had wished. I was prepared to travel somewhere far away, but where? That part I did not know. Or did I?

An unseen force pulled me further and faster into the Fold. I felt split between the two worlds and nowhere at the same time.

"Coop!!" Miles screamed out.

It was too late. His last words echoed, bouncing about as if

I were trapped in a sealed capsule. As the woods disappeared, the light grew brighter—then exploded all around me.

There was nothing but silence—I was gone.

CHAPTER five

CHANCELLOR BARTHOLOMEW ADIMUS

Standing motionless with my eyes tightly shut, I held my breath wondering if I had been blown to smithereens. Slowly, I opened one eye and then the next, letting out the built-up pressure in my lungs. I ran my hands across my chest, checking myself over, assuring all my extremities were intact. Nothing was missing. As a soft touch from a warm summer breeze brushed against my cheeks, I drew in a deep breath. The air smelled fresh and clean.

I stood in the middle of a swaying field of apple green grass that was speckled with vibrant wildflowers growing from the ground beneath. It was like nothing I had ever seen before, and I felt lost. But I knew I wasn't in the place I had once considered my home. Not the kind of home a child dreamt of living in, but the home I knew for the last ten years—on Earth. *Could this be where I am from? Was this Alyssum?*

Wherever it was, it was utterly amazing.

The empty space surrounding me let out a faint warning, as

if a rock had been dropped into a lake—breaking the once still surface. From out of nowhere, Aria had appeared, and she didn't look well.

"Oh my, I think I'm going to be sick," she said hunching over at the waist. She looked around. "Where are we?"

"Alyssum I suppose."

The air around Aria split and then rippled. Miles appeared alongside her, followed by Serra. He fell to the ground and clutched the grass below his palms.

"Are you okay?" I asked.

"That was—" Miles began before throwing his hands up in the air releasing grass clippings toward the sky, "—the coolest thing ever!" Then, he turned his head and threw up.

Serra shook her head. "You're all probably feeling a little sick. I should have warned you that could happen the first time," said Serra, rubbing her stomach. "I still get a slight tingle in my belly each time though. Well, shall we? Mom and Dad are probably beginning to wonder where I am."

Miles mocked Serra, flipping his hand across the side of his head as though he had pigtails himself. "I get a tingle in my belly, blah, blah, blah," whispered Miles under his breath.

"Does anything look familiar?" asked Aria.

"Not really."

As Aria, Miles, and I made our way through the meadow of tall, lush grass with our newfound friend, we reached a paved walkway at the entrance of a long bridge built over the massive body of indigo blue water, leading into a large city.

In the center of the city, a towering skyscraper, glistening with gold and silver, stretched into the clouds. Circling the towers were flying vessels appearing and disappearing in mid-flight, silhouetted by several planets, barely visible to the naked eye.

Miles said it best, "Whoa…"

"That is the city of Elise," Serra pointed out.

"Is that where you live?"

"No one lives in the city, silly," said Serra, looking out toward the vast blue sea.

We all paused for a moment to look out at the view of Elise—it was like nothing we had ever seen or even imagined before.

"Well, no time for sightseeing, we have to get home," Serra said, walking away from the majestic city. "This way, follow me."

Our journey took the four of us further away from the city of Elise, and led us to a clearing where a lone structure stood. What appeared to be a large block of solid concrete sat in the middle of a well-manicured landscape. If it hadn't been for the large doorway and a small porch in front of the structure, I would have thought it was nothing more than a massive rock, shaped into a two-story square.

"Home sweet home," said Serra.

As we got closer, I realized that it was more than just a solid lump of concrete. Far from it. It was truly a magnificent looking home, surrounded by potted tulips and roses throughout the yard.

Aria, Miles, and I followed Serra up the steps and to the front door. She entered. Seated in the living room near a bookshelf full of old books, were her mother and father, reading from tablets. On the inside, nothing extraordinary stood apart in this home from the ones I once lived in. Except for her parents of course. There were couches, with end tables, a dining room with a table large enough for four, walls of family photos, small strange plants, and decorations that filled the entire space.

"Hello mother. Hello father," said Serra standing at the edge of the room.

"Who do we have here?" her mother asked.

"Friends of yours from Grayson?" asked her father, putting down the tablet next to him in order to make a proper greeting. "How do you children do? I'm Mr. Penrose, and this is my wife Mrs. Penrose."

"Hello," we all mumbled at the same time.

"I have something to tell you, and I don't want you to get upset with me," said Serra, preparing her parents for the next part of her story. "You see, I found them. Well, they found me I suppose. I was out collecting flowers and I saw them all together talking, so I was curious and wanted to meet them—"

Mr. Penrose looked at the bracelets on Aria and Miles' wrists. His eyes widened. Serra did not have to go any further. He knew exactly where she had been. "—Serra Penelope Penrose, where did you meet these children?" asked her Father sternly.

"Earth, but let me explain—you see I started talking and this boy here, Cooper, understood me right away. Without a translator—"

"—That's impossible. Young lady, have you any idea what you have done?" asked Mrs. Penrose with concern.

"No, he really could, Mom! Then we were talking, and apparently, he is an orphan. That is when you don't have parents on Earth, and he was found like eleven years ago or something, wandering some town. It was like he came out of nowhere—"

"—How long ago did you say?" asked Mr. Penrose, lowering his voice.

"About ten years ago to be more accurate, sir," I added nervously, not wanting Serra to have to explain everything about me on her own. "Just showed up one day on the side of the road in a town called Cooper, Maine. They said I was alone, and my parents could never be found. So, they sent me off with a woman from Child Services named Ms. Pedigree."

"Ms. Pedigree?" asked Mrs. Penrose perplexed.

"See I told you—weird right?" said Serra.

"Oh dear… oh dear indeed… can it really be him?" muttered Mr. Penrose to himself.

"You three sit right there. Don't move," said Mrs. Penrose, as she rushed out of the room.

We all sat as quietly as possible, watching Mr. and Mrs. Penrose off in another room—talking amongst themselves. Mr. Penrose gave his wife a nod of approval, and she stepped aside, running her hands over one another. She spoke aloud to herself.

"We need to speak. It is urgent—it's the boy," said Mrs. Penrose, but who she was speaking to was a mystery.

Mr. Penrose sat down between me and Miles rubbing his hands nervously together. "Earth you say?" he asked, making small talk.

"Yes, sir. Cooper, Maine in the United States of America," I responded.

"Ah, the good ole U-S-of-A huh? They must have wonderful food there. You know, I do enjoy a good meal. "

"Um, I suppose," I said, not really too sure. I had never experienced anything too remarkable in terms of flavor, except for Mrs. Martin's meatloaf she always made on Sundays.

Abruptly, a knock on the front door sounded the arrival of a new guest. Mrs. Penrose quickly walked to the foyer and opened the door.

Standing on their porch was a tall older gentleman, dressed in a long, gray, wool overcoat. He wore a white dress shirt, buttoned up to a three-quarter collarless neckline, and brown wool trousers that matched his long coat.

"Good afternoon, Mr. and Mrs. Penrose. So good to see you again," the man spoke in a commanding voice.

"It's always our pleasure, Chancellor Adimus," said Mr. Penrose, greeting the man with a sturdy handshake. Standing beside him was a familiar face—Sister Elsa.

Serra, Aria, Miles, and I quickly stood up when we recognized our former headmistress from St. Mary's.

"Sister Elsa?" blurted out Miles. "You're an alien too?"

"You may call me Ms. Elsattera, Mr. O'Malley," she told him with a faint look of kindness.

"I shortened Uriel's name to make it easier for your young minds to comprehend. Clever if I do say so myself," said a memorable voice from behind the two.

Ms. Pedigree stepped in last, still dressed as though she was from the 1960's on Earth. She clasped her hands together and wore an affectionate expression. "You children gave us quite a fright when you didn't return home to St. Mary's after sunset.

"Don't fret, we've told the others you just didn't fit the image of the orphanage and were placed elsewhere. Somewhere more suitable."

Ms. Pedigree spoke as though it should all make sense to the three of us. That it was a brilliant cover up story, and we should be captivated by her quick-witted thinking. In any case, I am sure no one would have noticed had she not explained our absence.

"No introductions are needed then I see," said Chancellor Adimus, addressing the three of us in a delighted tone. "You have already met two of my finest Pedagogues. For those of you who do not know—I am Sir Bartholomew Adimus."

"Pedagogues, sir?" I asked.

"Yes Cooper, Pedagogues. They are what you would refer to as a teacher back on earth," said Chancellor Adimus kindly.

"Who else is from this place?" asked Aria in disbelief.

"You may or may not be pleased to discover this, but this is everyone, Aria," said Chancellor Adimus, placing his hand gently on her cheek. "The gig is up so to speak."

The Chancellor turned my way, and his eyes narrowed with pleasure as he looked upon me. There was a familiarity in his gray eyes. "I had looked forward to seeing you again sometime in the near future, but I am afraid to say it is a little sooner than I had hoped, *Cooper B.*," he said in a soft voice.

"*You* know who I am?"

"Of course I do," responded Chancellor Adimus in a matter of fact voice. "Afterall, I did help you Fold for the first time."

Mr. Penrose interrupted the formalities of the reintroductions. "We're terribly sorry, Chancellor. Serra has been told not to go to Earth, but she insists on gathering their flowers for her garden."

"Ah yes, tulips I believe?" he said tenderly, as he looked past Serra at a vase placed on their mantle—filled with bright yellow flowers.

"Yes, sir," said Serra, happy to hear him somewhat express his approval.

In another time or another place, I would expect this man to begin yelling and scolding Serra for her actions. She apparently broke their rules and grounding would be the least of her worries. Instead, he turned back toward me and motioned for me to sit down on the couch beside him.

"I'm sure you have many unanswered questions, Cooper. However, I ask that you trust that those questions will be answered in due time—but for now we must prepare our world for you and your friends' arrival," said Chancellor Adimus as he paused in thought, tilting his head toward Serra. "Quite an unexpected arrival at that."

Serra seemed to realize he was referring to *her* decision to bring them back and lowered her head.

"You see, we simply couldn't risk sending you back at this point," continued Chancellor Adimus. "Dear no. You are far too important. Now that you will undoubtedly be noticed, you cannot return home."

"Is this my home? Alyssum that is?"

I heard what he had said, but a million questions suddenly

entered my mind. Questions I wanted answers to, sooner than later, "Are my parents here too?"

"To answer those simple questions would require difficult answers. In the meantime, we must get you prepared for your studies at the Grayson Academy where, as you may have guessed, I am the Head Chancellor. There you will be enrolled as Second-Year Students, and I trust you will excel in all that you are tasked with."

"Second-Year, sir?"

"Yes, Cooper. Unfortunately, you have missed the first of seven years you will be joining our Academy for. However, I am quite confident you will have no trouble catching up with the rest of your class."

Chancellor Adimus now addressed Aria and Miles with a great deal of empathy, "Regretfully, I must be the one to remind you that you are not the same. Cooper may possess certain abilities the two of you do not. Therefore, you will at times be separated into different classrooms, studying different subjects."

Chancellor Adimus, standing back up off the couch, pointed to Miles' wrist, "Awe, I see you two have been fitted with voice translation bands. Crafty little invention, aren't they? Be mindful. Even our technology can't always translate every word or their meanings precisely."

Chancellor Adimus stood tall, straightening his overcoat. His attention was now turned back to the Penroses. "May I have a word with you all in private?"

The grownups all walked back into a large study and closed the sliding doors behind them—leaving us kids behind.

I desperately wanted to be in the room with them. I wanted to hear what they were discussing. They must have been discussing us. Why exclude me then? It was obviously private—but why couldn't we hear what needed to be said? *What didn't they want us or me to know?* I didn't have much time to deliberate all of those thoughts. The doors slid back open, and the five of them returned.

"Very well, then," said Chancellor Adimus, heading for the front door. "I shall see the three of you again tomorrow morning. Mr. Penrose will have the details you will require—good day to you all."

"Good day to you as well, Chancellor," said Mrs. Penrose, and she courteously opened the door for their departure.

"It is wonderful to see you again, children" said Ms. Pedigree as she passed over the threshold behind Chancellor Adimus and Ms. Elsattera. "So good indeed."

Chancellor Adimus stepped off the first step of the porch, and the Fold appeared in front of them. He vanished, with Ms. Elsattera following behind. Before Ms. Pedigree began to make her journey back to wherever they had come from, she stopped and turned toward me.

"Welcome home, Cooper B.," she said with a great smile. Then with one step forward, she was gone.

"Well that went better than I had expected," Mrs. Penrose said with relief, closing the door, "but that does not excuse your actions young lady. If you Fold without permission one more time, we will fit you permanently with a Dezma charm and see how you like traveling by streamliner."

"It won't happen again, I promise," said Serra, crossing her fingers behind her back.

"Fair enough. Now go along and play before it gets too late. Your father and I have things to do for our new guests," said Mrs. Penrose over her shoulder while returning to the study that had held the secret meeting.

Outside in the yard, we stayed close to Serra's home, afraid to venture too far out into this strange land. Serra told us about her parents and how they were scientists by trade. They Folded outside of their own universe. Exploring new worlds. But Serra didn't want to be a scientist, even though the idea of exploration seemed to fascinate her.

"Your planet isn't much different than ours. I mean other than those planets in the sky there," I said to Serra.

"Ya, totally not what I've read in comic books. Where's the space suits? You all seem to dress like us. Dated, but like us," chimed in Miles.

"How do you suppose we should dress, Miles?" Serra asked, sounding a bit disturbed by the conversation of aliens once again.

"Well, space suits. One-piece jumpers or some kind of alien material. You know, like I've read in graphic novels."

"That doesn't sound comfortable at all—"

"—How about the little green men? Do you have green men with bulging eyes here?" Aria asked, now joining the conversation.

"Well, we have many types of species here but no little green men. Don't those exist on Earth? 'Leprechauns' I think they're called?"

Miles began laughing. "Leprechauns? They're made up—no such thing."

"Well neither are little green men from outer space. At least not from here. So I wouldn't keep looking for things you would only find in one of those graphic novels you keep talking about," said Serra coldly.

"Well, is there anything you can do that we can't?" I asked.

"Dunno… can you do this?"

Serra outstretched her arms, and slowly wiggled her fingers in the air.

"I don't think you have to be from Alyssum to do that," Miles said, watching in anticipation as though Serra would begin shooting lasers from her fingertips. I had to agree with him though. Anyone could wiggle their fingers.

"Just give me a second! Geez."

We all scooted a little closer to Serra, watching intensely as she strained her face to make something, anything happen. Then suddenly, a rock from the yard below us began to move. It rolled to the left, then to the right. The rock began to lift from the ground trying to take flight before dropping back down to the spot it originated from.

"Whoa!" Miles shouted excitedly. "That was amazing!"

"It's just the Art of Ambriose. I discovered I possessed his ability last year," said Serra with a look of confidence about her, but she also looked exhausted from straining so hard her eyes nearly began to bleed. Figuratively speaking, of course.

"The art of what?" asked Aria as she leaned in closer with eagerness to learn more.

"Ambriose. He was one of the Seven Disciples of Imperium who discovered the Guild. I learned all about him last year."

"What is the Guild?" I asked.

"The abilities we have here are known as the Guild. There are seven different types of gifts we could possess, each named after the Disciple who discovered it. But no one really possesses them all. At least not their full power anyway—well, except maybe Chancellor Adimus. I hear he is super powerful."

"How about you, Coop? Can you do anything like that?" Aria asked—but before we could find that out, Mrs. Penrose called us inside for dinner.

"Get Tinselly from out back and bring her inside, please!" Mrs. Penrose shouted from the porch.

"Tinselly?" I asked.

"Yep, our family pet—think you call them dogs?"

The four of us made our way up to the porch as Serra began shouting for Tinselly. The sound of hooves galloping from a distance grew louder and louder. I slipped in behind Serra, afraid of what was about to make its appearance. Miles and Aria must have felt the same because they stood behind me, cowering. Finally, this may be the alien Miles had been waiting to see.

From around the bushes darted a strange looking beast. It was no larger than a miniature pony and certainly was like no dog I had ever seen. It was furless, and its legs were as long as the body it supported. Gray and white diamond-like patterns covered its hairless body. His eyes were large and black as night.

The creature paused, staring at the new flesh standing before it, ready to devour us. The feature that nearly brought a laugh out of me, had I not been so terrified of the alien beast that was about to feast upon my small body, were its ears drooping toward the ground.

"Tinselly, sit!" Serra commanded.

Tinselly sat and began wagging his tail. If you were to tell me a story of a creature that suddenly changed its colors, I wouldn't have believed you—but Tinsley did. The gray diamond patterned shapes became full of color and changed in front of my eyes. *There's your alien, Miles*, I thought.

"He likes you," Serra told us. "He gets quite colorful when he is happy you know."

"Well, no. I didn't know—but that's good I suppose," said Miles relieved.

I reached out and ran my hand through the bit of peach fuzz on Tinselly's head. I wasn't sure exactly what I had expected his soft coat to feel like. It reminded me of old velvet wallpaper I had once had in one of the many homes I lived in during my time on Earth. Tinselly began to drool, thick and slimy drool.

"Let's go eat!" Serra told Tinselly, and we all joined her— and raced back inside.

Inside their home, Mrs. Penrose was setting the dinner table that now had three extra chairs crammed against one another. Mr. Penrose sat at the end and gestured for the four of us to join them. I stood and just stared at the marvelous view. It was a family dinner table, just as I had always wished for.

"I hope you're hungry children," said Mr. Penrose rubbing

his palms together. "Tonight, is spagoon!"

"Spagoon?" asked Miles cautiously.

"You are going to love it, Red," said Serra as she crammed in next to her father.

My mouth dropped open and my eyes nearly bulged out of my head, when Mrs. Penrose spoke aloud and in the center of the table, food appeared out of thin air.

"How did you—"

"—It's a food replicator, Cooper. It's our way of preparing meals here," responded Mrs. Penrose as she scooped out a helping of Spagoon. It reminded me of noodles back home with a thick white sauce and several odd-looking vegetables on top.

"I want one of those in my room," said Miles through his watering mouth. The idea of food being replicated from a distant planet didn't curb Miles appetite. He dug in and seemed to truly be enjoying the meal prepared by Mrs. Penrose.

The others made quick work of their dinner and seemed very satisfied. I, on the other hand, wasn't hungry. It wasn't the fact the meal had been created with spectacular technology. I was thinking about the conversation I had earlier with Chancellor Adimus, and I wanted answers to my questions.

"Off to bed you four," ordered Mr. Penrose. "We have a very busy day ahead of us tomorrow."

Serra kissed both her parents on the cheeks and ran off for the stairs. As I made my way up behind the others, Mr. and Mrs. Penrose stood and watched. They had a peculiar look on their faces. It was a look in their eyes that reminded me of a time when foster parents would watch as I left their home, never to see one another again.

In Serra's room, which was a typical room for any girl her age, we sat and stared out her window at the millions of stars filling the night sky. We discussed Chancellor Adimus and what he had said about learning more in due time. I felt that wasn't enough. I needed to learn more, now that I had discovered my home. If Chancellor Adimus wouldn't give me those answers, we would have to do what kids do best—find them ourselves.

"Well it's quite simple really," I said.

"How's that?" Aria asked.

"We will find the answers ourselves. It'll be our new adventure."

"Oh, I like adventures!" said Serra excitedly.

"Hey Coop, you never did see if you could do what Serra did outside with that rock. Think you could move stuff around like she can? I mean, if you're actually from here, do you have these abilities too?" Miles asked eagerly.

"Ya, remember what Chancellor Adimus said to us? *Cooper possesses certain abilities you two do not*," reminded Aria.

Aria was right. Chancellor Adimus did say that, but was he referring to the Guild? If so, why didn't I ever show signs of this ability before, back on Earth? I rubbed my hands together with great anticipation, taking in a deep breath, wondering if I actually had this extraordinary gift.

I wiggled my fingers as Serra had done, but nothing happened.

I felt a great wave of disappointment overcome me, and I sensed that Serra, staring at me with a wary eye, had been disappointed at my failure too. I looked back at her and realized she wasn't staring at me, but rather the necklace I had worn from the time I could remember. It had slipped out over my shirt collar. The medallion itself often felt a bit heavy, but something about it made me not want to take it off.

"Hey! Why are you wearing that?" asked Serra.

"Don't know—I guess I've always liked it," I responded, tucking it carefully back into my shirt.

"That symbol there is a Dezma. It's normally given to those who are prevented from using the Guild. The circles on the Dezma are what binds your abilities," said Serra as she leaned in closer to me and lowered her voice, looking back over her shoulder. "If you get caught using it inappropriately, they use the charm to ground you."

"Take it off!" shouted Miles. "See if you can do it without that dizzy thing on."

I removed the necklace and felt as though the weight of the world had just been lifted off my shoulders. I felt free. *It had to be all in my mind.* It was just a necklace, after all. I looked over to the shelf on Serra's wall. It was a shelf with several tiny toys perched on the shelves. And before I could tell myself to move the figurine of a winged serpent, it flew across the room, hitting the wall and smashing into a hundred tiny pieces.

"Wow!" Miles said excitedly, sitting upright. "Did you see that?"

"How could I miss it, Miles?" said Aria.

"You broke my Alcoyi, Coop... but that was impressive!" Serra said. "I don't think I've seen a seventh-year Graysonian do it that well."

"I… I didn't mean to do that. I mean, make it fly across your room like that. I am sorry Serra for breaking it."

"Don't be sorry! Don't you see? You are from Alyssum!"

CHAPTER SIX

THE COUNCIL OF ALYSSUM

The following morning, the three of us awoke refreshed and ready for a new day. The air was filled with an abundant smell of something wonderful. Something I could never forget. It was a familiar scent, but one that had been out of my life for quite some time. It was bacon!

The three of us must have caught that blissful scent simultaneously. Aria, Miles, and I raced out of the guest room where the Penroses had put us up for the night. As we made our way to the kitchen, Mrs. Penrose was standing at the breakfast nook, looking pleased with herself.

Sprawled out on the table were stacks of pancakes, bacon, potatoes, and scrambled eggs. A large glass jug of orange juice with beads of condensation glistening down its sides was smack dab in the middle of it all. It was a meal like I had never seen before—only imagined, back when I raced down to get in line for oatmeal and toast.

"I hope this is acceptable," she said pleasantly. "I did a little research on the types of food you children would be accustomed to. You may find it more appetizing than dinner last night. I noticed you didn't touch your meal, Cooper."

Mrs. Penrose was right—I didn't eat. To be honest, I wasn't hungry and was overwhelmed by the day's events. I didn't know how to tell her or apologize to her for my bad manners. I was embarrassed.

"You made all of this?" I asked. My mouth was watering in anticipation of the huge banquet.

"Oh no, don't be silly. I programmed our replicator to produce it for you."

I didn't care how it was made. Whether it was cooked from scratch or created by a million molecules pulled together in a machine, I was famished and ready to dive in.

For the next several minutes, the only thing you could hear was the sound of our lips smacking together. Serra was eating so fast it caused her to snort in order to get air into her lungs.

"This is what you eat?" asked Serra with a mouth full of pancakes. "It's divine!"

"Hurry up with your meal, boys and girls. We have a long day ahead of us," said Mr. Penrose, as he made his way into the kitchen—reaching for a piece of bacon. "Hmmm, the meat of a piglet? I shouldn't."

Mr. Penrose sniffed the curled piece of pork belly, with his lips stretched from one ear to the next exposing his pearly whites. "Oh my, one bite won't hurt will it?" he said, pressing the piece of bacon against his nostrils.

"Fenton!" cried out Mrs. Penrose, but before she could stop

him, he placed it in his mouth.

"This is absolutely amazing," he said, reaching for seconds.

Mrs. Penrose, slapped his hand away and insisted, "That's enough, Fenton. Save the rest for the children."

After consuming a breakfast that was created by a fascinating piece of technology from this planet, we made our way to an empty room that had a circular platform, lit from beneath, and just as Serra had done on Earth, Mr. Penrose waved his hand through the air. A bright bundle of light appeared over the platform, sending out sparks that danced off the ground below.

"Alright, who is first?" he asked.

Serra stepped forward. "The red head will take too long. I'll go," she said, stepping onto the platform.

Serra instantly disappeared.

"Is that what it looked like when I Folded on Earth?" I asked with my mouth slightly hung open. I was completely amazed at what I was witnessing.

"Sure was," said Aria, stepping up onto the platform. Then, she too vanished into the vibrant light.

"Miles? Do you want to go next?" I asked.

Miles' hands trembled as he rubbed them together, taking a small step forward. "I don't think I am going to like this, again," he said, formulating his plan. He sucked in a deep rush of air and held his breath, as though he were about to jump into the deep end of a frigid swimming pool. With fists clenched and by his side, he stepped forward and disappeared.

"Now you my dear," Mrs. Penrose told me, placing her hand gently on my shoulder.

I stood motionless, staring at the bundle of energy that just consumed my friends.

"Um, Ms. Penrose?"

"Yes, Cooper?"

"How does the Fold know where you want to go, exactly?"

"Oh it's quite simple really. You just have to think of the exact spot you wish to travel to," she replied, leaning in a little closer. "It does help if you have been there before. Makes it easier to imagine it in your own mind. Does that answer your question? There really isn't anything to be afraid of."

"There's only been one or two examples of a time that someone was never seen after they—"

"—Fenton!"

"Oh… well… you heard what Ms. Penrose said. It is perfectly safe. Now, I'll be right behind you, Cooper," somewhat reassured Mr. Penrose.

Unlocking my ankles, I stepped into the bright, pure white sphere that hovered over the platform.

Immediately, I felt an enormous rush, but it didn't feel familiar this time. My body was being pulled violently in opposite directions, causing me to believe I was going to be pulled apart from the inside out. It stopped. I was alone. I had a foreboding sense I wasn't where Mr. Penrose had intended me to be.

Intense winds swirled around me, as if I were in the middle of a ferocious tornado. Scorching heat and sand were tearing at my flesh. From what I could make out through my obscured vision, I was standing in the belly of a rocky valley. The sky above was dark, engulfed by threatening clouds. I felt trapped in the middle of the Fold. Part of me was here, another piece of my soul elsewhere.

Whispers began to fill my ears. It wasn't one voice but multiple voices speaking at the same time. I couldn't understand what they were saying. It felt like an ancient and primal version of the language I had spoken when I first met Serra. It grew louder and louder and echoed throughout my skull. I felt pain. The sand began to feel like shards of glass peeling away my flesh.

The wind was blowing faster—fiercer. I couldn't breathe. Statues of men or beings taller than any buildings I had ever known, lined the rocky canyon walls. At the end of the desolate gorge was a superstructure built into the boulders that climbed the canyon walls, with crimson red sand pouring from every one of its openings. I dropped to my knees. Was I dying?

Suddenly, there was calm. I felt a solid surface under my knees, and I was no longer alone. I was with Aria, Miles, and our new friend Serra.

"Hey, Cooper. Didn't do so well this time did ya?" asked Miles sarcastically.

Mr. Penrose appeared next. He looked around, then down at me still on my hands and knees. "It takes some getting used to my boy," said Mr. Penrose helping me to my feet. "How do you say it on Earth—if first you don't succeed, try and try again?"

"Yes, something like that, sir," I responded shaken, brushing dirt off my knees.

Mr. Penrose led us to the entrance of the building directly ahead. I wanted to tell him what had happened to me, find out if it was a hallucination common with Folding, or some other explanation. Before I could decide whether or not to tell Mr. Penrose what had just happened, I became distracted by the sights around me.

"Welcome to the Council of Alyssum," said Mr. Penrose, revealing the largest building in the city.

When I first bared witness to this city from across the river, it looked large and intimidating from a distance. Up close, it was far more overwhelming than I had envisioned. The structures were menacing and appeared very old. Gold and black, hand forged steel columns reinforced the large stone blocks that made up the exterior walls. Every strike made from a masonry's hammer could be seen from the ground all the way to the tippy top of the last tower that reached into the clouds above.

I felt compelled to run my fingertips over the stone walls. The jagged material looked familiar, but I knew it wasn't from the Earth. It was some form of mineral, created by gas and liquid that were compressed over a millennium to form the perfect stone. It was rock but felt like cold hard steel. Carved in the stone over the entrance was—

VOX POPULI

"What does that mean?" asked Miles, straining his neck to look upwards.

"Vox Populi? It means the voice of the people," responded Mr. Penrose.

"Neat," said Miles, rubbing the back of his neck.

As the five of us headed inside, tarnished noble statues of two powerful looking winged creatures were perched on marble pedestals on each side of the entrance. These majestic beings were a cross between a lion's body, a ram's head, and an eagle's wings. I wanted to learn more about them, but Mr. Penrose apparently had more pressing matters at hand and hurried us inside.

We walked into a colossal, round hall, full of men and women making their way to different corridors that encapsulated the edges of the room. I looked up. There was no ceiling above me. As far as the eye could see, were the inside of the towers revealing the blue skies above. It was made of thick iron beams supporting the clear mosaic glass that amplified the sunlight beaming down upon us—onto the polished, white marble floors.

"Upstairs, to the balcony. I will meet you back here when you are done," Mr. Penrose said, pointing to a corridor with a stairwell.

Aria, Miles, and I headed for the stairs as Serra and her father stayed back, watching us walk away. I had an unsettling feeling when we disappeared into the crowd of those who called Alyssum their home. Losing sight of the only people recognizable to me on the entire planet filled me with a sense of dread.

At the top of the stairwell, there was an opening. The three of us stepped through it, out onto a balcony, overlooking a great chamber. Stretched down on both sides of the room were men and women seated alongside the walls in small observation boxes. Standing in the center of the room, on a small round stage, was Chancellor Adimus.

The group of men and women were speaking all at once, filling the stale room with white noise. *"This is unprecedented."* *"They must return to their home planet immediately."* *"Who let this happen?"* *"Is it really him?"* *"Mindless prophecies."*

"Please, council men and women of Alyssum. I will be more than happy to discuss this, but we must remain civil and speak in turn," urged Chancellor Adimus as he silenced the crowd. "As I was saying, this boy was sent to Earth for his own protection, and now he has returned."

"Have you any idea what you have done, allowing him to stay?" shouted a woman seated in one of the boxes. "This is absolutely reckless."

"I am quite aware of the dangers ahead, and now that he has returned—we have no choice but to watch over him. After all, we are Watchers are we not?" said Chancellor Adimus, eliciting a roar of mumbles amongst the council.

Silence descended upon the chamber, as a black orb appeared in the center of the grand room. It was a Fold, but this was not like the Fold we passed through moments ago. This one was dark, and menacing—without a welcoming light. It was made of pure blackness surrounded by a radiating cast of deep purples.

Suddenly, three large figures appeared, all dressed in shadowy cloaks which concealed their identity. I wasn't sure if I even wanted to see what was beneath those shrouds. The moment I began thinking about it, the one in the center looked over its shoulder in my direction—as if this thing had heard my thoughts. It stopped and turned back to Chancellor Adimus.

"We will take the boy back with us," snarled the cloaked figure in the center of the three. "Back with us he must come," the other two cloaked figures whispered in unison.

"I must deny your request, Lord Dominus Mortimer," responded Chancellor Adimus without hesitation.

The whispering became louder and more intense, bouncing off the polished stone walls and ceiling throughout the chamber.

Those whispers—I heard those whispers before.

"You dare interfere with the bidding of an Absolute?" said Dominus Mortimer in a near growl. His cloak began to sway.

"It would be foolish of us to challenge the Absolutes in this matter, Chancellor. I'm sure they mean the boy and his friends no harm," said a council member nervously.

"We only want the boy," snapped Dominus Mortimer. The other two cloaked figures echoed his statement.

"May I remind everyone, if we were to denote the old scrolls, I do believe I have control over the students in my school and until such time when they have become of age, you do not," Chancellor Adimus told the group of onlookers, unmoved by the maleficent cloaked figures.

"They are not students of yours—not students at all," whispered the other two cloaked figures.

"I beg to differ. As of this morning, they have been enrolled at the Grayson Academy as second-year Graysonians," Chancellor Adimus quickly rebutted, looking up at the three of us—nodding his head in approval of his decision.

The Absolute that seemed to be in charge glided in the direction of the Chancellor. The Chancellor did not waiver and stood his ground—seemingly the only one in the entire chamber not afraid of these unwelcoming cloaked visitors.

Without warning, dark matter exploded from behind Dominus Mortimer and engulfed the other two Absolutes. A loud thunderous clap raced through the chamber, and where they once stood was now empty. The three chilling figures had scattered into the black void that had surrounded them.

The room was quiet and the occupants had relaxed.

"I fear you have put us in great peril, Chancellor," said a short and plump older man who was wrapped in a golden robe.

"Then I implore you to help me bring truth to those willing to seek it, Tardivel. A truth I know many of you here today are in search of," persuaded Chancellor Adimus.

"This is blasphemy Adimus! We will not hear another word on this fairytale of yours," cried out Councilman Tardivel. He cleared his throat, "As far as this council is concerned, these children will now be your sole responsibility."

Chancellor Adimus looked around the room at the other councilmembers. The men and women all remained silent. Some members had a look of utter disbelief, while others hung their heads in shame.

An expression of sadness overcame the Chancellors face before he softly spoke, "If there will be nothing else, I shall bid you all a farewell." Without another word, he stepped backwards into a Fold that opened behind him.

Councilman Tardivel sat back in his chair looking up toward us. He appeared shaken and deep in thought. "You three children," he bellowed, "are now to report to Grayson Academy where you will stay until otherwise informed by this council. Do we make ourselves clear?"

"Yes sir," I responded, completely lost on what exactly we were agreeing to.

"The school will now be responsible for you, but heed our warning—should you decide to leave the confinement of the Grayson Academy, you are doing so at your own risk," spoke a younger councilwoman with short, blonde hair, wearing a purple velvet robe. Her words were spoken with dire urgency.

It felt like we were being scorned for something out of our control. We didn't choose to meet Serra the day she appeared. I didn't choose to be abandoned by my parents ten years ago in Cooper, Maine. I certainly didn't know I was a life form from another planet. We did however choose to step through the Fold. This much was our doing—but there was no way we could have known our presence here in Alyssum would cause so much concern or conflict. After all, we were just children. Children once orphaned on Earth and now alone in a distant world.

Mr. Penrose appeared behind us and placed his hands on my shoulder. "I do believe that is our cue to go," he exhaled.

Aria, Miles, Mr. Penrose, and I rushed back down the stairwell we had entered. He was hurrying us from behind.

"No time to go back to our home, children—I must get you to Grayson immediately," said Mr. Penrose. "This time we will use another means of transportation."

CHAPTER SEVEN

GRAYSON ACADEMY

Serra, Aria, Miles, and I followed Mr. Penrose back outside and past the noble winged statues guarding the entrance to the tower that held the council meeting. We all departed with haste, as Mr. Penrose informed us we could not Fold into Grayson Academy. Apparently, this fantastic way of traveling was not permitted on school grounds, at least not for Graysonians or their parents. But that was okay—I didn't fare well with the last time I had to enter that bright bundle of light, Folding from the Penrose home to here. I could still feel the sweltering heat and sand burning against my flesh. It was an uneasy feeling, and I was struggling to free myself from it.

My thoughts were disrupted when a gust of wind pushed down upon us. A soft hum filled the air and the sun was blocked, shrouding us in a shadow cast from a large craft above our heads. It was sleeker than any futuristic car that a young imagination could dream up. The crafts undercarriage had a series of ports that glowed brightly in the daylight. At first glance, the blue haze from the underbelly should have scorched us to the core, but it did not. In fact, the air felt cool and crisp like a gentle breeze.

"This here is a Streamliner, Cooper B. A Streamliner T1012 to be more precise. It's an alternative means of transportation here on Alyssum," Mr. Penrose told me.

The unmanned craft carefully navigated itself down beside the five of us and came to a rest a few inches from the ground. When suddenly, the doors slid back to the rear—inviting us inside.

"In we go children," said Mr. Penrose. "Must be going now."

We all hurried to the opening of this smoothly shaped, dark grey spacecraft, but Miles beat us to it as he pushed his way ahead of me and Aria.

"This is so cool!" shouted Miles with utter excitement. "I call shotgun!"

Miles excitement would be short lived since there were no front passenger seats, only a leather captain's chair in the front of the cavity. Behind the drivers' chair were bench seats lining the wall on the opposite side of the opened door. Since Miles was not licensed to drive on Earth or Alyssum for that matter, he was forced to take a seat on the bench with the rest of us passengers.

It didn't seem to faze Miles. He sat bouncing on the leather bench like a child would. The interior cab provided a three-hundred-and-sixty-degree view of the outside through its long narrow windows. It was roomy enough inside for a young boy or girl my age to stand tall, but an adult would have to hunch over to prevent hitting their head on the un-upholstered ceiling.

Aria, Serra, and I took our seats alongside Miles as Mr. Penrose sat down in the driver's seat—helming the craft for our journey ahead.

"Buckle up everyone," said Mr. Penrose looking around. "It's been a while since I've maneuvered one of these…"

We watched as Serra rested her hand on the side of her lap, initiating a safety harness that came out over the top of her shoulders and secured itself into the seat between her legs. Miles was next. He flinched at the near miss, as the buckle found its way between his legs—securely fastening him to the seat.

"Here goes nothing," mumbled Mr. Penrose under his breath.

Just as Aria and I were fastened into our seats, the craft jerked forward, then backward, and forward again, before lifting higher into the air. The crowd outside quickly stepped aside, avoiding becoming victims of a hit and run. We jerked side to side, then lost altitude and dropped back down, scraping against the pavement blow.

"Just use the auto navigation, please," Serra pleaded with her father.

"No, no, I think I got this," Mr. Penrose responded, unconvincingly. "Now just sit back and enjoy the ride."

Finally, the flying car leveled out, taking flight high into the clouds. Soaring through the sky, we were safely above the looming cityscape joining other Streamliners of different shapes and sizes. It should be smooth sailing from here—with clear blue skies ahead.

But Mr. Penrose had a different course in mind, and my

stomach twisted and turned as we dipped back down toward the solid surface below. The shear force hurled our bodies back against the seats, as the Streamliner sped ahead until the paved streets gave way to the crystal-clear water that surrounded the city of Elise. The reflection of the flying car leaped from one gentle roll of the sea to the next—never breaking the calm surface.

Mr. Penrose swung his chair around to face us, and a feeling of despair crept its way inside my body. I immediately thought to myself that it may have not been the wisest thing for him to do, considering we were zipping across just a few inches above the surface of the ocean.

"Your belongings will be sent to you later, my dear," Mr. Penrose told Serra. "Unfortunately, you three did not pack anything before running off with my daughter, so the Mrs. and I will gather a few things for you and make sure you have everything you need as well—now, please hold on, as this may get a bit bumpy."

Mr. Penrose swung back around, looking off into the blue skies ahead and said aloud, "Grayson Academy."

My stomach again began to churn. We were securely fastened to the bench, but there was nothing to hold onto as Mr. Penrose had instructed. I felt the craft pick up speed. I looked over at Miles, who had squeezed his eyes shut—mumbling to himself. But I didn't want to miss a thing, so I kept my blue eyes wide open.

My view became obstructed, as the air around us opened and swallowed us whole, like a great white whale consuming a small tug boat lost at sea. As quickly as it happened, we were pushed out the other end, rapidly slowing our approach. The sensation of a hand being firmly pressed against my chest was lifted, allowing me to take in a much-needed breath of air.

"Was that another Fold?" I asked Serra, rubbing my chest.

"Sure was, Coop, but look over there."

White clouds circled and brushed against an island sitting out in the middle of the vast cobalt sea. It was remarkable. I couldn't see any beaches, only tall trees at first. It was as though the lands were growing straight out of the water—emerging high above. Suddenly, off in the distance, in the middle of the lush green landscape were the peaks of a cathedral.

"Is that Grayson?" I asked in awe.

Mr. Penrose swung his chair back around. "Well, yes, yes it is Cooper. That will be your home for quite some time. It's rather extraordinary if I may say so myself, being an Alumni of course," Mr. Penrose responded, emulating my thoughts on its greatness.

He stared through me, as though he had found himself lost in his thoughts. Recalling his days as a young man, roaming throughout the grounds of the academy.

"Um Mr. Penrose… sir…" I said, pointing to the sandy sea walls that we were quickly approaching. "You may want to turn around."

My body lurched back. Without warning, we were on a collision course with the under belly of the island.

"We're going to die!" shouted Miles, pointing toward the massive cliff made of solid rock and sand.

A series of white capped waves crashed against the island's

jagged barrier reef, turning the rolling sea into a mist. Mr. Penrose turned his chair back around just as Aria tucked her head down onto my shoulder—letting out a shriek.

"Don't be silly my boy. We're on a perfect course," he responded, gripping the arms of his chair. "Right on course... I believe."

My eyes slammed shut, just at the moment we should have crashed into the rocky cliff.

When the end of my life didn't manifest, I opened them once again, one at a time. The craft must have pushed right through the rocky cliff. We were now safely inside the island, slowly making our way to a platform with a few other Streamliners, but not like the one we were in. They were a bit fancier looking then the one Mr. Penrose owned.

Scattered about on the platform were other children gathering their belongings and hugging their loved one's goodbye.

"Ah, I see we aren't the only ones getting an early start today," said Mr. Penrose, bringing the Streamliner to a halt near a sign above us that read:

NEW ARRIVALS

Mr. Penrose looked pleased as the door slid back. "I hope you children enjoyed your ride."

"I certainly did, sir," I responded with a white lie.

Miles still looked a bit green from our near-death experience. "Ya... It was just peachy," he said stepping out onto the platform, where he dropped to his knees and kissed the smooth glossy surface. "Thank you."

"You are such a drama queen, Miles," said Aria, stepping over the red headed heap on the ground. "Quit embarrassing us and get up."

"Oh, like you weren't scared out of your mind? I heard you whimpering," Miles countered.

"Greetings!" a voice came from off in the distance.

A short, overweight gentleman, with a long, gray beard made his way toward us. He stopped and looked at me through his round spectacles that were squished on the tip of his round nose.

"You must be Cooper B.," he said with a welcoming grin. "I had heard rumors that you would be joining us this year." He pressed his palm against his forehead. "Oh dear, my manners escape me." He reached out with his hand and paused for a moment, collecting himself. "I am Mr. Hordo. Might I say how delighted I am to make your acquaintance? I am one of your Pedagogues here at Grayson. That's what you refer to as a *teacher* I believe."

"Pleasure to meet you as well, sir," I responded, as he energetically shook my hand.

"Oh, quite the manners you have young man. Truly, quite the manners," said Mr. Hordo, turning his attention to Miles and Aria. "You two must be his friends from Earth... Liles and Arma?"

"I'm Aria, that's Miles," responded Aria in a slightly irritated voice.

"My apologies!" howled Mr. Hordo from the depth of his loins. "Please excuse me for that unfortunate gaffe, and welcome to Grayson Academy!" He turned to Serra. "Well hello there, young lady. I trust you enjoyed your break this year?"

"I did thank you."

"Hello, Seeminster, good to see you again," interjected Mr. Penrose. "The children were a bit rushed coming here today, and I didn't have a chance to prepare their belongings. I will make certain they are sent later today. Could I trouble you to be so kind as to see to it that they arrive and are delivered proper?"

"Certainly, I will. And it's always a pleasure seeing you again, Fenton."

Miles leaned in and softly spoke, shaking his wrist. "Is it just these translator bands, or is everyone a bit chipper here?" he asked. "Chancellor Adimus did say they could get a bit funky."

"I think he's just really nice," I whispered to Miles.

"That's just creepy. Like, a new level of creepy," Aria added, quietly.

"I think he's just excited to meet you Cooper. You'll find that a lot of people have heard about you three by now," said Serra.

"Geez, Coop. It's like we're famous," said Miles, raising his eyebrows.

Our private conversation was interrupted.

"This way please—I shall escort you to your rooms," Mr. Hordo said with great enthusiasm, gesturing toward a hallway. "I trust you will find them to your liking, Cooper B… and of course you as well *Miles* and *Aria*."

Mr. Penrose reached out and hugged Serra goodbye.

"You be well Serra," he told her. "Mind yourself and listen

to your Pedagogues this year."

Mr. Penrose turned his attention to me—placing his hand on my shoulder. "Well, I hope you enjoy your time here. If you ever need anything… anything at all… we will always be here for you."

"Thank you, Mr. Penrose," I responded as he removed his hand.

We followed behind Mr. Hordo to a hallway at the end of the platform. Beyond its arched threshold, was a massive set of stairs leading up to the unknown.

As we ascended onto a landing, that lead to another hallway, my legs were throbbing. Miles was groaning all the way, but Aria did not appear affected by our long upward trek. It was obvious she was in far better shape than the both of us.

"Hurry up, Miles, you're slowing us down," said Aria.

Miles was too winded to give her a witty response.

We continued our journey for what felt like an eternity through the high arched hallways made of both smooth stone and glossy metal beams. Every so often, the walls revealed long windows that looked out to the courtyard below—which was decorated with a variety of colorful plants and potted trees.

Finally, we reached a doorway, exhausted and with a glimmer of hope that it would lead the four of us to our destination. I had imagined in my mind that the doors here at Grayson would disappear into the ceiling with a simple greeting or command, revealing the rooms beyond its frame. But these did not. It was your standard double doors, equipped with hinges, and two tarnished brass handles. I was a tad disappointed, yet a part of me was relieved it was just your typical door.

"Well you two boys are here, and you girls are over there," said Mr. Hordo, pointing to another doorway across the hall. "When your things arrive from home, I shall see to it they are delivered straight away," he continued as he turned with the same grin he had welcomed me with on the platform for new arrivals. "It was really my pleasure to finally meet you Cooper B. If you need anything, you just ask."

"Um thank you, Mr. Hordo," I said, still shocked at the idea he seemed to know me even though this was the first time I had ever heard of his name. Then he turned and took one step forward as the space around him lit up—Folding him back to wherever it was he needed to be.

"Why couldn't we have just Folded to our rooms instead of traipsing all the way here?" asked Miles.

"He's a Pedagogue, you're not. Anyway, we will be right over as soon as I show Aria our room," said Serra stepping through their door.

Miles and I stepped through the doorway with great anticipation. Our room was exactly what one would expect it to be in such an amazing place. I had to imagine that Aria's room was just as perfect as ours. No more water stained ceiling tiles and dank floorboards. Oh no, not here. The floors were smooth granite looking stone and the walls were made from a polished material that closely resembled quartz from Earth—outlined with some sort of metal beams.

"Have you ever seen anything like this, Coop?" asked Miles spinning around gazing up into the ceilings above.

"Never."

The gathering room was massive, with seating enough for twenty or even thirty of us. High ceilings were adorned with large glass skylights that would surely provide us an impressive view of the stars at night. Straight back on the rear wall were five arched openings leading into shallow corridors. Inside the corridor were two cutouts on each side that had full beds with thick plush comforters over the top of them. There were even *two* pillows per bed. But the best part of our new room, there were no signs of Theodore and his gang.

Miles and I rushed to our beds and leapt onto them. We bounced up and down on the soft mattresses for several minutes—finally, a room we could call our own. With my heart pounding, I got down and walked to the large window overlooking a small portion of the academy's sprawling property. It was a beautiful sight to behold. It was then I knew I was going to like it here.

Back out in the gathering room, a group of children, no older or younger than Miles and me, crowded inside. They were led by a boy quite a bit taller than the two of us. He was looking at us for a few moments, long enough to begin making me feel a little uncomfortable. The rest of the group seemed to be waiting for this boy to speak first, but he didn't say a word. Now, he was really beginning to make me nervous with his stone-cold stare.

"Hello, I'm Cooper B., and this is Miles. Miles O'Malley," I said, reaching out to shake his hand.

No response. He just continued to glare, leaving my hand out to float in the air like a balloon drifting away from a child at the county fair.

"So, you're the aliens?" he asked in a low and deliberate voice.

Miles' eyes widened. He had to be asking himself, "*What do you mean, Aliens?*" The boy was right however. After all, we were on their planet now, so technically, we would be the aliens.

"Um, well I suppose we are, but we're not green if that's what you are wondering," I replied, trying to use a little humor to break the awkwardness of this gathering.

"We're from Earth," added Miles.

It was just awkward. No one spoke for what felt like a lifetime when suddenly, Aria and Serra came barging into the room laughing. There was nothing funny about this, and I wasn't sure if they realized Miles and I were amid a galactic standoff.

"Hiya boys!" Serra shouted out waving at everyone. "I see you met Cooper and Miles. The two aliens I told you about."

Serra's laughter was joined by the others, and they let down their guards. The galactic standoff had come to a peaceful end. They surrounded Miles and me, smiling and patting our backs, welcoming us to Grayson. I should have known. They were putting us on, initiating us in some cruel and inhumane way. It didn't matter. They all seemed very friendly, and I could not have been happier at that exact moment.

"I'm Bolliver," the taller boy told me, now shaking my hand. "You'll get to know the rest soon enough."

We all sat down on the couches in the gathering room as more of our classmates joined us from the girl's dormitory. Who would have thought first contact would be so easy. Had anyone been the wiser back home, I am sure they would have tried this years ago.

While I continued to meet new friends, Miles was really putting the replicator we had in our room to the test. He was generating everything from a popular drink at Grayson called Willow Whickle, to requesting good old-fashioned soda from Earth—sharing the experience with some of our other classmates. I will confess that Willow Whickle was probably one of the best things I had ever tasted. It was cold and had a creamy citrus flavor that was literally out of this world.

"So how do you like it on Alyssum?" Gwillian asked me.

"I think it's marvelous from what I've seen so far."

"Just wait until you see the rest," responded Bolliver. "This weekend we will give you the grand tour and take you out to the Nemus garden. Its endless!"

"And full of unfriendly little creatures," said Serra. "Besides that, you know you aren't allowed in the Nemus garden alone, *Bolliver.* If you get caught, you'll be banished to your room until winter."

"I don't plan on getting caught, *Serra*," said Bolliver snottily as he leaned back, putting his hands behind his head. "Plus, you'll be there too, and you can make sure no one follows us by using that keen sense of mind reading you bragged about last year."

Mind reading? Serra didn't tell us she could read minds. Miles and I looked at each other. Immediately, I began to wonder if she had been reading our minds all this time. The look on Miles' face told me he was thinking the same thing.

"You read minds?" asked Miles. "Like, you can crawl into other people's heads and just hang out and listen—uninvited? Okay, what am I thinking right now?"

"It's not like that, Miles. Well, not really. I can sense other people's thoughts… just not clear on what those thoughts are," said Serra, "and besides, if I crawled into your head—there'd be plenty of room for all of us."

We all laughed. Miles did not. He just glared at her for winning another battle of wits between the two of them.

"I heard you've possessed the Art of Eulalian your entire life," said Gwillian with his brows raised to the edge of his thick hairline.

"Eulalian? Was he one of the Seven Disciples you were telling us about?" I asked.

"Yes. *She* was a disciple too. And in my opinion the most powerful of them all. But I'm certainly not able to do what she could. So, don't bother listening to them or their lies."

"She's your favorite cause she's a girl. Anyway, if someone else is near, she can sense them and give us a warning—right, Serra?" asked Bolliver, leaning forward.

"I suppose—"

"—Then it's settled!" shouted Bolliver, not interested in continuing the discussion of the Seven Disciples. A subject I was becoming more and more interested in. "We're going to the Nemus garden. You'll love it, I swear."

"No, we aren't. It's not safe without a Pedagogue with us. We will find something else to show them."

Bolliver put up his hands, submitting to Serra.

"Okay, fine. You really need to lighten up a bit."

"Hello, children," a voice called out.

I nearly jumped out of my skin when from out of nowhere, Ms. Pedigree appeared—standing smack dab in the middle of Miles' lap.

"I would be delighted if Miles, Aria, and Cooper would join me in my study, please," Ms. Pedigree spoke, then vanished as quickly as she appeared—leaving a small orb of light behind.

"What—What was that!" a pale Miles asked.

The group of second-years began laughing. I was taken back by the sudden appearance of Ms. Pedigree in a somewhat transparent form.

"That was a Spectral. Pedagogues are able to project themselves anywhere in the school—at any time. Takes some getting used to," Bolliver answered, still chuckling.

"That was so wrong!" cried out Miles, still visibly shaken by the sudden appearance of a Pedagogue.

"Hey, you don't think she heard us talking to you?" Bolliver asked nervously.

"If she did, you would be going with them," replied Serra, turning her attention back to the three of us. "Just follow the orb and it will lead you to her study."

The tiny bright sphere that was left where Ms. Pedigree once stood was now hovering by the doorway.

We walked out of the boy's dormitory, following the bundle of light through the halls to Ms. Pedigree's study. I knocked gently on her door, not sure how badly the steel against my knuckles would feel.

The door opened.

Inside the study was a single desk made of glass. Standing alongside the desk, with a massive window pouring in beams of sunshine behind her, was Ms. Pedigree. Her red hair was pulled up in the shape of a beehive, and what looked to be glitter nestled in her hive, sparkled in the well-lit room.

High ceilings perched over her work space, and the only other furniture in her study was a chair behind her desk with two additional chairs facing toward the window. The room was quite sterile.

Ms. Pedigree's hands were clasped tightly to one another—her eyes were glowing with delight through the cat shaped lenses of her glasses.

"So good to see you children again! Splendid indeed!" she said, making her way over to properly greet us. "I hope you have enjoyed your time here with us thus far? And that everyone is treating you well?"

"Yes ma'am, we are," I said, happy to see her again as well.

Ms. Pedigree stood very close to me—now silent, giving me an uneasy feeling that she wanted to embrace me. But she didn't. I wondered if there was some school policy preventing her from doing such a thing. A policy I welcomed, because no matter how delighted I was to see her, I wasn't used to affection like that.

"You wanted to see us, Ms. Pedigree?" asked Aria, likely trying to save me from the uncomfortable silence and proximity of Ms. Pedigree.

"Oh yes, but of course," Ms. Pedigree responded, taking a step back—out of my personal space. "I would like to discuss your class schedule for the year. There are many things you normally would have been afforded during break to prepare yourselves, but since you are… let's just call it *late arrivals*," she said with air quotes, "I will need to do my best to prepare you. Now, first and foremost you will require these." Ms. Pedigree took three thin black rods off her desk. "Wonderful, aren't they?"

"Um sure… I guess, but what are they?" I asked with curiosity.

The sleek gadgets were no longer than a yellow standard pencil and no thicker than a dry erase marker. On each end, there were silver buttons. At first glance, they didn't appear as wonderful as she made them out to be.

"They're called Wuickens. Those are your school books for your time here at Grayson," she said, ecstatically. "You simply press that button there and voila!"

Of course, Miles was the first one to try it before she could finish her explanation. A small projected screen appeared from alongside the rounded edge. On the virtual screen, it said "Welcome."

To Miles and Aria, it apparently was a scrambled set of symbols or letters.

"What does that mean?" he asked, confused.

At first Ms. Pedigree was searching for a response. "*Could this boy not read?*" was written all over her face. Then, like a light bulb being turned on in a dark supply room—revealing all its mops, brooms, and buckets—it must've hit her.

"Oh dear, I nearly forgot! Okay you two. I will need you to look into your screens there," instructed Ms. Pedigree, and she pressed her finger to the virtual monitor and smiled. "There we go, now it should be working splendidly."

"Welcome? Is that all it said?" he asked as his eyes lit up.

"Your eyes have now been adjusted to read our text on these tablets or anywhere else for that matter. Not only do these Wuickens contain your assignments, class schedules, and everything you need for your studies, they also act as a map... In case you ever find yourself strolling through the halls of Grayson and need to find your way back to your gathering rooms," she snickered—then pursed her lips before speaking deliberately. "But, as you would have been reminded last year, had you been here, you are to only go where students are permitted."

We stood in silence. It sounded so ominous the way she spoke. What kind of dangers could possibly lurk in the shadows of a school such as this? *What was here they didn't want us to find?* These were the questions of a child who spent his summer on a series of fantasy quests with the two best friends he now stood side-by-side with in silence. My mind was always a bit too active for my own good. I was sure Ms. Pedigree only meant there were areas of the school children were not allowed, the same as it was back home.

"Ah, Uriel! So splendid to see you," said Ms. Pedigree, as Ms. Elsattera made her way into the study.

"Alannah," Ms. Elsattera simply responded as she swept past the three of us, taking a position alongside Ms. Pedigree.

"Welcome to Grayson Academy, children."

"Thank you," the three of us responded.

"While you are here, Ms. Elsattera will be your guidance

counselor—much like she was at St. Mary's," said Ms. Pedigree as she leaned in and blocked her mouth from Ms. Elsattera's view. "Maybe this time, she will be a bit more helpful and mindful of your whereabouts, hmm? But we shouldn't fault her for trying."

Ms. Elsattera let out a gasp.

"In any case, you may even be lucky enough to have her as one of your Pedagogues. Wouldn't that be just marvelous?"

We all agreed—afraid to disagree.

"May I suggest you get back to your common rooms and begin looking over your schedules? You have a full day tomorrow, and I would hate to see you fall behind on your first day of school… Assuming you decide to stay put and not find yourself another little girl to follow to strange planets?" said Ms. Elsattera, obviously making a point that we were responsible for putting her in a predicament when we left on her watch back home.

We stood in silence. Nodding.

"She is one hundred and ten percent correct, children—it is getting late. Run along, and we hope you have a most amazing day tomorrow!" said Ms. Pedigree.

Quickly making our way to the door, Miles bumped into me while looking over his shoulder.

"Do you think she holds a grudge?" he asked.

"I don't know."

"For your sake, you better hope not, Red," Aria added.

CHAPTER EIGHT

FIRST DAY OF SCHOOL

The feeling of knots twisting tightly in the pit of my stomach was no different than it was the other years I attended the first day of school. You woke up, wondered what you were going to wear to make a good first impression with your new classmates, and decide what you were willing to share with them about your summer break. Which in my case, never meant a great deal, other than the time I went to one of those amusement parks in Florida with the Martins on summer vacation.

Today was no different. I was as anxious, no matter what planet I was on—but at least I didn't need to worry about what I was going to wear. Here at Grayson, we wore a standard school uniform of white dress shirts, sleeveless V-neck sweaters, grey slacks, and matching blazer jackets—*proper attire for second years preparing their minds for greatness.* So I was told, when the school Famulus entered our rooms last night to deliver our wardrobe.

Luckily, Serra was still visiting us the prior evening when Avantha, our dormitory Famulus, made her debut. Serra explained that Avantha was one of numerous Famulus' at Grayson that was responsible for many things about the students, including preparing our belongings for our daily routines. I believe they were commonly known as nannies back home—but truthfully, Famulus sounded much better.

Neatly dressed and with our Wuickens in hand, Miles and I left the boy's gathering room and waited in the hallway for Aria and Serra.

"I'm famished!" shouted Serra, as she exited the girl's gathering room. "Do you think they can make us some of those pin-cakes?"

"Pancakes. They're called *pan*-cakes," Miles said, sounding irritated as he always seemed to be when it came to Serra.

"Whatever you want to call them, *Red*. I want some more."

Aria stepped out from behind Serra. The two of them wore black and gray plaid, pleated skirts that fell just below their knees and matching colorless pumps. Like the boys, they wore long-sleeved white shirts (which were somewhat messily hanging over their waistbands), sleeveless V-neck sweaters covered by their blazer jackets with Grayson's insignia embroidered on a patch, that matched ours. The only difference between Aria and Serra, was that Serra chose to adorn her outfit with pink, plaid socks instead of the seemingly school traditional black and grey over the calf socks.

"Look at you in a dress, Aria!" said Miles, shocked.

"It's a skirt. Got a problem with it?" asked Aria quickly.

"No. It's just—"

It appeared Aria was not comfortable outside of her normal

dress code of jeans and a T-shirt. I didn't want Miles to upset her. It was her first day of school here too, so I tried my best to change the subject. Truth be known, I thought she looked very nice and wanted to tell her—but I knew that would embarrass her even more.

"I wonder what they have to eat for breakfast here?" I asked.

"Anything you want, Coop. Anything you can imagine," Serra told me.

"That's the best thing you've said all morning!" said Miles, exploding with excitement.

We took our time walking through the corridors of the school toward the dining room. Unlike most school institutes I had attended, these hallways were welcoming and not claustrophobic at all. Floor to ceiling windows lined the path ahead of us, introducing a brilliant wave of light from the outside. It was as though the sunlight was charging our internal batteries as we made our way to the dining hall.

I had a great sense of relief not having to hurry to get leftover scraps from the breakfast table. Leaving the second-year wing, we grew closer to our destination, and the hallways became even more crowded.

Boys and girls of all ages filled the corridors. Some lingered, visiting with one another, as others rushed to their final destinations. One thing that they all had in common, they were watching our every move. It appeared word had spread that *Earthlings* had invaded the halls of Grayson. Somehow, they were able to sense it was the three of us. Most kids smiled, as others stepped away. It was like we carried a contagious plague to some, but to others, we were three normal kids. If I had ever wondered what it would be like for a little green man on its first day at my public school—this would be as close as it gets.

We entered a large open room with a large sitting area. It was another example of how spectacular this place was. Rows and rows of large tables made their way down the long hall. High above the vaulted ceiling, was a large glass dome, surrounded by metal beams, that gave way to the brilliant indigo skies outside.

Closer to the main entrance were children closer to our age, and they appeared to get older the further away the tables spread. We joined a table full of other eleven-year-old students enjoying the first meal of the day.

"Pancakes and syrup please," spoke Serra out loud as she plopped down.

Nothing.

"*Earth* pancakes and syrup, please," she said, really enunciating her words.

Still, nothing.

SMACK!

Serra slammed her palm down and let out a disgruntled groan, when gradually, a light appeared on the smooth, black tabletop. Right before our eyes, pancakes, covered in golden melted butter and sticky syrup stacked high on a plate, appeared in front of Serra.

Miles was watching Serra's every move, learning the ways of ordering a meal in this great room.

"Sausage and scrambled eggs," Miles said aloud—and within

moments, it appeared in front of him. There was enough to feed four of him. Miles ran his tongue across his lips. I had no doubt he was going to eat every bite as if it were the last meal of his life.

"I am going to really love it here."

"Oatmeal, please," I said softly. I wasn't about to overdo my first order. Besides, I never said I didn't like oatmeal—I just didn't like the company I had to eat my oatmeal with.

"That doesn't look very appetizing," said Serra, staring at the bowl of oats that just appeared.

"With a little milk and sugar, it's quite tasty actually," I said, unconvincingly. "Milk and sugar too, please."

My request was immediately fulfilled.

"Really, Coop. Anything you want and that's what you get?" said Miles, in sort of an irritated voice.

"Leave him alone. If he wants that, then he can eat whatever he wants," said Aria, coming to my defense for the choice I'd made.

"Just trying to help out," mumbled Miles.

"Better hurry if you wanna make it to class on time," a voice from behind us called out. It was Bolliver and Gwillian walking behind our seats, heading out.

"We'll be on time, Bolliver," responded Serra, never looking back at him. "I swear, he acts like he is the greatest student some-times. But don't pay him any attention, he's the champion of being late to class."

Aria shrugged her shoulders. "Maybe he's trying something new this year?" she said as she looked at Miles, who was shoveling food into the hole just below his nose. "I bet Miles could beat his attendance record."

With a mouthful of food, Miles looked back over at Aria, "Huh?"

As I was finishing my breakfast, trying to hurry so I would not be late for class, I looked across to the far end of the hall at the seventh-year Graysonians. For the most part, they were a happy bunch of older kids talking amongst themselves. Periodically they would look back to their younger classmates, pointing and giggling. It wasn't too different than what I had been accustomed to. There were also signs of blossoming relationships that were being shown through a public display of affection by some. I didn't understand what some boys saw in girls—it was nauseating.

As I continued to eat and observe the others throughout the hall, I had a sudden sense of being watched in return. Sitting together in a row of five were cloaked figures, staring back at me.

"Are those Absolutes?" I asked.

"Nope," said Serra with a mouthful of fluffy pancakes. "They're called Bollcrees. Wannabe Absolutes."

Whoever or whatever they were, they were terrifying. They looked as though the life had been drained from their bodies. Unlike the rest of us, dressed in school uniforms, these students were draped in deep red cloaks—with hoods that I wished they had pulled over their heads to hide their pale, sunken faces. Their soulless, cold stare made me feel truly unwelcomed for the first time here at Grayson.

"Don't mind them," said Serra—sensing my uneasy feeling

about them.

"What or who are they?" Aria asked.

"They're future slaves to the Absolutes," Serra responded sarcastically, starting on her second serving of pancakes. "I guess that would be the best way to describe them. Family tradition normally. But sometimes kids are unnaturally drawn to them. Against their families' wishes. They study the ways of the Absolutes in their seventh year—stay away from them. I heard they eat their young."

Miles stopped chewing a piece of sausage he had just shoved into his mouth. "They eat children?" he choked out. "That's absolutely disgusting."

Serra snorted, "No, Miles. They don't eat their young. Do you think we're savages?"

Miles gave her a dirty look and continued to devour the sausage link. Regardless if they were flesh eaters or not, I had no problem with the idea of staying away from them. Far away. I forced myself to take one more look to see if they were still watching me. Sizing me up for their family kitchen oven—but they were gone.

With our bellies expanding against our waistbands, we made our way down the well-lit corridors to our first class, Ancestry. We entered a lecture hall of sorts. It was half-moon shaped and four rows deep. A large desk and podium faced the watchful students, who were quietly seated in their chairs.

It was a tradition of mine to sit in the back of the classroom on my first day. Out of sight and out of mind. I wholeheartedly intended to do just that here as well, had there been any seats available in the back row that is. Bolliver was one of the second years that had beat me to the good seats. He sat and waved, almost taunting me that I had been too late to get the back row. It was just my luck that the only four seats open for Aria, Miles, Serra, and I were in the front row—directly in front of the Pedagogue's podium.

As we made ourselves as relaxed as we could, a large, brown-haired, flat-faced gorilla dressed in a brown suit and black tie made his way down the aisle. Apparently, no shoes were available to match his wool suit, as he was barefoot and carrying a briefcase. Miles's eyes nearly bulged out of his head.

"Holy cow, it's a monkey!"

"Miles!" Aria let out in a heavy whisper.

"What?" asked Miles, almost as though he didn't say anything offensive at all.

The monkey, as Miles put it, placed his briefcase onto the desk alongside the podium. Adjusting his spectacles that were resting on the bridge of his wide nose, clearing his throat, he looked directly at Miles.

"I am what you would call on Earth, a Bornean Orangutan, or Pongo if you would like to be more scientifically accurate. It is quite unfortunate that Primates from *your* world have yet to discover their true intellect and remain unevolved. However, I am. Therefore, you may call me Mr. Bonabos," he said, in a condescending manner with a bit of a British accent.

"Yes sir—Mr. Bonabos," said Miles, turning a slight shade of ruby red after being put in his place by a monkey dressed in a suit. A monkey that was clearly far more intelligent than he was.

"Unless anyone has anything further to add to this stimulating conversation, I would suggest you all open your Ancestry Apps on your Wuickens," said Mr. Bonabos.

Everyone quickly responded, as the lights in the room slowly dimmed. On my Wuicken stars appeared, taking us on a tour of the universe. Suddenly, those stars erupted out of our tablets and surrounded us in the room. I couldn't believe my eyes. I was seated in the middle of their galaxy, wrapped by stars and a piercing bright sun. I could almost feel the heat radiating from the flaming star. If all my classes were going to have this type of dynamic presentation, I was going to become a great student.

Green and yellow gases circled me. The mist began spiraling slowly at first, picking up speed, until it was rapidly spinning into a sphere. Mr. Bonabos stepped through the swirling gases.

"Our planet was formed nearly six billion years ago," Mr. Bonabos began. "However, I shall allow Ms. Elsattera to discuss her rudimentary syllabus on Planetarium Studies and focus on Alyssum billions of years after it was formed.

"As we discussed before the end of the last term, our planet wasn't always as peaceful as it was today." Mr. Bonabos stepped forward through the sun—addressing Miles, Aria, and me. "If you were sleeping through my lectures or you were not present—I suggest spending time with the Historian of Archives to otherwise correct your apparent deficiency of knowledge." He stepped back through the burning surface. "As I was saying, we were driven by war and control of our neighboring societies."

Alyssum was a beautiful planet. At least what I could tell

from the center of the classroom. Earthlike, but smaller. The surface was deep shades of blue and green. Peaceful looking from outer space. That all changed when small explosions erupted all over the surface of the planet.

"We were determined to eradicate ourselves off the planet. Death would be the only answer to the question of which species shall rule."

It was the most amazing and frightening thing I had ever witnessed. I was standing in the center of a magnificent city. It was much older than the city of Elise, but far beyond anything I had ever seen. Towering structures reached high into the skies and were built in the middle of beautiful meadows with green mountains with white caps filling the horizon from all around. People were abundant, dressed in silks and other materials I had never seen before. They looked happy. That was until the skies opened with bright flashes dissolving the white clouds that filled the atmosphere. Before the people of this city could react—everything and everyone was gone.

"Our Capital was destroyed, and nearly every citizen gone. We were defenseless, and the wars waged on for decades. We would have been lost if it were not for the rise of the Absolutes. They brokered peace when half of the planet was sent into total dismay. Elise rose out of the ashes along with seven other societies. Our scrolls were written, declaring peace, and our technology flourished, making Alyssum what it is today. We will begin our focus later in the term on the Torrian culture and what they contributed to our ways of life today."

The dramatic show ended, and the room was once again

filled with light. We were speechless. How could such an advanced society have been so cruel to one another? I suppose they were no different than we were at one time. Who they once were was definitely not the same as they appear to be today.

"That is all for now. We will begin our year with discovering the origins of single-cell life forms that inhabited our planet long before the wars. You are dismissed," Mr. Bonabos told the class.

Serra looked across the classroom to an eagerly waiving second-year student, Cornelius Grevengoed. "I'll catch up with you guys in a little while. I need to talk to Cornelius about something."

"That's okay, I got something to do anyway. I will see you back in our room later," Aria responded.

As we made our way out of the classroom, leaving Serra behind, I was still trying to comprehend everything I had just witnessed. If school lessons were as exciting as they were in Mr. Bonabos class, I would have been an "A" student for sure.

"That was terribly depressing," said Miles, breaking the silence.

"There's no way those creepy dudes in the cloaks are good," Aria pointed out, stopping us in our tracks.

"What do you mean? You heard what he said—if it wasn't for the Absolutes, the planet would have been destroyed," said Miles.

"I'm sure that's what they want us to believe, but there's just no way. Good guys don't wear spooky outfits."

"Well, what difference does it make? Sounds like they would've killed each other had the Absolutes not stepped in," said Miles, defending what he had just learned as fact.

"Whatever. I'm not buying it," Aria said, walking past both of us. "I'm gonna find this Historian of Archives."

"*Whatever*—What's her deal anyway?"

"I have no idea—but she sorta has a point," I said, running after Aria.

"Can't we just eat?" called out Miles.

I followed Aria for what felt like days until she finally reached her destination—the Grayson Library. It had to be the largest room in the entire school. Rising three stories high were wall to wall bookshelves dressed with all kinds of literature. And all about the room were children of all ages reading from their Wuickens while others were reading the old-fashioned way— with a book open in front of them.

At the end of the room was an opening to another corridor. Above it read:

HISTORIAN OF ARCHIVES

Together, the three of us made our way into the pitch-dark and somewhat ominous room.

As we entered, the room grew brighter. The walls had no edges. They were rounded from one side to the other. In the center was a small bench covered in a soft fabric. The three of us sat down, waiting for something to happen—but the room remained silent.

"So, where is this Historian?" Miles asked impatiently. "Maybe they're not open yet, and we should just come back after we get something to eat."

"Will you stop thinking about your stomach for a minute?" snipped Aria. "We can go as soon as I check something."

"What do you want to check, Aria?" I asked, curious as to why we had come here exactly.

Before Aria could answer, the walls lit up. Off in the distance, a figure made their way toward us. It was a tall woman with dark skin—dressed in a black, slender suit. She was not flesh and blood. She was just another Spectral, trapped within the walls.

"Good morning. I am Aurora, Historian of the Archives. What answers do you seek?" she asked in a proper manner.

"Who are the Absolutes?" asked Aria, without so much as even saying hello.

"They are the ones who brought Alyssum peace," Aurora responded.

"Where did they come from?"

"I am sorry young lady; those are questions not permitted to be asked by second-year students."

"Why not?" Miles asked, now seemingly interested in what Aria was doing here.

"As I have stated to your friend, those questions are not permitted to second-year students here at Grayson Academy," Aurora told Miles, never changing her tone. "I would be more than happy to answer any questions pertaining to your current curriculum, or how would you like to discuss the origins of the elusive Nemus? They are quite charming looking and elusive little creatures."

A forest appeared on the wall—surrounding us from all around. Little, white, furry animals with different colored spots, some brown and some gray, began appearing. They were no more than one or two feet tall, and just like Aurora had said, they were quite cute.

"They haven't been seen in years, but be warned—don't make any sudden movements. They are quite mischievous and can be very dangerous."

"Nemus? No, I want to know who the Absolutes are, and where did they come from?" insisted Aria, interrupting the lesson defiantly.

The forest disappeared. "I am sorry, those questions are not permitted to second-year students here at Grayson."

"I don't think she's going to tell you anything," I said to Aria in a whisper.

"Oh, forget it!"

Aria was apparently upset. The whole reason she had made the trip to the Historian of Archives was to prove something to me and Miles. Aria got up and headed toward the entrance to the room. "I'll find out on my own."

We followed as Aria stormed into the main library, letting out a heavy sigh of defeat—and the room dimmed to black once again.

CHAPTER NINE

THE NEMUS GARDEN

Miles and I didn't see much of Aria over the next couple of weeks, or Serra for that matter. From time to time, I would catch a glimpse of Aria heading to the library with our pink haired friend—walking with a purpose. When I asked what Aria was working on, she would just tell me she would let me know when she found what she was searching for.

Miles and I did find out one thing for sure. They spent a lot of their time in the History of Archives.

I offered to help with her secret expedition many times, but she never accepted my offer. Frustrating as it was, we gave the girls their space. Miles and I spent most of our lunches and dinners together—alone. When we did have the opportunity to visit with Aria and Serra, they never shared anything about their trips spent together at the library.

No matter. I was enjoying my time in the various classes I was assigned to and almost forgot about whatever it was the two of them had set out on their own to find.

My favorite class, by far, was the Art of Ambriose. Who would have imagined that I had the ability to move objects with simply my mind? I quickly found out I was pretty good at it and only wished I knew I could do this when that misfit Theodore was acting out. I may have been able to prevent many painful memories if it weren't for that necklace I had worn.

Ms. Pedigree taught the class, and she, by far, was one of the best teachers I ever had. She seemed to take her time with me, more so than the others. This didn't sit well with some of my classmates. I would occasionally find an animation delivered to my Wuicken, an animation of a fiery red headed woman wearing cat eyed glasses, leading me around the class—on a leash. A rudimentary comparison to a teacher's pet.

"Now class, please pay close attention to the objects in front of you," Ms. Pedigree told us. She walked up and down the aisle of the class, speaking in a comforting voice, "You have learned to move these objects from side to side and up and down. Spectacular as that is, I want you to really concentrate now, concentrate on manipulating the object and transforming its shape into another." Ms. Pedigree paused and took in a deep breath. "Please, children, don't be disappointed if you aren't able to perform this very difficult task. Most of you won't and that's quite alright. Okay? Wonderful. Now begin when you're ready."

On the tabletop in front of me was a metallic looking sphere. It was no bigger than a baseball. It held my shy expression in its reflection and looked as though it weighed as much as an elephant. I couldn't imagine lifting it off the table—let alone changing its structure. I closed my eyes and began to concentrate. The grunts and sounds of my fellow classmates straining all throughout the classroom told me they had begun their attempt to do the impossible.

"Oh dear, Vander… You'll pop a blood vessel in your head if you're not careful," Ms. Pedigree said off in the distance. "Oh, Briella! That looks… well, it looks—interesting. Interesting indeed," she told another student, making her way around the classroom.

I must have had my eyes closed for what felt like an eternity—when a familiar voice sounded from behind me.

"Splendid, just splendid Cooper B.," said Ms. Pedigree in an excited voice.

I opened my eyes, and what was once a perfect sphere was now crunched into a four-sided cube. It was not exactly geometrically perfect by any means, but I had done it. I only wished I had kept my eyes open to see it for myself.

Most of the class was as excited as I was. Besides a few feeble attempts by others, it seemed I was the only one to fully complete my task. Others, however, didn't seem too pleased that I had done what they couldn't. This was evident by some of the stares from a few classmates of mine who reminded me of the misfits back home. Future Absolute lackies for sure. Regardless, I kept practicing, and each time I was successful in transforming my sphere into a different shape.

Ms. Pedigree's classroom quickly began to spiral out of control, as objects flew throughout the room. Some seemingly by accident, others were certainly done so mischievously. There were even a few students transforming her classroom furniture into various shapes and sizes. I however, to my utter enjoyment, kept progressively getting better—each attempt I made to create a new shape was becoming easier and easier to do.

Before the class was dismissed, I received another anonymous image on my Wuicken. This one wasn't reminding me that Ms. Pedigree had taken a profound interest in my scholastics. Not at all. It was my head, being transformed into a cube.

"Now class, remember, no practicing outside of the classroom. We will not have another incident like we did last year in the boy's lavatory. Understood? Wonderful then, have a beautiful day—you are dismissed."

At the end of the lesson, I lingered until the room was emptied. I slowly approached Ms. Pedigree, who was now seated behind her desk. As I grew closer, I searched for the right words so I would not offend the one Pedagogue in this school who seemed to have taken such a great interest in me.

"Ms. Pedigree?" I said nervously.

"Yes Cooper?" she responded, folding her hands together and looking at me over her outdated glasses, that were balancing on the tip of her nose.

"Could I ask a favor?" I said, clearing my throat—still searching for the right words.

"Well, of course, my dear boy—what is it?"

"Um, you see... well... could you please not treat me any differently than the rest of the class?"

She paused. It didn't seem as though I needed to give her much more explanation on how I felt. She knew. "Oh dear, was I being that obvious? I am truly sorry," Ms. Pedigree responded in a very understanding and compassionate voice.

Suddenly, I was ashamed of myself for bringing this to her attention. I began second-guessing my decision to tell this nice woman how I felt.

"I shall be more mindful of your feelings from now on... It's just that... Well, to be honest, I have looked forward to this time with you for so long, finally witnessing your true potential."

What did she mean by my potential?

I wanted to ask more. Maybe Ms. Pedigree would help me find the answers to the questions I was asking for myself. *Maybe she knew my parents. Maybe she knew where I had come from and why I left Alyssum to begin with.*

"I will be more cognizant of how I am. Thank you for letting me know," she said gently.

Wait. *This could be the moment I needed to find out more about myself.* But I couldn't form the words quickly enough.

"You better run along—you don't want to be late to your next class," she said, ending my struggle to inquire more.

"Yes, ma'am. Thank you."

As I turned and walked out, I still had no more understanding of who I am, or who I was. I did know for certain she would do her best to treat me like every other kid in class. I hoped so anyway.

I entered the busy hallway, and Miles was already outside my class, waiting for me—with a bitter look. He had been introduced to Palatum Poppers. They were like sweet and sour candies that were far more tart than anything he was accustomed to. His lips puckered, and his nose was nearly turned inside out.

Unable to speak, he tried to offer me one. I refused, of course. Why in the world would I want to share in his experience? Miles's expression would lead you to believe he had learned his lesson and would toss the rest out. Apparently, he did not and popped another one in his mouth—immediately reacting to its pungent flavor.

"More for me," he said, barely audible.

"They're all yours, Miles," I told him. "We better hurry, or we will be late for Ancestry."

Besides Ancestry, Miles and Aria only had a few other lessons with me. We began studying the history of life on Alyssum, which was quite interesting. We mostly looked at images of fossils that were once creatures who roamed the surface, and in some cases, roamed deep below the ocean.

Serra had once said they didn't have monsters on her planet, but I would have to disagree with her. Maybe they weren't mythical giants to her or others here on Alyssum, but to me, they were far more interesting than the ones that Aria, Miles, and I invented when we went out on our grand adventures.

We were barely on time. Aria had already found her seat in front of the class, next to Serra. As Miles and I were settling in—activating our virtual screens on our Wuickens, Mr. Bonabos came striding in. He was dressed less refined than he had been in previous classes.

"Put those away. We are studying outside of the classroom today," he told us.

Miles and I looked at each other with pure joy—field trip!

We were finally able to get out of the classroom and get some fresh air. In all the time we've been enrolled here, we haven't really explored outside of the Academy. No matter if it was just within school grounds—it was still a gorgeous, sunny afternoon, and being outside would be a welcomed change.

The sun soared high above the lush green landscape as we made our way to the forest that surrounded the Academy. It must have been fall here on Alyssum since the trees had begun to transform into a multitude of wonderful colors. Shades of blue, red, green, and yellow painted the treetops. The gentle breeze made it look as if the foliage was performing a ritual dance for us. In fact, if one stared too long, you could find yourself swaying side to side, imitating their every move.

Miles walked alongside me, as Serra and Aria were together up ahead. The two girls were directly behind Mr. Bonabos—and I was beginning to get a complex. *Had I lost my best friend?* Was it more than just secret trips to the library, or had I said something that upset her and she no longer wished to spend time together? Could it really be all over their time in the Historian of Archives, or was it something else? What were the two of them up too?

"Hey, Coop?" Miles said, nearly out of breath from our long trek.

"Yes?"

"Do you know what time of year it is?" Miles asked with a great sense of enthusiasm. He didn't give me a chance to respond to him. "Halloween! It is almost Halloween!"

"I don't think they celebrate Halloween here, Miles. But you're right, it is almost that time of year, isn't it?"

"What do you mean they don't celebrate Halloween?" said Miles, shocked. He stopped and looked at me, perplexed. "Who doesn't celebrate All Hallows Eve? That's—That's just plain sacrilegious. I bet they do… I hope they do."

Miles was right. I didn't care where we were. It is a rite of passage for children our age to dress up any way we want and wreak havoc on our neighbors for just one evening, pounding on doors, collecting as much candy as we could fit into our pillowcases. Only to reap the rewards the following day, with our miserable and aching bellies.

But if not Halloween, what? What do the kids here do that is similar to our favorite time of year, next to Christmas that is.

"Let's just ask Serra. She'd know," I told Miles, just to give him a glimmer of hope on the subject.

"Would the two of you be so kind as to join the rest of your class? Or would you prefer we set up camp here and let you two take a retreat for the evening?" Mr. Bonabos called out. Apparently, we had fallen behind the pack—deep in conversation about truly important matters.

"No sir, we're coming," I said, turning back to Miles. "Let's look into this and figure something out. We can't miss Halloween."

"If not, we could always do that Fold thingy back to Earth. Just for one night and get our treats."

We caught up to the rest of the group and got a somewhat nasty look from Aria. It seemed as though we were holding her up from one of her more important meetings with Serra.

Just as I gathered up the courage to confront her and Serra

about her weird attitude toward Miles and me—we arrived at our location.

"This will be far enough, class—we don't want to wander into the Nemus Garden," said Mr. Bonabos, holding up his fury hand. "Let's spread out. I shall give further instructions on the proper method to search for a fossil, a technique I am sure your Paleontology Pedagogue will attempt to emulate."

As I made my way to a spot I thought suitable for our class experiment, I heard a series of whispers. The same voices I had encountered before the council meeting in the Fold. I looked around and noticed something barely visible in the wooded area that surrounded us. There appeared to be someone standing in the shadows—peering at me through a low hanging tree branch.

I spun to point the figure out to Miles, but he had walked off in the opposite direction. His head was still in the clouds about Halloween, I am sure. When I turned back, the figure was gone.

The breeze picked up. Hidden in the rustling of the multi-colored leaves, the sound of soft voices could be heard again. It seemed to be coming from somewhere off in the distance. It was subtle and faint. I couldn't make out what it was saying, but I felt it was trying to tell me something.

So, I did what anyone my age would do at that point—I began to follow it.

I made my way to the thick tree line, unseen by Mr. Bonabos—or he surely would have asked me where I thought I was going. As I entered the woods, I could see the shadow once again. It made its way deeper into the woods. I followed. The whispers echoed off the heavy bark that wrapped around the twisted gnarly trees, disguising its exact origin.

I turned to see how far I had gotten from the others. They were out of sight. Nowhere to be seen. My curiosity kept me moving away from the rest of my classmates, toward the sound of the soft voice.

I came to a clearing. Tall grass and colorful purple flowers were sprawled across the ground. Small, flying whimsical winged insects with long vibrant tails hovered over the blossoming purple flowers.

In the woods, on the other end of the clearing, the shadowed figure reappeared. Hiding. Still watching me.

"Hello?" I called out nervously. "Who are you?"

I moved closer. Taking small steps in the direction of the strange observer—unsure if I truly wanted to meet the tall form that kept itself shrouded from my view. Maybe it was Bolliver Winnington. After all, he was bound and determined to show me the Nemus Garden.

"Bolliver? Is that you?" I asked—hoping he would jump out and reveal himself. "What are you doing out here?"

No answer.

Before I could discover the mysterious figures' true identity, the ground gave way beneath my feet and I fell into an abyss. The sound of a large limb snapping under my weight could be heard as I hit the surface below—I was in agony.

I tried to stand back up and crawl out as quickly as I fell into this hole, but pain shot up my leg and throughout my entire body. It wasn't a limb that snapped below the weight of my small frame, it was my leg. Broken and throbbing. I could barely stand, let alone climb back out of the hollow cavern I had descended into.

Looking up through the hole I entered, I realized I had to have dropped at least twenty feet down. Maybe more. Measuring distance wasn't something I was ever really good at. One thing I did know, there was no way I could climb back out.

I frantically looked around, trying to find another way out. The walls were covered in thick roots from the massive trees above. I couldn't tell quite how large the cave was. I only knew I was barely able to stand without touching the tip of my head to the dirt ceiling.

Off in the distance was a faint blue haze. It wasn't the same as what filled the sky above the dirt ceiling I was under. It was unnatural—but may still hold the key to a way out.

Before I limped my way deep inside the chamber I had mistakenly discovered, I needed to try and find help from above. Hopefully, by now, the new kid's absence had been noticed. Maybe I was an oversight to my classmates, and I wouldn't be missed until later tonight after everyone had found their way to the dining hall. Or would it not be until after everyone had gone to bed and when they awoke, they'd notice my bed was empty.

Surely my best friend Miles would see that I wasn't with the class as they headed back to safety within the walls of the Grayson Academy. At that point, Miles would start asking questions. Aria, I wasn't so sure of since she has been preoccupied with her own thoughts lately. The idea of her not noticing hurt worse than my leg.

Someone. Anyone—must be looking for me. Even my

Pedagogue, Mr. Bonabos.

"Hello?" I called out, stretching my body toward the opening filled with sunlight from outside. "Can anyone hear me? Help!"

The only response came from my own voice echoing against the gnarly roots down the desolate chamber that dissipated into the darkness.

"Please! Help me!" I tried again.

Out of the corner of my eye, I noticed that the blue haze began to brighten. It was expanding as my voice repeated itself—tumbling down into the darkness. It gave me an eerie sense of discomfort. Why was this unnatural light reacting to my voice?

"Hey!" I called out, this time toward the strange lights. They doubled in size once again—like air filling into a deflated balloon.

You need to stay where you are. Someone will eventually find you—I thought to myself. But the limbs below my waist had other plans. I took a small step into the shadows, toward the mysterious glow. Each step was followed by immense misery.

A few years back I had taken a trip to the local fire department, where a firefighter gloated about what they did for a living. Besides the great meals they prepared, I recalled a time he spoke to us about being stuck in a smoke-filled room, unable to see. The large man in the fire-retardant suit explained to a group of children that they would find the outermost wall and feel their way through a room when they couldn't see anything.

Reaching out to the sidewalls of the cave, I rested my hand against the packed dirt—making my way down, further into the darkness.

I held my breath, inching closer toward what must have been some kinds of jewels decorating the walls ahead. The closer I got, I noticed what I thought or hoped were some magnificent minerals illuminating in the dark crevasse, begin to blink.

The glows weren't riches of the soil. They were full of life, and I was being watched by something from all around. The troubling part was they were slowly getting closer—sizing up this small, lost, and injured boy.

My sight was slow to adjust to the darkness as my sense of sound magnified. Over the deafening noise of my heavy breathing and rapid heartbeat pounding in my ears, I could hear the scuffling of claws scratching and digging at the roots and dirt all around me. I strained my eyes to find what was creating the unsettling commotion.

Standing no taller than I did when I was an infant, were little creatures with large ears, huge blue eyes, and spots all over their fur-covered bodies. They could only be one thing—the Nemus. And there were hundreds of them.

They were making their way toward me like hungry wolves positioning themselves to circle a young girl dressed in a red cloak—lost in a forest of nightmares.

Slowly, I began walking backwards, making my way back to where I started. Maybe they couldn't see me. Nonsense, they were staring right into my eyes—and I was surely to become their next meal.

I spun around with haste and ran as fast as I could for a boy with a busted leg. The strange part was, I couldn't feel that pain any longer. It must have been the adrenaline pulsing through my veins—giving me the boost I needed to outrun these small bloodthirsty rodents. However, they were faster than I could have imagined. How a small animal could be so fast with such tiny legs was beyond me.

Up ahead, I could see the light shining down on the ground from where I fell. I was almost there. I could feel those little monsters gaining on me. Nipping at the space my feet had just left.

Suddenly, I remembered—Aurora! What was it she said? *Be still.* Aurora said if you ever encounter one of these little, furry monstrosities, just remain still, and they wouldn't attack.

I fought with myself as I hobbled to safety wondering what was better, stop… freeze… and hope they go away or make my way to the light. Hoping I had made the right decision, I stopped in my tracks.

I tightly contracted every muscle in my body to prevent even the slightest twitch. The Nemus had also stopped their advance, but they were much closer than I had thought they were. But to my surprise, I had made it to the outer ring of the light—shining down from my sanctuary above.

The light provided me with a better view of my assailants. They were all around me—hundreds of them, far more than I had initially thought.

If I were back home, visiting a shelter for forgotten animals, I would fall in love with one of these soft and cuddly looking furballs. Something to take home as a pet. A part of me wanted to reach down and pick one up. To pet its furry coat and smell the new puppy breath on my skin. Just before it mauled my face off of course. But I knew better and didn't make a move.

Doubling in their numbers and forming ranks, they continued to swarm—exposing their razor-sharp teeth. The Nemus were circling me from all sides, unsure of their next move, while waiting for me to make mine. The low—and high—pitched cackles were unsettling. It was as though they were communicating with one another, arguing over who would test my ability to remain still. What they couldn't have possibly known, was that I was the champion of freeze tag. There was no one better than I when it came to remaining fixed as a statue.

The only problem was—the adrenaline I had initially felt was beginning to wear off and the pain slowly began to return. I wondered just how long I could stand completely still.

"Cooper?" a voice shouted through the small opening that delivered me into this predicament.

It was Miles. He had found me! But I was too nervous to call back to him and let him know I was trapped and to go get help.

"Copper B.! Are you down there? Hello?" Miles called out again. "Can you hear anything?"

"No, because you keep talking," another voice responded—with attitude. It was Aria! She was with Miles looking for me.

The Nemus stepped back—now focused on their dessert. I had to somehow let my friends know I was down here. I had to somehow warn them I wasn't alone. But I knew if I spoke, or if air passed through my lips, if I so much as blinked—I was certain they would attack.

I had to take a chance.

"I'm here," I said—softly.

But no one responded.

"Down here," I said a little louder this time—to the disapproval of the Nemus, who didn't seem to appreciate me making any sounds. They appeared to be growing irritated with me, climbing over one another preparing their assault.

"Coop!" Miles shouted back. "What are you doing down there? Don't you remember the Nemus Garden is off limits to students?"

Sigh. Obviously—but I didn't know where I was wandering into when I followed that shadow into the woods. "Get me out of here," I said, with a tremble in my voice. There was no time to explain just how I got here.

"Hang in there, Cooper! We'll go get help," Serra called down.

I felt a sense of relief knowing that someone who knew more about this area was with Aria and Miles. But during their attempt to rescue me, either Aria, Miles, or Serra must have been dangerously close to the edge of the opening when they pushed back to head for help. Loose rocks slid down into the hole—bouncing off the sides of the wall like a game chip hitting a row of pegs leading down into a game winning slot.

It was then that I made my one fatal mistake—one that would cost me my reigning championship of freeze tag and bragging rights for years to come. I turned my head to watch as a rock bounced off the dirt surface of the chamber that I had become entrapped in.

With that, the Nemus had their go ahead to commence their

feeding frenzy. I closed my eyes in anticipation of their final move.

The Nemus overcame me from every direction. Like a tsunami sending wave after wave of sea water, battering the shoreline of a small village, they attacked. The pain in my leg was replaced with the feeling of hundreds of papercuts slicing open every square inch of my body.

I did everything I could to cover up and protect myself from the onslaught of their claws and fangs—but there were too many of them. I was helpless and could feel the warmth of my own blood running down my skin. I was surely finished, and I became angry. Angry that I was unable to protect myself.

When suddenly, I felt an intense surge of energy leave my body, like a rush I had never experienced before. *Had it been my soul ripped from my small adolescent body? Had they won and stole my short-lived life from me?* It couldn't have been. Hidden behind the extraordinary burst from within, I still could feel the residual numbing pain from their razor like fingertips that had dug deep into my flesh.

What I no longer felt was the weight of their tiny bodies pressing down on me.

I slowly opened my eyes. The Nemus were now scattered throughout the cave—unconscious, tucked up into little balls of white and brown spotted fur. *Did I make that happen*, or had Mr. Bonabos come to my rescue? I looked all around—but I still was alone.

Before I could wrap my mind around what had just taken place, a great sense of pain started slithering down from my head to my toes. The adrenaline had finally worn off, and the pain grew worse. My muscles began to contract. The pain was masked by numbness tingling throughout my extremities. I could no longer feel my fingertips or toes for that matter.

The thick roots that covered the ceiling of the small cavern—the tomb I had become trapped in—were fading. Darkness converged from all around. I could no longer keep my eyes open and fear took over as I descended into sleep.

The next thing I remembered was waking up in the school infirmary—no longer in pain. Gradually, a figure seated across my bed came into focus. It was Chancellor Adimus, reading. The Chancellor noticed that I was awake and gently closed the book and placed it on his lap.

"Ah, Cooper B. You have had quite the adventure," he said in a comforting voice.

"Um, yes I guess so," I said, a bit confused on how I ended up in bed.

"I heard you had an unpleasant first encounter with the elusive Nemus. Nasty little critters, aren't they? I do have to admit to you, as a child, I had wanted one as a pet, but my parents would not allow it. For good reason I suppose."

Inside I chuckled—that was my thought exactly when I came face to face with them for the first time.

"No matter. It will take a day or so before you can get back to your feet. Your leg was badly broken, and Nurse Grangard has instructed you to remain in bed. She was rambling on about how you are not permitted to, how did she put it? Undo her medical miracle? Hmm, everything is a miracle to her.

"In any case, you are lucky to have survived a swarm attack as you did. You see, the Nemus contain very dangerous levels of toxins in their bite. In fact, for as tiny as they are, they've been known to take down a full-grown Phorlaxton if it had the unfortunate encounter with an entire pack as was the case for you. Nonetheless, you did well today. Very well."

"I don't really remember anything, to be honest," I said, still a bit fuzzy on the events that led me to this bed. "Am I in trouble, sir?"

"Trouble? Goodness no. I would not expect anything less than a boy your age inquisitively discovering unknown places. I will say this, however. You must always assume there are things in this world that mean you harm, and for that reason, I ask that you do not venture too far from school—alone," Chancellor Adimus told me in a compassionate voice.

"No, sir. I won't, I promise."

He stood for a moment and then made his way toward me, placing his hand on my shoulder. "Thank you for understanding," he said. Then like a light going off in his head, he pointed his finger upward and recalled another matter. "You may be pleased to know Ms. Pedigree had some Willow Whickle brought to your bedside. I trust you will be able to enjoy some when you're ready to. That is if your friend Miles doesn't help himself to them first. He has quite the appetite I've learned."

I agreed with a smile and sat up in my bed as he removed his hand from my shoulder.

"Sir? I heard voices in the woods—" I said, hoping to find

out if I was going crazy and hearing things. Not willing quite yet to tell him about the strange figure that led me into the woods.

He said nothing and placed a very short brim, black felt hat on his head. Then Chancellor Adimus looked at me. It felt as though he was about to tell me something. Something important—but he didn't. He simply smiled and headed for the door.

"I've selfishly taken most of your allotted time, and your friends are eagerly awaiting your audience. I shall send them in to see you now… Goodnight, Cooper."

"Goodnight, sir."

CHAPTER TEN

NURSE GRANGARD AND THE INFIRMARY

The infirmary was still, and it was slightly frightening being left there all alone. There were no murmurs from Graysonians talking, no sounds of laughter—nothing. It seemed far too large of a room for one child to be left alone in for an extended period of time. One's imagination could easily get the best of them—from shadows lurking in the corners to bumps in the night. Each instance manifesting itself into something terrifying.

I tried desperately not to think of the events that led me to my new sleeping quarters. Tucked away in the most uncomfortable bed, at least since coming here. The sheets were sterile, and the pillow was firm. Too firm for my liking. As hard as I tried, I couldn't put that horrifying experience behind me.

What were those whispers I heard? Who or what was making them? I shook my head. Trying to force those thoughts in my mind out through my ears. On top of it all, I blew it. I had an opportunity to press Chancellor Adimus for answers—but I gave up far too easily. Even if I could stop thinking about the *what if's*, I knew for sure I couldn't shake one thing. Every time I closed my eyes, I could see the flashes of large, black eyes—glowing a brilliant blue haze—followed by razor sharp teeth all around me.

I ran my hands over my arms—the scratches were nearly gone, and the bite marks were just as faded. Back home, these cuts and bruises would take weeks to heal, and for that, I was grateful and extremely impressed with Nurse Grangard.

"Now, you children cannot be here for long… I'm not interested in what Chancellor Adimus told you, those are the infirmary rules and you shall mind them… I have several other patients that need me as well… Don't get lippy with me, young man," shrieked Nurse Grangard, just outside my room.

Nurse Grangard was apparently having a heated discussion about her policies with some unruly visitors, and I was pretty sure I knew who the young man was.

"Have your visit, but mind you, by the time I am done with my rounds, you shall be on your way. And for the love of all, keep your voices down. Everyone, but you three, is trying to sleep around here. Understood?"

"Yes, ma'am—thank you," replied Miles, somewhat sarcastically, as he pushed through the door and into my room.

"Coop!" yelled Miles, already disregarding the rules of inside voices set forth by Nurse Grangard.

"Hiya, Miles!" I said—just as happy to see him.

Aria and Serra followed behind the disorderly redhead. Nurse Grangard gave them a very strict look as she began to close the door behind her. I will say this, I believe she actually smiled at me just before the door closed all the way behind my friends. Maybe that woman dressed in her long white robe with matching pale hair wasn't so bad after all.

Aria pushed Miles to the side as she ran to my bed—as though she were about to hug me. But instead, she froze just at the edge of my mattress and punched me in my arm. Thankfully, the medication Nurse Grangard had given me dulled the pain. It was okay. I knew she meant it as a loving gesture.

"Dummy," said Aria with squinted glossy eyes.

"The Nemus? You really survived the Nemus?" Serra said, shocked—approaching my bedside next. "I'm not sure anyone has ever lived to tell their story about a Nemus swarm attack. Everyone is talking about it. You're going to be even more talked about then you already are!"

"If they're so dangerous, why are they allowed so close to the school?" asked Aria.

"Ya, they even have a garden named after them. Who does that? And when I think of gardens, I think of tomatoes and yellow flowers. Maybe even harmless little bees flying around. Harmless of course if you're not allergic to them. Remember Timothy—"

"—Okay Miles, we get it," said Aria, interrupting his trip down memory lane.

"They've never attacked a student before. Never," said Serra.

"Then why did they attack me?"

Serra shrugged her shoulders. "No one knows. I overheard Mr. Zalophus telling Mr. Ceberus that Chancellor Adimus was looking into it. Apparently, the day after you were attacked, they relocated the Nemus—"

"—Is that Willow Whickle?" Miles interrupted—looking hard at the several bottles on a table next to me.

"I think so—" I told him.

"—Do you mind if I have one? I am pretty thirsty and haven't eaten yet today. Waiting for you to wake up and all," Miles said, making his way over to the table before I could respond.

"Sure," I told Miles before turning my attention back to Aria and Serra. "What do you mean the day after? How long have I been here?" I said, confused. I was absolutely certain my near fatal attack happened just today.

"You've been lying in that bed for two weeks now, Coop," said Miles—taking a large gulp of the Willow Whickle.

Two weeks? I have been in this room and bed for *two whole weeks?* That would explain why my arms have healed the way they have. I sat back. Trying to grasp the fact I've missed two entire weeks from my life, and I didn't even know.

"The Nemus are quite poisonous, you know," said Serra.

"Actually, no, I didn't know that," I responded. How would I have? I just got here a few months ago, and before that, I had never even heard of those little beasts.

"After we came back to that hole with Mr. Bonabos, he carried you over his shoulder all the way back here. That giant gorilla is fast! I could hardly keep up with him," said Miles, impressed—as he sat down in the only chair off to the side of my bed—once occupied by Chancellor Adimus. Miles hadn't quite learned yet to offer a lady a seat first.

"Miles, you couldn't keep up with a Sanaffaloop," said Serra.

I didn't know what a Sanaffaloop was, but I assume it moved

as quickly as a snapping turtle dragging a ball and chain the way Serra compared it. Miles scowled at her—he too must have believed it to be a slight to his athleticism.

But Miles was quickly distracted by a bowl of little red candies I hadn't noticed myself.

"Hey Coop? Are those Alcoyi Breaths?" Miles asked, digging his hand into the bowl and taking a handful out before popping them into his mouth. "I love these things," he mumbled, with his mouth full. His eyes began to water. They were meant to be eaten one at a time, considering they pack a fiery punch.

"If it wasn't for Serra sensing your presence, we would have never found you," said Aria, looking at Serra with gratitude.

"Nah, I am sure we would've found you—in a week or two," Serra responded, causing us all to giggle.

"You were covered in so much blood. I thought—I thought you were dead when Mr. Bonabos leaped out of the ground holding your body," Aria said in a soft voice, no longer finding humor in the conversation.

"How did you stop them anyway? The Nemus. How did you get them to stop?" asked Serra.

"I don't know, to be honest. I closed my eyes when they attacked. Next thing I knew, they were scattered all over the place. Knocked out or something," I told Serra—wondering the same thing. I finally remembered another detail. One I had honestly forgotten about. "Oh… while they were attacking me, I felt something weird. I don't know how to explain it, but it was like I exploded, or something."

That sounded better in my head, and I wished I could pull

back the words that just left my lips. The idea of exploding seemed a bit ludicrous.

"Cool," said Miles.

"Do you think you used the Guild to push them away?" Aria asked.

One of the reasons Aria and Miles were my dearest friends, was because no matter what came out of my mouth, they always seemed to accept it as my truth. Never leaving me to feel I was suited for a mental health evaluation. Well, not all the time anyway.

"That would be remarkable if he did. Some kids our age can only move small objects across the desk—if they're lucky. But to stop a hundred Nemus? That's Chancellor Adimus level type of the Guild. No one our age could do that," said Serra looking at me with skepticism.

"He made that toy fly across your room, remember?" Miles added—now with the bowl on his lap, popping Alcoyi Breaths into his mouth one at a time.

"It wasn't a toy! It was a figurine—big difference—"

"—Toy—figurine—whatever. Coop still made it fly, and if he could do that, why couldn't he do the same thing with a bunch of angry rabbits?" said Miles, in a matter of fact way.

Aria stared at Miles for a moment. "Don't get upset with me, but I agree with Miles. People can do some amazing things when they are put in situations of life or death. Little old ladies can lift a car off a child if they had to."

The room was silent for a minute or two. Serra was either trying to figure out what a car was, or she was contemplating what Aria had just said. It wasn't totally out of the question that I could have used my new found ability to save my life. On the other hand, I wasn't sure what actually caused the Nemus to stop—being I was too terrified to watch the outcome.

"Well, Cooper B. If you did do that, then you are quite remarkable," said Serra—sitting down at the foot of my bed.

"Hey Coop? What were you doing in the garden all by yourself anyway?" Aria asked.

"Ya, Coop. You were standing beside me one minute, and the next thing I knew, you were gone," added Miles. I quickly wondered just how long did it take Miles to discover my absence.

"You really shouldn't have gone off on your own like that. The area is full of things none of you are used to," chimed in Serra.

I stared silently at the three friends sharing my hospital room, waiting to have a chance to answer at least one of their questions.

"Can I explain now?"

"Just waiting on you, Cooper," said Miles.

I spent the next several minutes explaining about the whispers I heard and the mysterious figure I followed out into the garden. I have to admit I felt strange telling them I was hearing things, and maybe even seeing things, but that's what I remembered from two weeks ago. I wondered if they would believe me or had I finally told one too many grand tales.

"Who was it do you think?" Aria asked, apparently not as suspicious of my story as I thought she would be.

"Bolliver."

"Bolliver? Why would you think Bolliver lured you out into the woods? I've known him my whole life. He'd never intentionally hurt anyone," Serra responded.

"Well, he did want to take Cooper to the Nemus Garden in the first place. So why not?" said Aria.

I am glad someone remembered our first day here at the Academy. Bolliver was very insistent that he would take me to the Nemus Garden. It was obviously off limits for a good reason. It was a very dangerous place to be, so why would Bolliver be so interested in sending me into harm's way. It had to be him, no matter what Serra thought. But why did he want to hurt me?

"True—but Bolliver was with Mr. Bonabos the whole time. Sucking up to the Pedagogues is what he has mastered. I couldn't get a question answered all day because he was stuck to his side," said Serra.

That small detail could have put a damper on my conspiracy theory with Bolliver. Not sure anyone could argue with the facts Serra was giving us, regardless of how much I wanted to believe I was right when it came to my now, mortal enemy.

Miles leaned forward in his chair, "Well, if not Bolliver, then who? Who did Cooper see? And who was whispering to him?"

"Did any of you hear anything?" I asked, in hopes that they too had heard the soft whispers calling from the woods. They looked around at each other. It was clear they hadn't.

"No—but that doesn't mean you didn't. If you say you heard something, then I believe you," said Aria.

"Can't say I did. I'm not going to lie—I was more interested in figuring out this Halloween issue we have," said Miles.

"Halloween?" Serra asked.

"So, you don't know, huh? We'll explain it later."

"Well Coop, we will figure this all out. Serra and I have been doing some research at the History of Archives, and Aurora has given us some pretty interesting stuff to share with you," said Aria somewhat excitedly.

"You found my parents?" I quickly asked.

"No, but there's something odd going on around here ever since you showed up," said Serra.

"You think?" Miles quickly interjected.

I was overcome with a sense of disappointment learning I was no closer to discovering who my parents were. At the same time, I was happy to hear my three friends weren't planning an intervention to have me committed for a psychological evaluation. It felt good knowing I could discuss my experience with them and not be judged in return. Maybe, just maybe, with the help of these amazing allies, I would start getting answers to so many unanswered questions. Unfortunately, it would have to wait until another time.

"That's long enough. Time for Cooper B. to get some rest," said Nurse Grangard, as she walked through the doors, apparently done with her rounds. But I had enough rest and wasn't ready to let them go. After all, I've been stuck in this bed for quite some time.

"Hey—we will be back before breakfast. Then we can talk about that one thing," Aria added with a wink.

I couldn't tell you how great that felt. Hearing that the girl I was introduced to at St. Mary's Academy for Exceptional Youth not so long ago, with long, curly, black hair—and the one who truly gave me hope once again—was planning to come back first thing in the morning. I had missed our daily conversations, running like children throughout the halls, laughing, and playing. But mostly, I missed my friend.

As the three of them were escorted out of my room, Nurse Grangard motioned her hand over a small area on the wall shutting off the lights. My eyes weren't quick to adjust, and it was an unnerving feeling being plunged back into darkness for the first time since that day in the forbidding chamber of death.

I know that I was being dramatic. I knew I had nothing to fear. I was safe now. What I feared most was hidden in the confines of my small head—in the darkness of my thoughts. *Were nightmares in store for me when I closed my eyes to fall asleep? Was the comfort of Aria's words enough for me to get past it?* It had to be. If not, I would drive myself into insanity.

I lay there for several minutes—looking out at the millions of stars. Observing those other planets—scattered in the night sky—through the panes of glass in the massive window that spanned from floor to ceiling. I don't recall much after that. I must have been in desperate need of more rest like Nurse Grangard suggested. Or the thought of my friends being there for me brought forth the peaceful resolution I yearned.

My eyes closed, and I slept—free of any nightmares.

CHAPTER ELEVEN

THE VESTIGE

My eyes slowly opened. The stars had been replaced by Alyssums massive sun—shining brightly through the window of my room. I could feel the beams of heat gently warming my skin. It was a welcomed sensation, one that replaced the pain of days past. That morning, I knew I was on my way to a full recovery. That delightful news came when Nurse Grangard informed me she was preparing to send me back to my school lessons shortly after breakfast.

As Nurse Grangard made her way out of my room, Ms. Elsattera entered. The two spoke softly to one another for a few seconds, every so often looking in my direction. If it had not been for the fact I was just informed about my full recovery, I would begin to wonder if Nurse Grangard was passing on a ghastly medical prognosis about my condition. The two finally separated, and Ms. Elsattera made her way toward me. There was kindness in her eyes.

"Cooper B., you seem to be making remarkable progress, so

I've been told by Nurse Grangard. Regardless, I shall still ask— how are you feeling?"

"I feel much better thank you."

It seemed as though Ms. Elsattera was both pleased to see me but concerned at the same time. She stood at the foot of my bed, staring at me through her nearly black eyes—dressed in a long, button down dress more suitable for a funeral.

As seconds passed by, I was beginning to feel uncomfortable once again, as though I should say something to break the silence. She came around and sat at the edge of my bed, resting her hand on my leg. She finally spoke.

"Glad to hear that," she said, patting me motherly like. "As I am sure you've already been told, you were quite lucky to have escaped with just the injuries you had. The Nemus don't take kindly to unwelcome visitors in their habitat. I trust you have come to realize this?"

"Yes ma'am," I said, while searching for words to justify that I had not known where I was. Maybe I should have told her about the sinister phantom that led me there, but I chose not to.

"If I had known—I certainly wouldn't have gone in there."

"I'm sure you wouldn't have," she said, patting my shin one last time. "Well now, we shouldn't dwell on the past, should we? I came here this morning to inform you that you have been given a reprieve by your Pedagogues and will not be required to make up any lost assignments. They all seem very pleased with how well you are doing. How did Ms. Pedigree put it? Ah yes, you are like a sponge, absorbing knowledge."

That was typical of Ms. Pedigree to praise me, as she has done so often. To use whacky analogies, nonetheless. At least now, it seems she was doing so, not with other students but my other Pedagogues instead. Honestly, I could live with that.

"That's great news. So no homework then?"

"No homework. You have a clean slate once you get back to your classes—starting today."

Suddenly, something clunky hit just outside the door—taking me by surprise.

"I do believe your breakfast has arrived," Ms. Elsattera told me, looking back at the sound of the tray on wheels being shoved through the threshold.

It was my friends. They had returned as promised, and they brought nourishment.

"Hiya Coop!" Miles shouted.

"Voices!" Nurse Grangard called out from beyond.

"Oh ya—hey Coop, we brought breakfast," Miles said quietly, as if he were in a library.

Miles, Aria, and Serra made their way into my room. Miles must have ordered everything imaginable you could order from a café menu back home. Scattered about on a medical trolley, made into a crude room service cart, were chocolate chip pancakes, scrambled eggs, sausage, bacon, waffles, butter, syrup, and orange juice. It was enough to serve all of the second-years.

"We didn't know what you would be hungry for, so we just got you everything you like," Miles said, as he presented the feast with arms wide open.

"More like everything *he* likes," Serra added—taking a strip of bacon off a plate.

"It all looks marvelous," I said while sniffing at the aroma of food in the air for the first time in what felt like forever.

"Hello, Ms. Elsattera," Aria said politely, being the only one to acknowledge my guest.

"Good morning, Aria," she replied, with a pleasant smile, as she got up off the edge of my bed. "I shall leave you children to visit. I will see you all again very soon."

We all told Ms. Elsattera goodbye as she left the room.

Miles quickly replaced Ms. Elsattera by taking her spot on the bed. Miles, of course, did not sit as softly as she had. Instead, he just plopped down, pulling the cart closer to him.

"I'm famished," he said, grabbing a plate and filling it with each item. "Aria wouldn't let me eat until we got here."

"I told you after Cooper eats, you buffoon," Aria told Miles through scorched eyes.

"It's okay. All of you have to be hungry too. Let's eat," I said, reaching for a piece of sausage.

The rest joined in as we just sat there—forgetting everything that brought us together in the infirmary in the first place. It was just what I needed. The funny thing about kids, we could put behind the worst of times by simply finding something to make us forget long enough to move onto the next chapter in our lives. For me, that something was these two friends of mine. No matter what I had been through in my short-lived life, I could count on them to make me forget. To heal. Even if it was for just a moment. And now, Serra was part of that circle. Sure, I would likely recall those events again in the near future, but for now, it had been forgotten.

"Are you really going to be able to leave today?" Serra asked.

"That's what they said. Apparently, I'm all healed up, and I don't have to be here any longer. And it's about time—my butt is getting sore from sitting here for so long."

Miles laid back, holding his belly. "I'm stuffed," he told us.

"I couldn't imagine why? You ate everything on your plate… twice," said Serra.

"We call that seconds," Miles said without skipping a beat. He let out a deep sigh.

"When can you leave?" Aria asked, impatiently looking at the door—ignoring Miles. "I thought for sure, Nurse Grangard would have been here by now, to release you? And, we have so much to tell you."

I replayed the word "release" several times in my head. Aria made it sound as though I had been imprisoned in my room in the infirmary for the past several days. There was some truth to that thought. It wasn't as though I was free to leave. Besides that, I was very eager to learn what they had found out.

Before anyone could say another word, Nurse Grangard returned. "I thought you would have left by now? I have other patients, you know," she said matter of fact like, with her back to the open door. "Now, on your way."

We didn't need to hear another word. I got up off the bed for the first time in a long while. I stood for a moment to catch my balance. But I was young, so it didn't take long. Once I was stable, the four of us walked quickly by Nurse Grangard—toward freedom.

"Nice and easy Cooper B. I wouldn't want you to fall and end up back in that bed," Nurse Grangard told me.

"No ma'am, neither would I," I responded with an expression of gratitude on my face for all she had done for me. "Thank you."

Soon after, I returned to the boy's common room to what felt like a hero's welcome. My classmates were patiently awaiting my return to congratulate me on my recovery. There were even faces I hadn't seen before, likely upperclassmen who stopped in to see who this boy was that survived a vicious attack. Serra was right, they had obviously been talking about my near-death experience and wanted to hear firsthand what had happened.

"Glad you aren't dead, Cooper," Bolliver told me as he patted me on the back.

Aria may have pointed out the fact that Bolliver couldn't have been the one I followed into the Nemus Garden, but I still had an uneasy feeling about him. There was something about Bolliver that made the hairs on the back of my neck stand tall. I truly hoped I was just over reacting. I had to put it behind me.

"Thank you, Bolliver," I told him—still unable to shake that feeling.

"Where did they get you?" Gwillian asked, examining me from head to toe. "Did they bite off any of your fingers? I heard they like fingers. Is that true?"

"Um, no I don't think so," I said, pulling my hand away from Gwillian who had taken hold of it to count each finger. "They mostly scratched and clawed at me."

"Come on now, give him some space guys," said Serra,

stepping in to save me from the onslaught of questions. "Let's let Cooper get some rest."

I knew Serra was just telling everyone that to get the four of us alone. After all, I had been getting plenty of rest in the infirmary. It didn't bother me that my big return was cut short. I was okay with the room thinning out so I could find out more about Serra and Aria's trips to the History of Archives.

When the last of our classmates left the room, we took a seat on the couch, huddling close together as though we had a guarded secret to share.

"I thought they'd never leave," said Miles.

"Okay, so what did you find out?" I asked the girls with great anticipation.

"Well, not a whole lot," said Aria. "Aurora talks in riddles half the time when you ask questions she doesn't want to answer or isn't allowed to tell us."

"What do you mean, not a whole lot?" argued Miles. "You've been building this up like you found out the meaning of life or something."

"Let her finish," I said—assuming that there was something more worth hearing if she wanted to talk in private.

"Ya, Miles let me finish," Aria said with a roll of her eyes. "According to Aurora, about ten years ago, something was discovered where the capital once stood. What did she call it?"

"A Vestige," Serra answered.

"Ya, a Vestige. Apparently, this thing is like a relic or something and is very powerful. So powerful, the Absolutes fear it and are searching for it. From what I could tell, they're not the only ones looking for it."

"What is it?" I asked.

Aria lifted her shoulders and Serra leaned in.

"No one knows. But rumor has it that Chancellor Adimus set off to the ruins of Imperium to recover it, and since then, no one has heard anything about it or even seen it since. It just disappeared—without a trace."

"Isn't that about the time you were found, Coop?" Miles asked.

"Ya, I guess so. But what would that have to do with me?"

"Well, Aurora gave a clue that Chancellor Adimus wasn't alone. With a little persuasive questioning, Aurora let it slip that whoever was with Chancellor Adimus, disappeared as well," said Aria.

"Like they died or something?" Miles asked.

Aria and Serra both shrugged. It was obvious they didn't have all of the answers to our questions and that Aurora gave them information in small bits and pieces. My mind began to race. It really didn't make any sense. What did I have to do with any of that, or was it just a coincidence that I ended up on Earth about the same time this relic was found?

"Or maybe, your parents were with him, Coop?" said Miles, adding to the list of unanswered questions.

Serra nodded her head feverishly. "That's what we thought too. Maybe, when Chancellor Adimus went to recover this Vestige, your parents went with him, and something terrible happened. Then, Chancellor Adimus sent you away to protect you.

"Everyone knows that Chancellor Adimus doesn't trust the

Absolutes, and I've heard there's a secret order that is plotting against them. These people say the Absolutes aren't who they claim to be." Serra looked around the empty room—and lowered her voice. "Some even say, Chancellor Adimus is the head of that order."

"That's what he was telling Councilman Tardivel that day. He said, *you know the truth*," I told Aria and Miles. "What's the truth though?" I asked, now speaking to Serra.

"Dunno, my parents won't talk about it. They say it's very dangerous to even repeat what some believe when it comes to the Absolutes."

"Okay, but why would he protect me then?" I asked. "I was just a baby."

"People were disappearing all over, according to Aurora," said Aria quietly.

Aria spoke in a way that made me believe she was afraid to speak out against the Absolutes. Doing so, would cause them to Fold right into our room—snatching her. "What if your parents were two of those that simply vanished?"

"Or maybe they have it and are keeping it safe?" Serra added.

I stood up and began pacing the room. Thoughts fluttered in my head. If this Vestige was hidden somewhere, and the Absolutes wanted it, then Chancellor Adimus wouldn't just leave it unattended—easily found. He must have put it in the hands of someone he trusted. If my parents traveled with him to recover it, then he would most certainly have trusted them.

"Then that's it—" I said.

"What's it?" asked Miles.

It was simple. I stopped and turned to face my closest friends. "We have to find this *Vestige*. If my parents have it, then I will find them at the same time."

As soon as the words left my mouth, I realized it sounded far easier than it would be to locate this relic. But if that meant finding my parents, then I would stop at nothing to set off and look.

I stepped toward my friends, hoping to get a sense that they too thought this was the best idea, the only way to get the answers I needed. Surely, they would be just as excited at the idea that we would once and for all solve the mystery. The mystery behind the boy who was left alone on that desolate highway so many years ago—but they just stared at me with blank expressions.

Slowly, they began looking back and forth to one another.

"How do you suppose we do that?" Miles asked.

Other than knowing it was the right thing to do—I hadn't thought that out quite yet. We were in a strange place, and I couldn't imagine where we would begin to look. Even if we had an idea, this relic would most likely not be on the school grounds. Since we were just students, we couldn't go too far. At most, we were probably allowed to visit Serra's home.

"I got it," said Serra. "We'll look for it during the *Scavenger Hunt*."

"Scavenger hunt?" asked Miles—intrigued.

"Yes. Every year Grayson has a scavenger hunt at the start of the second semester. You're given clues to certain items that you must set off to find. Most of the students that stay back during breaks are usually the ones who find everything. It's cheating, if you ask me," said Serra, drifting off into her thoughts. "Anyway, those with the most, are given extra credit to be applied to their overall scores for the year. Helps them pass their required Torts."

"Torts?" Aria asked.

"Yes, Torts. It's the points you earn at the end of your term to make you eligible to move onto the next year," said Serra.

"You're going to need that, Miles," said Aria, sarcastically.

"I'd kill it," Miles said, leaning back, folding his arms.

"But how does that help us?" I said—not quite as impressed with the idea as Serra was. "That's great and all for Miles, but how does that help get us out of Grayson? I'm sure the things that everyone is looking for are right here at school."

"Who said anything about just looking here at the school? It would be a good excuse for us to leave and not be expected back right away. Then, we will go wherever we need to in order to find your parents," Serra responded.

"Okay, but how do we leave the school? We're trapped on a giant island," Aria said.

"Hmmm, good point. I haven't thought that far," Serra added, scratching her bright pink hair. "My parents aren't going to be home during break, so we can't go there…"

Aria sat upright. "Who needs to know your parents won't be home?" she said. "We will just tell Ms. Pedigree that's where we're going. How is she going to find out anything different?"

"I guess they wouldn't," said Serra, with a look of concern. "Are you saying we would lie?"

"Ya," Aria quickly answered.

"Great, Aria," said Miles, shaking his head. "You're a terrible influence on Serra. Turning her into a delinquent and all."

I hated to agree with Miles, but I did. "Miles is right. You don't have to do this if you aren't comfortable with it," I added, hoping she wouldn't take advantage of my offer to get out of a small white lie.

Serra looked as though she was studying a map of the arctic ocean, navigating her route to land after months at sea. Then, with a grin from ear to ear, she gave her answer, "I'm in!"

CHAPTER TWELVE

PARTY PLANNERS

Over the next few weeks, I was barely able to concentrate on my studies. I kept wondering what we were going to find when we set off to look for my parents and the Vestige. Miles, however, spent his time telling all of our other second-year classmates about his favorite holiday on Earth—*Halloween*.

Word spread like wildfire throughout Grayson Academy. Everyone wanted to learn more about All Hallows Eve's ghostly stories and the costumes we wore, but more importantly—about the candy we collected once a year from homes throughout the neighborhoods we visited. The only problem was, we did not have neighbors here, and that was going to be our biggest hurdle. *Where* were we going to trick-or-treat?

The answer to our riddle came from an unlikely source. Chancellor Adimus. He was pleased with how quickly we made new friends and how we shared our earthly experiences with others, and he wanted to help. He spoke with his Pedagogues, and they agreed that for one night, they would allow students in the

restricted area of the school that was reserved for our Pedagogues only. We would be permitted to knock on doors for a
few hours on the night Miles's watch read October 31st.

"That is great news!" Aria told Miles.

"I know. But what are we going to go as?" Miles asked the
both of us as we sat in the dining hall eating our breakfast. "It's
not like there is a costume shop around the corner to check out."

"We will just have to be creative, Miles. I'm sure we can figure out something to dress up as," I said.

Miles sat quietly, staring off into the giant, round, glass ceiling above us. "I think I will go as a zombie. I always liked dress-
ing up like a zombie."

Serra looked at Miles, void of any expression. "What is a
zombie?" she asked.

Miles's eyes widened. His look said it all—how could anyone
not know what a zombie is? In the weeks past, Miles had taken
a great deal of time explaining the concept of Halloween to Serra
and the others. But he would have to forgive her ignorance on
this particular subject—after all, they probably had never seen
any dead Alyssiums roaming the streets of Elise before. But he
didn't. In typical Miles fashion, he was quick to point out her
lack of knowledge with Earth's nostalgic need for gore.

"What is a zombie? Are you kidding me? The dead, the walking dead! Come on. You gotta be joking!"

Serra still looked as though she had no idea what Miles was
trying to enlighten her with. She began spooning oatmeal into
her mouth, watching Miles throw his tantrum.

"Nope, I've got no idea what you mean," Serra responded

with a mouthful of mashed oats.

Miles's eyes darted left then right, and he set his sights on three Bollcrees as they passed their head Pedagogue, making their way into the dining hall.

"Mr. Versarius and his mindless followers. That's what they look like," Miles said, pointing to the group.

The head of the Bollcrees was Pedagogue Crassus Versarius. He was tall, skeletal, and pale, with a look that was beyond approach—far more terrifying than Theodore or any of his cranks. He was draped in a long crimson red robe—matching that of his seventh-year believers.

Mr. Versarius glared wickedly at the red headed boy.

It appeared as if the Bollcrees Pedagogue did not like being pointed at or being the subject of anyone's tale. With a large gulp, Miles was quick to turn away and focus back on Serra, sliding down into his seat.

"Nope, still don't know what you're talking about," Serra responded.

"Zombies are people that crawl out of their graves after they've died and then walk around," I told Serra in the simplest way possible.

"Why do they walk around?" she asked.

"Looking for someone living… to eat their brains. They like brains," Aria added.

Serra stopped chewing. The idea of someone eating brains didn't seem to sit well with her or her breakfast. "Brains?" Serra turned to Miles, unable to swallow the last spoonful she consumed. "Why—why would they eat someone's brain?"

"Cause they're zombies, that's why," said Miles in a ghoulish tone.

Serra sat quietly for a moment. Thinking—about what, I would never have guessed. "I want to be a *zombie*," she said as she began chewing rapidly once again.

"Well, we still have a couple of days to decide. I'm not sure what I'll dress up as. Maybe a Nemus?" I added.

Everyone got a chuckle out of that idea—everyone that is except Aria. Throughout the rest of our first meal of the day, Aria kept to herself, not joining in any of our silly conversations about nothing important.

We finished our breakfast and hustled through the halls of Grayson to head to our classes. Now that Miles and I finally knew what Serra and Aria were off doing on their own, we were back together as a group. But I could tell Aria had something on her mind, and it had nothing to do with me.

"What's going on, Aria? Is everything okay?"

"Nothing," she replied, walking a bit faster.

"But you're awfully quiet," I pointed out, catching back up to her.

Aria gave me her infamous look of "mind your own business." I had known her for almost a year and had come to learn when something was bothering her, but at the same time, I had also learned when and when not to push this spunky, dark-haired girl and just drop the subject.

"Oh okay, well… What are you going to dress up as for Halloween?" I asked.

"I don't celebrate Halloween."

"What? Why not?"

"It's a dumb day, and I don't have anything to celebrate. That's why," she said with fire in her eyes.

Aria was obviously upset about something, but she was my best friend. If she didn't want to celebrate Halloween, then neither would I. As much as I wanted to, I owed her that much. Even if it meant missing out on gorging myself on chocolate, and other unworldly sweets.

"Okay, then we won't celebrate it," I said, walking off to my lessons in the Art of Ambriose.

Aria remained frozen in the spot I had just left her, before speaking softly, "It's my birthday."

I stopped dead in my tracks. How could I have not known? I guess in some ways we were still strangers. I turned back to my friend.

"Your birthday is coming up? On Halloween? That's great! We can throw you a birthday party and then go trick or treating—"

"—No, that's okay. Don't make a big deal out of it, Coop," she said. "No one has really ever done anything for me on that day so there's no sense in starting now."

"Are you kidding me? Of course, we're going to make a big deal out of it," I told her, excited to learn something new about her. "This year will be different. I promise."

Aria stood still, looking at the flagstone below her feet, then slowly her eyes met mine as her lips quivered in the corners of her mouth, "Really?"

"Yup."

"Thank you."

She wiped what I bet was a tear of joy from her cheek, then turned and ran off.

I stood there for a moment, as I watched Aria catch up to Miles. They were heading off to their class together, language arts or something boring like that, and suddenly—my heart began pounding hard against my chest. I was only eleven. How was I going to prepare a birthday party for my best friend in less than two days? The answer came in the form of a pink-haired girl, just as spunky as ever—Serra.

"I need your help," I told Serra in a flustered voice.

"Sure, Coop. Whatever ya need."

We walked to class, and I explained to Serra about what I had discovered. It was then I learned on Alyssum, they didn't celebrate the same way we did with cakes, gifts, and streamers.

"It's going to be a great night," Serra promised me, as we reached Ms. Pedigree's classroom. "Don't worry about a thing, Coop. I will take care of it."

I had a strange sinking feeling in the pit of my stomach about leaving the party planning to someone that had never actually celebrated a birthday before. At least not the way we did back on Earth. Then again, I had never planned a party myself, so I had to give her the benefit of the doubt.

The following morning, I was abruptly awakened by Miles. He had torn two holes in a white T-shirt and placed it over his head. Not exactly what I would call a terrifying mask, being he had the head of a white-sheeted ghost and the body of a shirtless eleven-year-old. Miles was already celebrating Halloween a day early.

"Boo," he said to me.

"Good morning, Miles."

"Hey, Coop—how did you know it was me?" he asked, as he removed the shirt revealing his mangled red hair.

I ignored him and gently shoved him out of my face. While Miles dreamt of ghouls and goblins, I tossed and turned—thinking about Aria and her birthday, praying that Serra was able to do some research on what exactly she needed to make this a great night for Aria.

The replicator was the solution to a cake, but gifts couldn't be generated, and we had to find something to give to Aria as a present. The real question was, what would an eleven-year-old girl want? Again, Serra had assured me that she would take care of those details, so I needed to focus on what was important to Miles—what costume I would wear for Halloween.

I skipped breakfast and headed straight to my Art of Ambriose class to meet Serra. She wasn't there yet. Beads of sweat formed on my forehead, and my fingers began to twitch. Maybe she couldn't find a gift or couldn't convince anyone to come to the birthday or Halloween party. I heard so many stories of kids sitting at an empty table with no gifts or friends on their special day. I should know, that was me.

Finally, Serra came in.

"Everything is taken care of for tomorrow."

"Really? I mean, that's great! I knew I could count on you," I replied, trying to sound as though I had never doubted her ability. "So… what did we get her for a gift?"

Serra reached into her pocket and pulled out a blue, button-sized object. Are you kidding me? What kind of gift is that? We all know the bigger the better when it comes to gifts. Aria just might hate it—and her day will be ruined because of me.

"Um, what is it?"

"A beacon chip," Serra replied. "She can tell it who she wants to be able to find her *anywhere,* and they will always be able to track her. Mom and Dad gave me one when I first started Grayson. A bit intrusive if you ask me, but at least she can decide on her own who she wants to know where she is at all times."

I stand corrected—Aria is most definitely going to hate it. But there was no time to find something else. It would have to do.

Students began to fill the empty chairs in the classroom as Ms. Pedigree took to the center of the class. With the tip of her forefinger, she prevented her glasses from falling off of her nose—then, she cleared her throat to capture the attention of her unruly class. Her upright stance and narrow stare meant she had something important to discuss with the class.

"Now children. I am sure you all are quite aware that tomorrow we will be celebrating what is known as Hallows Eve," she said.

The class began to clap and cheer, causing Ms. Pedigree to raise her hand in protest so she could continue.

"This is a tradition on Earth that originated with the ancient Celtic Festival of Samhain. During this event, humans would dress in costumes and light giant fires to create a barrier between the living and the dead. A way to ward off ghosts if you will—"

"—Excuse me, Ms. Pedigree?" interrupted Panera Tudore, a clumsy looking girl with a ponytail and thick black-framed glasses. "What is a ghost?"

"Ahh, yes, a ghost," Ms. Pedigree began her explanation. "Very good question, Panera. A ghost is what Earth humans refer to as the souls of their previous form, that walk amongst the living. Although they are transparent, I believe—so I am not sure how anyone sees them... Nonetheless, a splendid story indeed."

An outburst of jabbering and laughter erupted in class.

"Quiet please, thank you kindly. In any case, that tradition soon converted into what is known as *Halloween* to most on Earth. And tomorrow is the day that it is observed on Earth's calendar," she continued. "The typical way to pay homage to this event is for adults to provide the children who are dressed in a disguise with sweet candies. Which we shall do for those of you willing to participate—and if you are undecided, I implore you to do so."

Chatter filled the air once again. It sounded as though the majority of the class was excited, and most of them had already heard about how this night was meant to be celebrated from Miles.

Ms. Pedigree cleared her throat, a little louder this time. She began walking up and down the aisles of her classroom until she came to rest behind her desk. She reached down and lifted an object up into plain view—placing it on her desktop. It was a large orange pumpkin.

"This my fine children is my personal favorite—it's called a pumpkin. Simple, right? On Earth they carve these into *jack-o-*

lanterns and place them out in front of their homes for all to see and admire."

Ms. Pedigree was peering over the giant squash on her desk, when Serra caught my attention, showing me her virtual tablet. There was an image scrolling across the screen. It was an invitation of sorts, inviting everyone to our Halloween party and Aria's birthday celebration.

An image of a zombie holding a brain was chasing a young girl with long, black, curly hair, dressed in a pink gown—I assumed to be Aria. Above them was the caption:

COME JOIN US IN THE SECOND-YEAR BOY'S GATHERING ROOM FOR A GHOULISH GOOD TIME!

At the end of the chase, the screen flashed:

ARIA TURNS 12!

I loved it. When I gave her my nod of approval, she sent it out to every Graysonian in the school, except for Aria, of course. Serra had made her first invitation, and it was evident in her gleaming smile—she was proud of her efforts. Now we would just have to wait until sundown tomorrow to see if anyone would attend.

Ms. Pedigree motioned her hand over the orange fruit on her desk and portions of the flesh caved in—leaving three triangles for eyes and a nose. Then, a mouth appeared last. The lights in the room dimmed, and the eyes, mouth, and nose began to glow.

She had just transformed her first jack-o-lantern, and I will have to admit it was one of the coolest things I had ever seen with my own two eyes.

"Oh marvelous, marvelous indeed," Ms. Pedigree said, as she rapidly clapped her hands together. The lights came back up—and her moment of glee ended. "Oh dear, I must press one more issue per Chancellor Adimus. There is a terrible tradition on this day. It is known as the *trick*. I know I do not have to remind you that you are not to indulge in this particular activity. Doing so would regrettably result in points taken away from you on your yearly Torts. Points I'm afraid to say that some of you are in desperate need of."

There was some mumbling in the classroom, mostly from the boys and girls you would have expected to hear from. Those kids like Miles, that needed all the help they could get.

"For today's assignment, we shall all make our own jack-o-lanterns," said Ms. Pedigree.

As we made our way to the front of the class to retrieve our pumpkins, I leaned over to Serra and whispered, "Those are great."

"Thanks, Coop. I think we should have a great turn out. Almost everyone I talked to will be there. Mostly for the candy, but Aria too."

I wished they would all be there just because of Aria, but I understood. We were new, and even though we were second-year students, this was only our first year at Grayson Academy. Regardless, I had a plan to celebrate. Celebrate Aria and the day she was brought into another world—light-years away.

CHAPTER THIRTEEN

AN ALL HALLOWS EVE BIRTHDAY

The day we had been waiting for had finally come. There was a sense of excitement in the air from all around. Both the boys and girls were in the common room, holding up different articles of clothing discussing what could be made out of what. Even our Famulus, Avantha, was getting into the spirit. There was no doubt this was a great day, even more so because it fell on our three-day break. Through the crowd, I could see Miles. He seemed to be the ambassador of the holiday, answering questions, and thoughtfully sharing his expertise.

Miles must have gotten up at first light, or he hadn't slept at all so he could lend his knowledge to the others. It was nice to see him fitting in so well—bouncing from one group to another.

"Cooper!" the redheaded Ambassador of Halloween shouted out in my direction.

Miles held in his hands a torn-up class robe. I didn't want to guess how Chancellor Adimus would feel about Miles destroying school property, but I remember being told by Mr. Martin once:

It's easier to ask forgiveness than it is to get permission.

"Have you decided what you're going to be tonight?" Miles asked excitedly.

"No, not yet. I am having a hard time deciding to tell you the truth."

I looked outside the window and witnessed thick, dark, and menacing clouds—settling low upon the peaks of the great school. In all the time I had been at Grayson Academy, I had only seen brilliant blue skies during the day and clear nights with bright stars peppered high above. "It's a good day for Halloween," I told him.

As the morning turned into the afternoon, Serra arrived with Aria. They weren't dressed in their costumes yet—but they seemed to be in good spirits nonetheless. I looked over at the pink-haired girl, and she gave me a thumbs up behind Aria's back. I knew she was ready to put our plan into action, but what really impressed me was how well a group of kids kept the party for Aria a secret. They were either on board or had no interest in helping us make this a special day for my dear friend.

The hair on my neck stood up as Bolliver made his way over to the four of us.

"Do you think the Pedagogues will all have candy for us tonight?" he asked.

"If not, they'll get a trick—won't they Miles?" replied Quentin Liemeer, joining our private gathering. Quentin was a fourth-year student and was already taller than the seventh-years. "Isn't that what we do if they don't give out any treats?"

"Well, technically yes, but it's not really done that way," said Miles. "I think it would be best to accept the fact they didn't give you anything and move onto the next."

"Besides, Chancellor Adimus made it clear that we were not to pull any funny business while we were out tonight—or this will be the first and last time we do this," added Gwillian, listening in as he made his way into the group.

"Always the worrywart aren't you, Gwillian?" said Quentin in a condescending voice.

For a moment, I thought Quentin would try and persuade us to do something that would surely hurt our overall Torts this year, but he smiled and agreed it was best not to ruin it for anyone else.

Quentin walked away, right through a Spectral of Chancellor Adimus that had appeared in the middle of our room. I think it took Quentin by surprise the most. He leapt from the ground, nearly toppling over. Admittingly, I had to agree with his reaction. I was not quite used to these sudden visits.

"Greetings Graysonians," boomed Chancellor Adimus. "As you are all quite aware, tonight shall be open to all who wish to participate in Halloween. Shortly after sundown, the bells will ring three chimes to commence your time has begun. For two hours, you will be granted access to areas normally reserved for your Pedagogues, to seek a fortune in sweets.

"Unfortunately, all good things must come to an end, and that will be known when you hear three more chimes. Please enjoy, and be on your best behavior."

Chancellor Adimus vanished into thin air—but before he

did, I felt as though he looked right at me. It was crazy to think that way, and I am sure many others had gotten the same impression. In any case, his words resonated in my mind, and I was slightly on edge, wondering whether anyone would try to ruin our night.

Those thoughts soon dissipated, and I concentrated on what I believed to be the most important issue—Aria's birthday party. Now that she had left the room with Serra to get into her costume, I had a moment to decorate. Luckily, Avantha was there to help and help she did.

Avantha apparently had visited the library and found some books on Earth's cultures. She prepared everything from streamers to party foods. With the assistance of the food replicator from our room, Aria's cake had been decorated with white buttercream frosting layered over a decadent chocolate cake, with tiny purple flowers around the edges, and her name written in large, bright-colored letters. It all looked amazing, and I couldn't have been happier. The only problem was—other than those typically found in our gathering room, no one had shown up yet.

I took a deep breath and went into my room. Miles had just finished applying face paint to his pale, freckled skin—making himself resemble something straight out of a horror film. Miles looked fantastically gruesome.

"Hurry up, Coop!" Miles shouted at me as he tore the shoulder of his school uniform sleeve. "Serra will be back anytime with Aria, and you still don't have your costume ready yet."

"I'm not concerned about that right now! There's no one here yet, and I promised Aria this would be the best birthday she has ever had. But if no one shows up, she'll be devastated."

"It's going to be okay, Coop. They'll show—just get your costume on," said Miles, reassuringly.

I had no choice but to trust in his words. Kids back home were cruel, and I've yet to fully experience that here on Alyssum. Then again, they had never been invited to a birthday party, and they knew just as much about birthdays as they did Halloween.

After searching my closet for something to wear, I settled on a black cloak that hung next to my uniform. It could be scary I suppose—if you thought about a group of kids roaming the school halls all dressed in black. With a little white face paint from Miles's clutter of make-up, I could pull something together—quickly.

I finished applying the pasty white cream on my face—adding a little touch of black under my eyes. I rushed back out into the gathering room. My heart was pounding. I was overcome with fear that I would begin to sweat, and the make-up I just applied would run down my cheeks.

I gasped and couldn't believe my eyes. The gathering room was packed with not only second-year students but classmates from all years. I shouldn't have doubted Serra. More than that, I shouldn't have doubted the children at Grayson Academy. Not only did they come to help celebrate Aria, but they were all dressed stunningly. It was every kids' dream who was born on the day of Halloween—a costume party!

"You look great!" Miles told me as he examined me up close and personal. "You're the creepiest skeleton I've ever seen."

"Thanks, Miles," I responded, happy to hear he approved.

"Don't they all look Spooktacular?" Miles said, in a poor attempt to sound scary.

He was right though. Some of the costumes were neat. One girl had painted her face to be what I would imagine a cat on this planet would look like. Spotted markings, white mouth, and even whiskers to top it off. Another boy was painted to look like a Nemus. I immediately decided I would stay clear of him—after I complimented him, of course. They all looked fantastic, except for Bolliver Winnington. I shouldn't have been surprised at the fact he wore a red hooded cloak—mimicking the Bollcrees. Regardless, by the look of the room, nearly everyone felt that Miles's disguise as a zombie was by far the best choice, including Serra.

Serra had walked in just before Aria, who was dressed in a long pink gown, wearing a tiara atop her black, curly hair that had been put up for the occasion. She looked like a princess. Before I could make my way to her and tell her how great she looked, everyone surrounded her—and began wishing her a happy birthday. The look of joy upon her face removed every reservation I had about whether or not we would be able to pull this off in such short notice.

Serra moved Aria through the crowd like she was royalty, introducing her to other Graysonians from all years—many of them I had yet to meet myself. Aria was on cloud nine, and she played the role of a princess well.

"Cooper, this is amazing!" Aria told me when she finally found her way to me. "You did all of this?"

"Well, no," I said—wishing I could take all of the credit.

"Serra did most of it. But I helped with the decorations... Sort of."

"Thank you," Aria told me softly. "It's the best birthday ever."

Success. Those were the only words I wanted to hear from Aria that night. Knowing I helped my best friend have a special birthday meant the world to me. Miles, on the other hand, only wanted to hear the bells chime three times consecutively—sounding the commencement of Halloween and trick-or-treating.

He didn't have to wait long. The bells began reverberating throughout the school. The sounds of cheers drowned out the last two chimes, but we faintly heard them and knew it was time to head out. With our pillowcases in hand, we followed a group of zombies and others out the doors.

Chancellor Adimus must have done some research of his own. Holograms of candles lined the hallways and lit the way through the corridors. The candles even had streams of wax dripping down the sides. Ms. Pedigree added a touch of Halloween herself with jack-o-lanterns strung throughout the corridors adding a bit more allure. Another fine example of just how great the Academy was.

"Trick-or-treat," echoed all around, as each student made their way from one door to the next in the areas commonly off limits to students. Off in the distance, you couldn't miss the distinct voice of Ms. Pedigree—complimenting each child who had approached her room. When it was our turn, she seemed just as excited to see us as we were to see her. She was dressed in a black cat-like outfit, ears and all.

"Trick-or-treat!" shouted Ms. Pedigree.

"Actually, we're supposed to tell you that," said Miles, arms outstretched holding his pillowcase in front of him.

"Oh dear, you are right," Ms. Pedigree responded while leaning in closer to the red-headed zombie, "but truthfully, I wanted to be part of this marvelous experience too. I hope you don't mind?"

"Not at all," said Aria with a curtsey.

Ms. Pedigree filled our bags, and off we went down the hallway we had never visited before.

Time flew by, and I felt it had to be nearing the end of our adventure. Soon, the bells would ring once again, and the night would sadly be over.

Windows began to rattle and the stone walls rumbled, as blinding bursts of light erupted from all around inside the narrow hallway. The weather outside had turned for the worse, causing the lights in the school to flicker—adding a dramatic effect to the evening's festivities.

Far away from the others where the candles ended, someone dressed in a red hooded cloak disappeared around a corner. The student had made its way down a hallway that had been considered off limits.

"Did you see that?" I asked.

"Ya, wasn't that the costume Bolliver was wearing," Miles responded, taking a piece of candy from his bag.

"Where do you think he's going?" I asked.

Miles wasn't nearly as curious as I was. He was already reaching for another piece of candy that he had procured from his night out.

"Well, wherever he is going he's not supposed to be there—I can tell you that," Serra added. "Come on, let's tell him to get out of there before he ruins it for everyone else."

We made our way to the end of the hall where Bolliver had just stepped out of sight. As we turned the corner, he was gone. Left was a long empty hallway that was void of any holographic candles or carved pumpkins, making it clear, this was not part of the path set out by Chancellor Adimus.

"Well, where did he go?" Aria asked.

Up ahead, a few doors lined both sides of the hall. Any one of them could have been used by Bolliver to disappear behind. We decided to keep pushing forward. If Bolliver was up to no good, I wanted to see firsthand and prove to my friends he had been the one responsible for my attack in the Nemus Garden.

The building shook again as thunder crashed outside. When I was younger, I was taught that you could count the time between lightning and thunder to gauge how close a storm was. Considering the lights flickered at each crash of thunder, the storm must have been on top of us.

Suddenly, with another grand eruption of thunder, the power was lost, leaving us in the dark hallway. Blind and alone.

"Oh great," Miles said, in a higher than normal pitch. "I can't see anything."

"Give it a second," Serra told him.

The lights came back on, but we were no longer alone. At

the far end of the desolate hallway was the figure we had been searching for. I felt my heart pounding in my throat. My palms began to sweat. I had a bad feeling about him.

"Hey there!" Serra shouted down the hallway. "You know we're not supposed to be down here?"

Serra began to take a few steps toward the ominous figure and against my better judgment, we followed her. I could feel the warmth from Miles pressing up against me.

"Great costume—Absolute, right?" Serra added, trying to make small talk.

I no longer felt the presence of Miles against my back.

"Hey guys?" said Miles as he took a step back—his voice suddenly changed. "Is it me, or is he floating in midair?"

Miles was right. Just below the bottom of the blood red cloak was a gap between the floor and where his shoes would have been. But that would be impossible. Then again, we were on a distant planet, so who were we to decide what was and what was not possible.

Whispers filled my head once again. I froze with fear. Was this unsettling and frightful looking figure behind the murmuring voices I've been hearing? The cloak that shrouded the figure in darkness began to sway—and he or it began floating toward us.

That was our cue to turn and run away. Run as far as we could. Aria grabbed my arm and pulled me with her. Otherwise, I may not have been able to move on my own free will.

No. No way. A wall now stood where the entrance to the hallway once was. A terrifying thought flooded my mind that we had become entombed—and we were surely going to die. The lights went out again, as lightning let out a cry of anger in the sky above the school. Aria screamed, causing my heart to nearly pump out of my chest.

The lights regained their strength, and the figure had cut its distance between us in half. We were trapped between the sudden appearance of a daunting wall on one side and a blood curdling fiend on the other.

"In here!" Miles shouted as he pushed open one of the hallway doors directly alongside us. I was so preoccupied with the thought of dying that I didn't see the potential escape route right next to us.

The four of us piled in through the door to salvation. However, it was merely a supply closet—just large enough for the four of us to hide. As I stood in the closet breathing rapidly, I realized this was probably the worst hiding place we could have found.

As best we could, we stood perfectly still. Deep inside me, there was a small glimmer of hope—since we couldn't see him, he couldn't see us. It was a long shot, but for a moment, it made me feel we had a chance. It gave me hope we weren't going to live out our last precious moments stuck in a closet.

A few seconds later, the door handle jiggled. Miles grabbed my shoulder and pulled me closer to him—shielding himself from what was waiting for us outside the door. In his defense, he used his free hand to guard Aria and Serra, who were trapped with us.

The door slowly began to open—we did nothing to pull it

shut. That would have at least been a feeble attempt to give us a few more minutes to live. As light entered the dark room, a tall silhouette filled the narrow doorway.

"Well, what do we have here?" Mr. Versarius spoke slowly in a cold whining voice.

I was not sure if I was glad to see him, or if we stood a better chance with the ghoulish cloaked figure. Truthfully, he was nearly as frightening as the other.

"Why would the four of you be in here?" he continued to ask, taking a closer look at Aria, Miles, and me through his piercing squinted eyes. "Oh? *It's you*? I am sure Chancellor Adimus will not be pleased to learn his newest pet pupils were the first to break his rules."

Serra began her plea, "It's not our fault, Mr. Versarius. Honest, we were trying—"

"—Silence, child! I did not permit you to talk," growled Mr. Versarius. "I will not have you speak on behalf of these—*mutants*."

"What's the meaning of this, Crassus?" a voice bellowed from outside the closet. "Who are you speaking to?"

It was Mr. Bonabos. Never in my wildest imagination did I think I would be as glad as I was in that moment to see this massive orangutan.

"These students have found themselves outside of the permitted area for this ludicrous spectacle of an event," Mr. Versarius responded, stepping aside to allow him to view the four of us huddled in the closet. "I shall be taking them straight away to Chancellor Adimus for corrective behavior."

"For what? What's the matter with you? They haven't practiced that barbaric method in a millennium," Mr. Bonabos said, as he reached in gently escorting us out of the closet. "I'll take it from here."

"You will do no such thing—"

"—Good evening, Crassus."

Mr. Versarius seemed not too pleased at the interference by Mr. Bonabos, but he was no match for the imposing Pedagogue—and he stepped aside. Mr. Bonabos motioned down the hallway with his fur-covered paws, to where we had entered. The wall that had blocked our escape was now gone. We all looked puzzled at the large opening that once stood between us and death.

As we made our way down the permitted area of the Academy, three chimes could be heard echoing throughout the school. Halloween was officially over, and we were about to meet our fate for breaking the rules, or so we thought.

"I trust you four can find your way back to your common rooms from here," Mr. Bonabos told us as he approached the door to his room. He peered over his spectacles, "That pompous ass will likely assume you have been properly disciplined for your infraction, and we will allow him to think just that. Good night."

He walked into his room and closed the door behind him, leaving the four of us speechless. How would we explain to anyone what just happened? We walked in silence as we made our way back to our room. I was certain I wasn't the only one still feeling the effects of pure fear. But more than that, I had wondered if anyone else had heard the whispers. *Had I still been the only one who was being haunted by sounds from the abyss? Was I going crazy?*

"I'm not sure what just happened here, but those whispers are going to give me nightmares," said Serra, to my astonishment, just outside the girl's gathering room.

"You heard them too?"

"We all did, Coop," said Aria.

I was genuinely shocked and pleased I wasn't going crazy. My friends heard the voices that had been haunting me in my sleep. I still didn't know what they were or who they were from, but knowing they had shared in my experience was good enough for now.

Aria and Serra went into their rooms, as Miles and I headed to ours. Suddenly, a sense that I had forgotten something quickly overcame me, and I brushed my hand over my pocket—feeling what was to be given to Aria still kept safe in my pocket.

"Aria, wait!" I called back to her, before she shut the door.

"Yes, Coop?"

"I almost forgot," I told her as I pulled the gift out of my pocket. "Here you go."

"What is it?"

"It's your gift. You can open it later—happy birthday."

Aria looked it over and smiled. She appeared speechless. Never taking her eyes off her gift, she headed back into her room.

SNOW DAY

I sat on the floor in the room I shared with Miles—sliding my Wuicken back and forth with merely my thoughts. I found that I could achieve this without much effort anymore—something I am sure would make Ms. Pedigree pleased.

Outside the frost covered windows, snow fell from the sunless gray skies. Beyond the frame that once held a beautiful glass canvas of a sunlit scene painted in cool blues, was now dreary and void of any color. There was something about this time of year that brought on a feeling of sorrow, no matter where you lived. Our activities had been restricted to inside the walls of Grayson—only allowed to roam free outdoors for a short period of time. In the last couple of months, we were constantly reminded of how dangerous the unsympathetic air was, and how quickly we could succumb to the elements. The winter months on Alyssum were bitterly cold.

I had learned that winter was known as the tri-quartam, summer was the first quartam, fall was the second, and the spring months were the last quartam of the year. During the time Ms. Pedigree was teaching me all about the four seasons on Alyssum—it was dreadfully obvious she enjoyed the tri-quartam the most. Mainly because it allowed her to wear a thick black and white spotted coat. A coat that was a painful reminder of the first Nemus that attacked me the day I was introduced to those vulgar little creatures.

Miles was sitting on the bench just under the window. He was lost deep in thought—staring off into the horizon at Alyssum's first snowfall of the year.

"I've really never seen snow before you know. Growing up in Florida and all," he said—snapping out of his trance. "I want to go out and play in it. How about you, Coop?"

"You heard what Chancellor Adimus told the rest of the school—it's too dangerous," I told Miles—still fixated on my Wuicken. "Besides, it's nothing special. It's cold, and then it melts. When it does, you're wet and still cold."

"Who cares—I still want to go out and see for myself," Miles said, climbing out of the window sill. He walked over to his closet doors and looked inside. "There's gotta be something in here that will keep us warm."

Aria and Serra came barging into our room and leapt onto my bed. It was typical behavior for the two girls to just appear unannounced and make themselves comfortable in our space. I didn't mind that so much—except the time I was in my underwear still getting dressed. Even then, they simply ignored me and made themselves at home, banishing me to my closet to finish making myself presentable.

"Isn't the snow absolutely amazing?" asked Aria excitedly.

Amazing? I thought. Aria grew up in Colorado, so I know she had seen snow before, and it wasn't her first time like it was for Miles. I figured, of all people, Aria would be just as miserable at the sight of the white fluffy specks—that had grounded us to our rooms.

"What's so great about it?" I asked miserably.

"Gee Coop, why so moody?" Serra asked.

"It's snowing, and like I told Miles—we're not allowed outside. If we can't go outside, how are we going to get to your house to start looking for my parents?"

"Well, the snow won't last forever," she said reassuringly. "Besides we're still going to sneak away during the break, and we won't have to follow any rules then. That's when we will look for your mom and dad."

Serra was an optimist, never seeing a glass half empty but always half full, and that is what I had grown to love about her. I needed to trust in her and know that she wanted to discover my origins as much as I did. The same could be said for Aria— Miles, on the other hand, was still tossing clothes out onto the floor of our room in search of the perfect tri-quartam outfit.

"Don't forget the scavenger hunt. I really need to find whatever it is they tell us to so I can ace my classes," Miles added.

"You only get so many points, Red. And no matter how well you do, you aren't going to get enough to *ace* anything," Aria told him sarcastically.

"Hey, now! I'm not doing that bad," said Miles—still buried

deep in the closet.

"Not bad if you were a first year," said Serra.

"Whatever. So, when are they going to release the clues for this thing anyway? I've been mapping out the whole school preparing for it," said Miles, reappearing from inside the closet, holding a long heavy looking jacket.

"Should be anytime now," said Serra. "It'll appear on your Wuicken when the time comes, and you'll have till the end of the term to find it."

"Just be prepared for me to be the first to find mine," said Miles.

"If you say so," said Serra, turning back to me. "It might help us if we can get more information on this Vestige. Aurora isn't helping Aria and me, and I think she's figured out we sort of tricked her into telling us more than she should have."

Aurora may have been just a Spectral, but she was programmed with every emotion we had. She was vulnerable to making mistakes when it came to having a general conversation—if you knew how to ask the right questions. The fact she was imperfect, was the perfect part about her.

"What did you have in mind?" I asked—getting up off the floor and sitting on my bed.

"Why not ask Ms. Pedigree?" said Aria. "Maybe she will help you since it could mean finding the whereabouts of your mom and dad."

"Ya, Coop, Ms. Pedigree thinks you're the greatest," said Miles. "I bet she'd help us."

"You think she would?" I asked, pondering whether or not

Ms. Pedigree would make a good ally in our quest to find the truth—if she agreed to help that was.

"Why not?" Aria responded. "Hasn't she been following you for essentially your whole life? She's been with you as long as you can remember. I bet she was there the first time they found you."

"Ya, I guess so."

"Then she obviously knows. She knows what happened to your parents and whether or not they are alive protecting this Vestige thingy—" Aria said—stopping herself in mid-sentence. "I'm sorry, Coop. I didn't mean... I mean, they are alive. I just know it, and she knows it too."

"It's okay, Aria. I know what you meant," I told her as kindly as I could. I knew her words weren't meant to hurt me.

I had never really thought about just how long Ms. Pedigree had been in my life. Deep down inside I know she was there with me in Cooper, Maine, after I was found—alone. She is the first face I so vividly remember. Why I remember only her, is still uncertain.

"I think what Aria is trying to say is that Ms. Pedigree probably knows what happened and why you were sent to Earth. Which means, she knows a lot more about you than you think she does," said Serra.

"Just ask her," added Miles.

Serra looked at Miles for a brief moment and rolled her eyes—taking a deep breath, and letting out a hefty sigh. "You know, I hate when I have to say this, but Red is right. You just have to ask her."

In reality, it was a no brainer. Just ask the one person who could answer all of my questions at one time. It's not like I hadn't been thinking about doing it for so long. It just took a little help from my dear friends to give me the courage I needed. Besides, Ms. Pedigree would be easier to talk to than Chancellor Adimus. I was sure of it.

"Okay, I will," I said with a bit of enthusiasm. The idea of Ms. Pedigree being the one to shed some light on my very own mystery gave me a good feeling. "When?"

"Not today," Miles said, putting on his long, thick winter coat made of some sort of Alyssum wool. "Today, we are going to go outside so I can see what I've been missing—snow."

"Ya, I think we need to get out of here too. I'm getting all claustrophobic being stuck inside for so long," said Aria, to my surprise. I suppose I had hoped she would become the voice of reason and thwart Miles's request.

"I'm game," Serra chimed in—this much I had expected.

The four of us met up again in the hallway outside of our gathering rooms, all bundled up from head to toe with the warmest clothing we could find. Being that the girls had skirts for school uniforms, they had doubled up their knee-high socks in order to fend off the crisp air.

As we made our way through the halls to the doors leading outside, we were met by skeptical onlookers. Miles tried to brush them off by complaining how cold he was, and that he wished the school would turn up the heat. I am not sure anyone truly bought his lame excuse for being overly dressed, but no one said a word to us. Thankfully, being it was our three days off from our studies, not a single Pedagogue was in sight.

We stood at a two-story high doorway that led to the outside and the doors slowly creaked open, revealing the snow-covered courtyard. Miles stepped out first. His head tilted back as he caught small snowflakes on the tip of his tongue. He inched further outside, savoring every bit of this moment. I gazed endlessly, as I watched Miles take his first step onto the snow packed ground. It was light, fluffy, and undisturbed. His feet and ankles disappeared down into at least six inches of freshly made snow.

Miles turned and glanced at my admiration, free of any expression. He raised his arms out from his sides, and without a word—he let go.

His red hair waved through the air before he landed softly onto his back. Miles began to laugh as he fluttered his arms and legs, side to side.

"This is so amazing!" Miles shouted. "Look! I'm making a snow angel, Coop!"

I stood there and watched for a moment—allowing him his own time to feel what it was like to be a school student during the best part of winter—a snow day. I don't remember my first encounter with snow, but I am sure it would have looked a lot like his. I began to think about how I had tried to minimize this time of year and suddenly was overcome with sorrow for—

—*SMACK!*

What first began as a stinging sensation, quickly turned into a fiery one across my face—caused by a well packed snowball. A snowball that had made a direct hit onto my cheek. I turned to see who dared strike first, and I shouldn't have been surprised. It was Aria, bent over at the waist laughing uncontrollably, preparing a second snowball.

"Snowball fight!" Aria shouted out.

The four of us quickly spread out, taking sides on this battlefield of adolescence. I wound up becoming teammates with the one person in our group who likely had no idea what Aria was talking about—Serra. If she had never participated in this form of barbaric fun, she was a quick learner. Serra threw one snowball after another. All in the direction of Miles, who was doing everything he could to avoid the barrage of flying frozen projectiles. He stumbled—tripping over his own two feet—and flew through the air, landing directly on his nose in the fresh subzero powder.

"Time out!" Miles called out to Serra—who was relentless in her attack.

"Quit being a baby, Red!" Serra shouted back, unwilling to ease up on him.

The war we had waged led us quite a longways away from our school. We didn't care. We were once again having fun—experiencing childhood antics together.

With a truce agreed to, we walked alongside the barren trees. I began to question the warnings put out by our school officials on the dangers of the tri-season. Sure, it was cold, maybe even frostier than I had remembered winter being back home—but it wasn't completely intolerable.

Suddenly, a deafening roar from deep within the woods added a new sense of excitement. The ground shook, and a grumble resembling a locomotive thundered. Something was bearing down on the four of us and taking every leafless tree in its path along with it. Without forewarning, the air around us picked up speed—nearly toppling me over. A rolling wave of snow was making its way in our direction.

It was a tornado made of ice and sleet barreling right toward us, throwing unpacked snow fifty feet in the air. Why would Chancellor Adimus only warn us of the bitterly cold air, and not about this?

"Get back to the school!" Serra yelled out over the blowing wind. "Run!"

Serra only had to tell me once. As our legs carried us with purpose, my lungs began to burn from the chilled air. Off in the horizon, I could see the peaks of Grayson Academy—barely visible through the whiteout we were surrounded by.

It was no use. Aria, Serra, Miles, and I would never make it. Grayson was too far away, and the spiraling winds made of ice and snow were gaining on us, nipping at our feet. Our clothing whipped with such anger—swirling around our tiny bodies. My face began to crystallize, and we were losing the race of our lives. The tornado was now upon us, about to swallow us whole. Our bodies were about to be crumpled into twist ties made of flesh and bone.

I turned my head and glanced over my shoulder to get one last image of the phenomenon when it suddenly blew apart. Left in its wake were huge snowflakes gently falling to the ground. We all stopped. What could possibly have destroyed something so powerful?

The answer was bittersweet.

Standing on the balcony overlooking our escape route was Ms. Elsattera with her arms still extended—fingertips reaching out toward us. She had used an unseen and formidable force to save the four of us.

It was the first time I had found that Ms. Elsattera had an incredible ability with the Guild she possessed that I, nor any other second-year student had. I was in awe with what she had just done. Ms. Elsattera on the other hand, didn't look too pleased, and she wasn't alone. Students of all years had gathered at the window—witnessing our near fatal encounter.

"Children! Inside, now!" she shouted down to us.

I followed Aria, Serra, and Miles as they made their way back into the sanctuary within the walls of Grayson. I felt safe for the time being—until I spotted Bolliver, inside a lone window high up on one of the cathedral peaks, glaring down at the four of us.

I was certain this was no coincidence.

"Why couldn't you just do that? That thing Ms. Elsattera did?" Miles asked Serra, taking my attention away from the one responsible for our misfortune.

"She's a bit more powerful than I am, dummy," Serra said, irritated with Miles. "One day I hope I can be as strong as she——"

"—Shh, I think she's coming," I told them.

The heavy clanks against the floor heading our way silenced the two and their continuous bickering. A silhouette—on a collision course to run smack dab into the four of us—came into view.

"What in the world of Alyssum were you four thinking?" she demanded to know before she even reached us. "You could have been killed—"

"—It's my fault," said Miles quickly. "I wanted to see the snow. I made them come along, but they tried to talk me out of it... I didn't listen to them."

"How did you get through the front gates?" asked Ms. Elsattera—her fiery eyes fixed on Serra.

"They just opened, like they always do," Serra responded.

"That's not possible, young lady. The grounds have been secured to prevent such a thing from happening. So, tell me... how were the four of you able to get past what no one else could?"

"No, really they did, Ms. Elsattera. She's not lying," I said, placing myself in her terrifying glare—pleading for her to believe me.

The look in Ms. Elsattera's eyes began to cool. I had hoped she could see in my eyes I was telling the truth. We hadn't done anything to sneak out. We simply walked to the front doors, and they swung open for us as they normally did when they were closed. Her posture relaxed, and she turned her attention back to Miles.

Miles lowered his head. He was ready for the punishment that was surely about to be delivered. I watched, as Ms. Elsattera gathered her composure.

"Very well. You are grounded to your gathering rooms for the next two weeks. You are permitted only to leave for your meals and studies. Maybe that will give you enough time to think about why our rules are in place and why you, as students, are to follow them," Ms. Elsattera said, nearly out of breath.

I reached over and placed my hand on the back of my best friend—now wet from the melted snow. Providing him a sense that I had felt bad he had been the one punished for something easily avoided, had I been more outspoken with my concern to venture out in the weather. Aria and Serra must have felt the same, reaching out to Miles to provide their condolences as well. Even though they were mostly to blame for encouraging him to do so.

"The three of you should be consoling yourselves, as you too will be suffering the same consequence as your friend," said Ms. Elsattera.

I couldn't say I was shocked. The look on Serra's face, however, said she had been taken aback by Ms. Elsattera's decision. Serra began to speak—but she was met by a look from our Pedagogue that changed her mind for the better. It was the kind of look that screamed, *"make that two more weeks for talking back,"* without having to actually say it. Thankfully, Serra didn't challenge the decision of Ms. Elsattera. My mind filled with images of the powerful Pedagogue raising her arms, twinkling her fingers, and Serra dissipating into thin air.

One thing was for sure, and we would all have to agree, Ms. Elsattera's sentence was a fair one. The three of us participated in Miles's first encounter in the snow. For all intents and purposes, we were willing participants. Another thing was for sure—Miles would never forget his first snow day.

CHAPTER FIFTEEN

BREAKING AURORA

E very free moment for the next two weeks was spent either in our rooms or the boys gathering area. From the sounds of it, Serra and Aria were doing just fine, and in fact, seemed to be enjoying a little quality time with the other second-year girls. Miles and I, on the other hand, were growing restless.

Bolliver and Gwillian annoyingly made it a point to come in and sit down—then immediately would get up and leave, telling us something exciting was going on in different parts of Grayson. Making matters worse, Bolliver would invite all of the other boys to join him, leaving the two of us behind. There wasn't really anything going on of course, they were just rubbing it in that they could leave any time they wished—and we couldn't.

Word had spread about our little winter excursion. Some of our classmates thought we were courageous for our daring escape, while others believed we were selfish and had ruined any chance they would have had to go out and enjoy the tri-quartam weather for themselves.

In any case, I wasn't excited about either side knowing how we had snuck outside and would have preferred that none of them had known what we did. But like a small town, the minute you did anything out of the ordinary, the entire school heard about it, long before sunset.

Late in the evening, while everyone was asleep, I found myself longing for the nights where all four of us would sit around and share our stories, keeping each other distracted from some of the older students' shenanigans until it was time for bed. Thanks to Serra's birthday gift, I would lay awake, looking at the screen of my Wuicken. Watching the tiny red dot provided me a glimpse into Aria's whereabouts because Aria had chosen me as the guardian of her location beacon. I imagined the things we would be talking about had we not been banished to our rooms—only to visit with one another during meal times and classes that we shared.

The day finally arrived when Miles and I woke, knowing that after we walked out of the gathering room, we never had to return. The quarantine had finally been lifted. We had nowhere else to go, of course, but the idea we could stay away from the boys common room if we so desired felt pretty good.

We quickly dressed into our school uniforms and darted out of our rooms as fast as possible—nearly crashing into Aria and Serra out in the hallway.

"Free at last!" Miles yelled.

"You're so dramatic, Red," said Serra, as she whisked by.

"Ya well, I'm never going back in there until curfew from

this point forward," Miles responded. "If you had to smell Gwillian's body odor day in and day out, you'd feel the same way."

"Gross," said Aria—catching up to me. "Hey, Coop? Since we don't have to come straight back after the last period, are you going to stay behind and talk to Ms. Pedigree today?"

"I don't know."

"What do you mean you don't know? That was the plan— you gotta keep to the plan," said Serra.

"Ya, Coop. There are only two more days before break, and we won't get another chance before then. If you don't talk to her now, we'll aimlessly walk around trying to figure it out," said Aria.

"I know, I know, it's just that I think I will be nervous," I told them as we reached the dining hall.

"Then we'll help. After class is over, we will head to Ms. Pedigree's room and go in with you," said Miles—walking straight into Mr. Versarius.

Miles looked up and made eye contact with the most dreadful Pedagogue at the school. The red-head was speechless and stood with slumped shoulders and his mouth half-open, trying to form a sentence. Instead, only short gasps of air left his lips.

"Haven't you a closet to be hiding in, Mr. O'Malley?" Mr. Versarius said, in his usual chilling voice. "Preferably, back on Earth—where you belong?"

His minions, dressed alike in long blood red robes, began to chuckle at Mr. Versarius's attempt at insulting humor, but he didn't need their support. Slowly, Mr. Versarius raised his hand

—shushing them back to the mindless drones they were.

Miles finally formed a couple of words, but his voice remained broken. "Sorry, sir."

"Mind your step. All of you," snapped Mr. Versarius.

The Bollcrees Pedagogue swiftly passed us, with his seventh-year believers following him away from the dining hall.

"Making friends are ya, Red?" asked Serra.

"Bite me, Serra," said Miles walking away, trembling.

The morning passed like any other morning for the four of us. After breakfast, Serra and I had our morning studies together. Miles and Aria spent their time in their non-guilded classes. My mind was elsewhere, and I was in a daze for the entire session of the Art of Ambriose—dreading what was sure to follow. Knowing I would have to muster up all of the courage I could, in order to talk to Ms. Pedigree about my parents, and the Vestige. In terms of my parents, I had come so close on other occasions to do so but never had the needed nerve to follow through. This attempt would be different. This time my friends were going to be by my side.

"Dismissed, class," said Ms. Pedigree.

Those were probably the only words I heard during the entire class. I took in a deep breath and immediately began second guessing myself and my decision to involve this kind woman. I closed my Wuicken and sat up, turning to Serra. Her brows were raised, and her lips were pursed. Her expression didn't feed me the nourishing confidence I was desperately in need of. My skin became cold and clammy, and beads of sweat formed on my forehead. My knees were weak and were shaking uncontrollably—the room began to spin. I was about to pass out.

I had to pull it together.

Aria and Miles had finally made their way into our classroom, and they approached, taking their positions alongside me. A voice in my head told me I could do this—my subconscious was trying to give me the self-assurance I needed.

"Ms. Pedigree?" I said softly. "Can we speak with you for a minute?"

Ms. Pedigree looked up and seemed genuinely surprised at the four of us standing in front of her desk. She had been too preoccupied to notice me and Serra had not yet left. Let alone that Aria and Miles had made their entrance into her classroom.

"Well hello there, Miles and Aria. So good to see you indeed," said Ms. Pedigree. "How may I help you all on this wonderful tri-quartam day?"

This was the time. I had run this scenario in my head for months now. I had practiced just what I would say to her when I finally had the much-needed fortitude to ask.

"I… I mean, we—were wondering if you could help us with something. You see, Aria and Serra found out something, and I was hoping you could help us understand what it is," I said—unable to get to the point.

"Well, of course, my dear boy. What is it that is on your curious minds?" said Ms. Pedigree as she sat upright and clasped her hands together.

I stood motionless, staring at Ms. Pedigree through the cat shaped glasses she always balanced on the tip of her nose. I searched my mind for the words, the words that suddenly disappeared the moment the time came to share them.

"I got this, Coop," said Serra, gently pushing me to the side.

Serra wouldn't let me down. I was sure my other two other friends were about to save me from ruining this prime opportunity to ask the right questions had Serra not.

"What Cooper is trying to tell you, Ms. Pedigree, is that Aria and I found out that Cooper ended up on Earth about the same time some Vestige thing was discovered. We were wondering if it had anything to do with Cooper leaving Alyssum and whether or not his parents were involved.

"Cooper would really like to find his parents, you know, and well, we'd like to help him too," said Serra, a little more robustly than I had expected, but straight to the point.

Ms. Pedigree didn't respond immediately. Like I had hoped she would have. No. Instead, she just stared upon us, void of any expression.

She remained still until her hands slowly began to unclasp. I had an odd feeling. She didn't seem to be her normal upbeat self. If I were to guess, I'd say she was speechless for the first time since I had made her acquaintance many years ago. And not in a good way.

"How did you come to learn this?"

"We prefer not to tell you, Ms. Pedigree. If it's all the same to you. Is there anything about this Vestige thing that can help Cooper?" asked Serra—still unrelenting in her approach on the subject matter.

"Ya, like where is it?" Miles asked.

"Well, that is a matter I cannot speak to you children about, and I suggest you immediately put an end to this—this inquiry you have begun," Ms. Pedigree said sternly.

I started to make my argument. "But Ms. Pedigree—"

"—Not another word, Cooper B. I mean it, stop this now... I will not hear another word about it... Please, children... Have a nice day."

We turned to head out of her classroom—defeated. It was not the answer we had expected to hear from Ms. Pedigree. Neither of us looked at one another as we walked out. Deep down, I was shocked. Shocked at how quickly Ms. Pedigree abruptly ended our conversation, but then my shock turned to disappointment. Disappointed with the fact, I had finally been able to ask the question I've been wanting to since the day I arrived. Only to have learned no more than I had already known.

"Cooper B.?" said Ms. Pedigree in a gentle voice—just as I took a step out of her class.

I turned. My heart sped up in anticipation that she had changed her mind. She stood up and placed her hands together down by the thin buckle of the belt on her bright yellow dress.

"Please know that I only wish you well, and I am truly sorry. I am not the one who can give you the answers you are in search of. When the time is right... You shall know... That time, however, is not now, and I shall end with this... Always be cautious of all that is new, and be mindful of that which is old. Be well, Cooper B."

Aria, Serra, Miles, and I went to the library—a place far away from our gathering rooms. The four of us sat together in the study on plush red velvet couches reserved for readers in an area full of bookshelves lined with leather-bound books. Aria's eyes were sunken, as she held her chin in the palm of her hands, sitting motionless.

"What kind of riddle is that?" Serra asked.

"I don't know. I've never understood riddles to be honest, so I am not sure what she meant by that."

"We're no closer than we were before today. Why isn't anyone willing to just tell us what we need to know? Why all the mystery?" said Aria—sitting upright.

She was right. We were no closer to discovering the truth about me, my parents, or this Vestige then we were before. But we hadn't asked the one person that would have the answers. The one that would be able to tell me, should he elect to. Chancellor Adimus. From the first day in this new world, he had told me that I likely had questions that would be answered in time. When was that time?

"Why don't you go talk to Aurora, Coop?" Miles said, reaching into a bag of Palatum Poppers he smuggled into the library. "Maybe, she'll answer your questions."

"It wouldn't hurt if you tried. Aurora may tell you things she wouldn't me or Serra."

The three of them looked to me for my reaction. It couldn't hurt. Aurora gave them the only clues we had so far, and she might have more to share—if asked. I rubbed my hands on my pant legs—gearing up the strength to just get this done. I stood up and nodded my head. I was ready. Chancellor Adimus would have to wait.

Past the sign above the entrance that read Historian of Archives, was the dark circular room. Inside, a lonely bench sat in the middle—surrounded by lifeless walls that waited to be awoken with a single word. I sat on the bench that was lit by a single light source high above in the ceiling.

"Aurora."

Lights swirled around me as the room came to life. I was encompassed by a beautiful landscape of lush green fields and colorful treetops. Off in the horizon and over the meadow appeared a figure walking toward me. Aurora had a way of making the grandest entrances. Dressed in her slender black suit, she came to rest directly in front of me. I was close enough to reach out and feel her Spectral skin.

"Good afternoon, Cooper B. How may I be of assistance to you today?" Aurora asked.

She must have been programmed to recognize previous encounters because before, she only referred to me as a second-year student.

"Where can I find the Vestige?" I asked—getting right to the point.

"A Vestige is an ancient relic that has many forms and meanings. Many relics can be found in the museum of history—"

"—Not any Vestige that has been found. The Vestige sought out by Chancellor Adimus roughly ten Earth years ago," I said.

"I am not showing any records of such an event. Please ask another question."

My leg began to bounce. I should have spent more time understanding what exactly Serra and Aria had said to Aurora to get the answers they did.

"Do you have any information on me, Cooper B.," I asked, trying to get some sort of grasp on what Aurora may know.

"Approximately two quartam's ago, Cooper B., accompanied by two of his friends, were brought to Alyssum from Earth—"

"—Before that, Aurora. Can you tell me about Cooper B. before he came to Alyssum? Before he was sent away from this planet ten years ago," I said—growing frustrated with this chess game between flesh and technology.

"I am not finding anything in my archives to support your question. Please ask another," said Aurora, but this time her nearly transparent form flickered—like a glitch I would find on a handheld game console.

"Did Chancellor Adimus find a Vestige?" I asked, in a last-ditch effort to have one of my questions answered, but Aurora stood still, staring through me as if she was frozen in time.

Aurora, along with the images surrounding me began to rapidly flicker and the wall was lifeless once again. For a moment, I was scared I had just crashed the entire Historian of Archives. Had I said something that short-circuited this advanced piece of technology or had she simply powered down, refusing to answer any more of my questions? In any case, my session with Aurora was obviously over, and once again, I was left without any answers, a common theme as of late.

I walked out and was greeted by my three eagerly awaiting friends. With my hands in my pockets, studying the laces on my shoes, I explained to them how none of my questions had meaning to Aurora, and that she vanished before I was through.

"What is it about you they don't want you to know?" Aria asked.

"Everything," I snapped, with furrowed brows. "They don't want me to know anything about me, my parents, or where I am from."

Everything I tried to do to find those answers was backfiring on me. It was as though I was never meant to uncover any of this. But why? Why was it such a guarded secret? I was only eleven years old and was beginning to think I should never have stepped through that Fold with Serra to come to this place. I was better off fending away Theodore and his crummy friends then I was here searching for the meaning of my existence.

"Don't give up yet, Coop," Serra said, placing her hand on my shoulder. Her words and touch were consoling. "We're going to get to the bottom of this."

"Ya, Coop, we are," said Aria as she leaned in and put her hand on my other shoulder.

Aria, Serra, Miles, and I walked out of the library and began our long journey down the corridors—back to our rooms. Through the arched walkway of glass and metal, the skies mimicked my mood, gray and foreboding. A day that should have been celebrated with knowledge and freedom from our penance was tarnished and fruitless. The one thought that should have brought me a feeling of hope was that it couldn't get any worse.

"Is that Chancellor Adimus?' Miles asked as I was looking off at the silhouettes of the planets in the sky.

"And Ms. Elsattera too," Serra added.

Up ahead, both were talking to one another until Chancellor Adimus saw us approaching. They stopped talking—waiting for us to make our way to them. Hopefully, this was merely a coincidence, but when it came to the Chancellor—nothing was ever without purpose.

"Ah, yes. I am glad I have found the four of you together," said Chancellor Adimus—in his slow deliberate voice. "Ms. Penrose, I must regretfully inform you that your parents send their regards and want you to know they will be away during the tri-quartam break. It appears they have pressing matters to attend and asked that we make your stay here as comfortable as possible. That, of course, goes for the three of you as well, being that I am under the impression you had all planned to stay with the Penrose family during that time?"

Apparently, it could get worse. I could hear it in the Chancellors voice. He knew we had planned to sneak away, and he wanted to be the one to let us know it wasn't going to happen. He never actually confirmed my suspicions, but I just knew. So did the others. As if we were synchronized in an orchestra of sorrow, the four of us let out a collective sigh.

"Now, please don't be too disappointed, children. There are plenty of things here at Grayson to keep your busy—yet curious—minds occupied for that time," said Chancellor Adimus with a slight smile. "And I understand that the scavenger hunt is soon to be revealed, giving you all a chance to stay one step ahead of your fellow classmates."

"Yes, sir," I said—not feeling any better than I had.

"Very well… Ms. Elsattera, may I continue to have a word

with you in private?" said Chancellor Adimus. The two walked off in the direction we had just come from.

My eyes were wide open, but I must have been dreaming. A dream! That had to be it. I was dreaming. After all, how much worse could it have gotten? It even appeared as though the gray clouds above us were looking down and smiling. Smiling at others' misfortunes and the mere fact they were the definition of our meek outlook in life.

We shuffled our heavy feet in a direction unknown, when suddenly, like an alarm going off in the early morning hours, our Wuickens began to sound.

Miles quickly reached into his pocket and pulled his out, revealing his virtual screen. Scrolling across the screen were a few words that brought a smile to Miles' face.

It read:

LET THE HUNT BEGIN

CHAPTER SIXTEEN

THE SCAVENGER HUNT

The halls of Grayson Academy were nearly empty. Only a handful of students remained behind during the tri-quartam break. Many children were now home enjoying their time with family—sharing all that they have learned thus far. Serra seemed down. Unlike Miles, Aria, and I, she had never truly felt the pain of not being with her family when others were. The three of us were experts in this field and did everything we could to pay a little extra attention to her.

We sat in the girl's gathering room. Only Serra and Aria were left behind, and our room still had Bolliver and another student, Quentin Liemeer, who had stayed behind as well. The two of them vowed to team up together and be the first to solve their riddles to their own Scavenger Hunt. Miles and I were invited to tag along, but I quickly declined due to the fact Bolliver was still my number one suspect for the misery that seemed to follow me throughout the year. Even though Aria said I was crazy for thinking so, I couldn't shake that feeling. I had to be right—all he was missing was a blood red cloak.

Frankly, I really didn't mind self-banishing ourselves from our common area. The girls room seemed much swankier than ours. It was the same size, full of the same furniture, and the infamous food replicator, but what really made it stand out was the fact it had a fireplace that burned actual wood. Miles was jealous and immediately complained that they had one, and we did not. Truthfully, it made sense. Boys were far likelier to burn things that weren't meant to be.

We sat in the comfort and warmth of the large plush couch directly in front of the crackling fire—studying our Wuickens. We each had our own clue and made a pact that we would help one another find what we were sent off to—during our scavenger hunt.

"What does this actually mean, though? The first to be hung in the halls that molded the minds of the young? What kind of clue is that?" asked Miles, complaining of his scavenger hunt riddle already. "You don't think they mean someone was actually hung, do you? I mean, we don't even do that back home anymore."

"We don't either, Miles. Geez, it's a riddle—you have to read between the lines."

Serra read her clue quietly to herself, "A charm worn over the heart of the sea gives those true believers the right to see."

"How about you, Aria?" said Miles, turning his attention away from Serra. "What do you think it means?"

"I've got my own to solve, Red," Aria responded. "It has to be the library—where else would you find classic tales? But how am I supposed to grow?"

Aria was overthinking her riddle. Hearing her read it several times—caused the words to echo in my head, *Classic tales are found within these rows, take nine steps then begin to grow.* Before I could solve my own, I knew what hers meant. I realized the answer wasn't to grow. She needed to make herself grow.

"On your tippy-toes," I told her—still examining my own clue.

"Say what?" Arias asked, confused by my sudden outburst.

"You don't actually grow. You have to make yourself grow. Whatever you are meant to find will probably be just high enough for you to find by standing on your *tippy toes.*"

"You're a mad genius, Coop!" Miles said excitedly. "How about mine? Figure mine out, would ya?"

He was wrong. I wasn't a genius. It was actually quite easy to figure out, and deep down inside, I felt that Aria got the easiest of the four clues. Maybe it was because she was new to this world, *but what about Miles*, I thought. Why would his be more difficult than Aria's?

"You sure bragged a lot about being the first to get yours solved, Miles. Remember? 'Don't be crying when I'm the first to an answer' blah blah blah," said Serra, mimicking Miles.

Miles put down his Wuicken and swung his legs off the arm-rest of the couch he had so effortlessly made himself at home on. He leaned over to Serra and nearly pressed his nose against hers. It looked as though he was about to push her off the couch—but I knew Miles well enough to know he would never put his hands on a girl. Instead, his expression turned to that of a young adolescent brat, popping his new found favorite treat into his mouth.

"Whatever, Serra," said Miles, as he began to suck on a Palatum Popper. "I don't see you racing outside to jump into the frozen sea… You know… it'd be a good day for an ice bath, so give it a try."

"Hush, you two!" shouted Aria. "So, I need to go to the library then? Unless you can find classic tales somewhere else, Serra?"

"Nope, that would be my guess," responded Serra—shoving Miles out of her personal space.

The four of us got up and headed out the door of the girl's gathering room, making our journey through the once-bustling halls of Grayson.

"Are you children enjoying your break?" asked Ms. Elsattera, coming from the area off limits to all Graysonians.

"Yes, ma'am," I replied.

"Good, and what have you in store for today? Have you begun your scavenger hunt?" she asked.

"We have, and I think I am going to be the first to find my answer," Aria told Ms. Elsattera, with a sense of pride.

"Only because Cooper helped you," said Miles, snarkily.

"Well, it's not meant to be an individual achievement, Miles," Ms. Elsattera reminded him—as though to put him in his place for being so quick to cast a shadow over Aria's moment in the light. "The best way to solve these is to sometimes look beyond your own clue and find a part of your answer within another," she continued—turning her gaze upon me. "With that said, happy hunting, Cooper B."

"Thank you."

As we continued our trek toward the library, we made our way past the dining hall. It was an odd feeling to see it so barren and lifeless at this particular hour. It was lunchtime and we normally would be seated enjoying a nourishing meal that was materialized for our consumption. Today, however, we were on a mission—and eating was the last thing on our minds.

We entered the long corridor that had framed paintings of former Pedagogues lining the walls. It was amazing to think that all of these men and women had once walked the path we were now on, forever gone and now only remembered with oils and acrylics.

Miles must have been thinking the same thing, as he looked all around him—taking in the history of Grayson and its Pedagogues. He fell further behind as his pace slowed. When suddenly, he stopped.

"That's it!" Miles shouted out. "The halls that molded the minds of the young. It's in here!"

We all stopped and turned to see Miles standing in the center of the corridor, looking all around. While searching for answers to his own riddle, he had figured it out—but a part of me was not as exuberant as Miles. Aria had also been excited and she had what she needed to take her to the answer she sought. Instead, now Miles would be the first, as he promised to be.

"The paintings are hung. Not the person I am looking for—well not really, since whoever it is, is hung in these halls. But it's a painting, you get what I am saying, right?"

"Ya, I guess," said Aria in a voice full of despair.

One thing about Miles, he was always competitive. In fact, he boasted about his athleticism in his previous schools. However, he also had an uncanny ability to sense when one of us wasn't ourselves. No matter how quick he was to accept an insult and give it back—he could always empathize with those closest to him. He never put himself above others he cared about.

Miles looked over at Aria, and his expression of enthusiasm drained away.

"Um—maybe when we're done with the library, we can come back here and find this dead guy," suggested Miles.

"Really?" said Aria, with a bit of joy coming back to her.

"Why not? It's not like they're going anywhere," responded Miles.

The four of us let out a collective laugh and agreed with Miles. I was laughing on the outside, but inside—inside I was beaming with a feeling of admiration. Proud of Miles for doing the right thing, and I wasn't the only one feeling that way.

"You know, you're not that bad, Red," I overheard Serra tell Miles, as Aria and I walked off ahead of the two of them.

"Thanks, Serra!"

"But I still think you're an idiot," added Serra, as she walked ahead of Miles, joining Aria and me.

Shortly after, we found our way back to the study area within the library walls. I could see the entryway to the Historian of Archives and wondered to myself if Aurora was still broken.

Aria made her way up and down the rows of leather-bound books, books that had become somewhat obsolete due to the creation of the Wuicken. Some students and Pedagogues preferred the old method, and because of that, they were still available for those who favored them.

"What would be a classic tale?" Aria asked—more so to herself than Serra, Miles, or me.

"I don't know," Serra responded. "There are hundreds to choose from... I got an idea. Why don't we each pick a row and take nine steps and see what we find?"

"I think the steps are spaced out for Aria. These riddles are all specifically made for each of us, right?"

"Ya, you're right, Coop. Grayson specifically designs these riddles for each student," Serra told us.

"You mean someone here at *Grayson* writes all of these riddles every year for the Scavenger Hunt?" asked Aria.

"No, the school itself."

"Now that's creepy," replied Miles.

No matter who was responsible for these clues, we needed to follow them. We all looked around, contemplating a way to solve this quicker than having Aria walk down every aisle in the library—taking nine steps designed off her own stride.

"I got it!" Miles shouted. "Aria you walk like... um... like you know... in your normal awkward sort of way, and we will copy you. This way, we can all spread out and help you look."

Aria had a look about her that was either confusion that Miles had for once come up with a pretty good idea, or because he thought she had an awkward swagger about her.

"Good idea... I guess," Aria said—seemingly still uncertain if she had just been insulted, or if Miles truly had a great solution to our problem.

For a minute or two, the three of us walked side by side with Aria, adjusting our steps to match those of hers. I had never thought much about it—but Miles may have been right. Aria's legs were a bit shorter than mine, but she had a long stride. Nonetheless, we were set to go.

I made my way to a section that contained literature all about Grayson Academy. It was full of books about different Pedagogues and the evolving courses offered. There was no way what Aria needed to find was in this row, but we had to try them all.

I began counting... one, two, three, four, five, six, seven, eight—and nine. I stopped. I was surrounded by old books on both sides of me. I looked around to find something, anything that would catch my attention. Nothing. I decided to bend my knees slightly to match Aria's height, and then slowly raised myself to a point that I imagined Aria would reach on her tippy toes.

The books all appeared to be the same, nothing jumped out at me. I turned around and checked the other shelf. It was more of the same—identical looking books from one end of the row to the other. My legs began to sting. I must have had used muscles I didn't even know existed. I stood back up.

I hoped the others were having better luck than I was—I had given up. As I turned to walk away and accept defeat, something out of the corner of my eye caught my attention. It wasn't like the rest of the books. In fact, I don't think it was a book at all. It was flat and barely visible, protruding between the History of Ancestry and The Evolution of the Pongo, by Batari Bonabos. I reached out to grab it—but quickly withdrew my hand. At that moment, I wondered if it was the seeker who must discover their own clue or no points would be rewarded.

"Aria! I think I found it!" I called out.

Aria, Serra, and Miles ran to my location. Miles was the furthest away, so he was the most winded. They all shared the same expressions—a look of curiosity about what I had located. I stared back at them, hopeful it was what Aria needed to score the points and add to her already perfect Torts.

"Well? What did you find?" Aria asked impatiently.

"Ya Coop, the suspense is killing us," said Miles, still catching his breath.

"I'm not sure if it's right or not, but it sure looked out of place," I told them. I began to second guess myself as to whether it had indeed been the answer to Aria's riddle.

"Where is it?" demanded Serra.

I pointed to the shelf and the folded sheet of paper between the two books. Aria stepped forward and stood on the tips of her toes to get a better look. Her riddle was right. She needed to grow and that she did, at least another two or three inches in all.

Aria cautiously reached out, unsure herself what would happen once she took hold of it. Her hand hovered over the slot between the leather-bound novels—carefully gripping the paper between her thumb and index finger—it slid out. Then the room filled with the sound of three piercing chimes.

Startled, we jumped back. Aria must have set off some sort of alarm for being in the library at this late hour, and now we were all about to be sent back to our rooms once again.

"Simmer down, you guys," said Serra sharply. "That just

means Aria found the answer to her Scavenger Hunt. Great job!"

Aria pulled the sheet out and unfolded it. It was a map, and it was old, delicate, and full of dust that had been neglected for what appeared to have been decades, if not more. The map was of Grayson Academy—but the school seemed much smaller than I would have guessed it to be. Serra took it from Aria and scrutinized it.

"It's Grayson Academy from like eons ago," she said, looking perplexed. "Look, the library isn't even on the map."

We all took our turns looking it over. Serra was right. Several areas of the school we had come to know as our home were not on the map. As I continued to scan the old parchment paper, I quickly noticed something else, something glaring up at me. It was the area on the map marked: *The Nemus Garden.*

"That settles it then," said Miles. "Now it's my turn, and I bet we can find mine before dinner. I'm starving."

We hurried and made our way back to the halls of those that molded the minds of the young. The corridor paid homage to the Pedagogues of the past. Miles was more than likely correct that his hunt ended there. The only problem was—which Pedagogue was it?

"What am I supposed to do now, Serra?" asked Miles—unsure of what his next step would be. "Do I need to find the painting that's the correct answer and take the whole thing with me?"

"No, Miles. You don't *steal* the paining. You just need to touch the right one," responded Serra.

"Whatever. I guess I'll just touch all of them then," said

Miles—reaching out to the first painting on the wall.

"Stop!" shouted Serra, grabbing his hand. "If you touch the wrong one, you lose, dummy. Geez, don't you know anything?"

Serra must have had a lapse in judgment earlier when she complimented Miles for being kind to Aria. She had gone back to her old ways, quickly becoming irritated at the smallest thing Miles did. Those things that reminded her he wasn't from Alyssum.

Nonetheless, my earlier suspicions were right. The seeker must be the one to find the article.

"Thank you," said Miles. "That would have really sucked if I lost over a silly technicality."

Aria, Serra, Miles, and I just stood in the long hallway—carefully studying each painting on the wall. They all looked nearly identical—wrinkled old men and plump women who taught long ago here at Grayson. It could have been any one of them. I scratched my head, trying to help Miles solve his crazy riddle.

"I got it," said Aria excitedly. "The *first* to be hung—it's the *first* painting to be put on the wall!"

"That doesn't help," said Miles. "How am I supposed to know who got put up here first? They might as well have asked me who built this school. I'd have a better chance figuring that one out—than which old geezer was hung first."

"I think I know the answer, Miles," Serra said, smirking. "It's not just whose painting went up first, but also who was painted first. I think."

"Now you're talking in riddles," said Miles—slapping his palm to his forehead.

"Who would have been painted first, Serra?" I asked—trying to give her a chance to help solve this.

We had agreed to work together, and even Ms. Elsattera told us we were better sharing our clues. Even if that meant sharing in our understanding of what those clues meant. We would be foolish not to listen to the one person who may hold the last piece to the puzzle—the one pink-haired girl who had actually grown up here.

"Go on…," I urged Serra.

"I would guess that would be—" said Serra, pausing a moment to scan the walls. Then, she pointed to a painting, "—*Emmisar Augtor*."

Framed in a wooden frame, dusted in pewter and gold was an older gentleman, dressed in a red cloak. He was visible from the waist up, standing in an old classroom full of books and wooden chairs. Like so many paintings, this one had beady eyes that seemed to be watching our every step—cautioning Miles to foolhardy touch the Pedagogues last pose, frozen in time.

"He's creepier than Mr. Versarius," said Miles intensely. "And why does it look like he's supposed to be holding something?"

It was true. The unknown artist portrayed a man with his arm strung across his chest with an empty hand. A hand that appeared to be holding something and that something was unfinished.

"He may be creepy, but Mr. Augtor was the first Pedagogue to teach the Art of Ambriose here at Grayson. Not to mention he was also its first Chancellor. I guess you could say he was the first of everything," said Serra, with certainty.

"How do you know all of this, Serra," I asked with curiosity. I had hoped she had an answer that would convince Miles she was right, and the way to solve his riddle was staring back at him.

"You weren't here last year, Coop. The first book we got in Ms. Pedigree's class was *the Art of Ambriose*, written by Sir Emmisar Augtor. It was required reading, and that's when we learned he had become Chancellor, the *first* Chancellor of Grayson Academy," said Serra.

That was all I needed to hear. She had a good reason why she felt this was the right answer, so I had to trust her, as I had many times before. Miles needed the points, that was for sure, so he needed to put his faith in our friend as well.

"Go on, Miles. Touch it," I told him, gently pushing him from behind.

Miles stepped forward and reached out. With the tip of his finger, he softly pressed against the bottom of the painting, sounding off a series of three loud chimes, like it had in the library for Aria.

Miles dropped to his knees and raised his hands.

"Yes! I did it! I did it!" yelled Miles as his voice echoed down the empty halls.

"Seriously? *You* did it?" Serra asked, with fumes steaming out from her ears.

"Well, you helped too, I guess," said Miles, as he picked himself up off the floor.

Miles had done it, with the help of his friends, of course. The best part was—this meant he would likely pass his Torts for the year, which would allow him to move on with the rest of us. The smile on his face said it all. He also knew he would make it past his first year at the Grayson Academy.

"How about you, Coop? You ready to work on your hunt?" Miles asked—holding his stomach.

It was obvious he was ready to eat. I couldn't blame him. It was getting late, and my stomach was tied in a knot, demanding to be fed.

"Nah, that's okay. Let's call it a day and try another time," I told them. "Besides, I'm starving."

"Ya, I'm thinking Miles is right," said Serra. There was a hint of disappointment in her voice. "I can't do anything about mine until the next quartam. Especially if it actually has to do with the sea, since it is frozen and all. Plus, we have until the end of term, I suppose."

"What was yours again, Coop?" asked Aria with interest.

I was trying to remember it word for word as we headed toward the dining hall. It was a peculiar riddle, to be honest. Something I had given some thought to, but couldn't figure it out as easily as I did with Aria's.

"The truth is found in the hands of he who first came, bonded to the chosen one who speaks his name."

CHAPTER SEVENTEEN

THE NIGHTMARE

Miles had a glow about him for the next several days, bragging to anyone who had stayed behind that he had discovered the answer to his scavenger hunt riddle. Some seemed genuinely interested to hear about his grand expedition while others dismissed him. Bolliver was one that wasn't impressed at all, telling Miles he simply got lucky, or his clue was so easy even a tiny baby Ventoox could figure it out.

I, on the other hand, hadn't been so lucky. My clue seemed unfair and impossible to solve for someone that had never stepped foot in Grayson Academy before this year. To be honest, I hadn't given it much more thought. A part of me realized it wouldn't really matter if I was awarded extra points or not since I was doing well in my classes. But another part of me wanted to locate the answer before Bolliver found his own. Regardless, I was starving, and my thoughts were directed to the pancakes, sausage, and scrambled eggs on Miles's plate.

"Aren't you excited, Coop?" asked Serra, sitting down next

to me in the dining hall. "It's nearly the Solace of Imperium!"

"The what?" Miles asked, drowning his entire plate full of maple syrup.

"I'm with Miles, Serra. I am not sure what you mean by *Solace of Imperium*," I said, confused.

Serra stared at both of us for a moment. I often wondered how difficult it would have been for someone to always have to explain everything about their day to day lives and the events in them. Like teaching a baby to walk for the first time, fun at first, but increasingly more and more frustrating.

"It's only the greatest day of the year!" shouted Serra, causing the handful of students in our row to stop eating and look our way. "We decorate—eat a huge feast—and the best part of it all, we get presents!"

"Christmas—" said Miles. "—that's called Christmas on Earth. What's the big deal? We do that every year?"

"Sometimes without the gifts, though. Depending on which home you're in," I said without really knowing I had said it out loud.

Aria came and sat down beside us for breakfast. She began conjuring her daily helping of oatmeal and orange juice. Some things never change.

"What about gifts?" she asked.

"They celebrate Christmas here too," said Miles, with a mouth full of sausages. The fact Miles often spoke with a full mouth still hadn't settled well with Serra. She gave him a disgusted look.

"It's the Solace of Imperium, not Christmas," said Serra

bitterly.

"Whatever, *the Solace of Imperium*, and they give presents," said Miles sarcastically.

"I love Christmas trees—do you have Christmas trees?" asked Aria.

Serra was overcome with a look of confusion.

"Not sure I understand what a tree has to do with any of this?"

"I guess I am not sure what they have to do with Christmas, either. But you can decorate them with lights, red, blue, and green ornaments, garland, and tinsel—I love icicle tinsel! And you put all your presents under them."

"That sounds divine! We have to get a Christmas tree," Serra said, with her eyes wide open. Then reality appeared to set in. She had no idea what Christmas even looked like. "But where would we find one?"

"I know. Let's ask Mr. Hordo. I'm sure he could help us find a tree to decorate. It doesn't have to be an actual pine tree, just something to hang decorations on," said Aria.

"That's a perfect idea," I responded with a big smile.

Leaving our plates, nearly full, the four of us ran out of the dining hall, as quickly as we could. The nice thing about the school being nearly empty, was we had the space to run around freely—without bumping into other students. However, it was still frowned upon to race through the corridors, but the Pedagogues had all but disappeared themselves this time of year.

We made our way to the far end of the academy, to Mr. Hordo's study. I had never had a reason to go there myself and was in utter awe when I arrived. Inside were old books, skeletal remains of mythical looking creatures, and empty mason jars that lined the tables. I could only imagine what once filled them. It was somewhat dreary but fitting for the man who occupied it.

Sitting in an old leather chair atop a massive animal fur, was Mr. Hordo looking through his thick-lensed glasses at an open book perched in his hands. He was illuminated by a crackling and roaring fire burning inside a stone fireplace. Mr. Hordo seemed completely oblivious to our sudden arrival.

"Um, excuse me, sir?" I said with a lump in my throat.

No response.

"Mr. Hordo? Can we ask you a question?" said Serra softly.

Mr. Hordo still didn't respond.

I immediately began to wonder to myself if he was dead. Had we stumbled upon the corpse of the student advisor and Pedagogue of Zoology, sitting in his final resting spot? Or had we come across a gruesome murder scene and would surely have the blame put on us because we were the ones to have found him?

The fairytale I had concocted came to an end when the room rattled from the sound of Mr. Hordo snoring. His breathing was loud and powerful. In a way, it was a great relief to hear he was breathing, but also slightly disturbing to see an older gentleman sleeping with his eyes open.

"Good gracious that is loud," said Miles, stunned. "He's going to bring the roof down on our heads!"

A painful memory flashed in my head, *remember when you tried to wake up Mr. Martin's father-in-law, fast asleep in his recliner?* That was when I learned older people hated to be disturbed while they slept.

I softly stepped over and gently placed my hand on the shoulder of the sleeping Pedagogue. "Mr. Hordo?"

"Yes, yes, what is it?" asked Mr. Hordo, sounding panicked. He cleared his throat and slammed shut the book. "Who is it?"

"It's us, Mr. Hordo. Miles, Serra, Aria and I," I said, shuffling back to avoid any flailing limbs.

"Oh, Mr. Cooper B. So good to see you again," said Mr. Hordo. He straightened his glasses and looked around for a moment to each of us standing in his private study. A perplexed look glossed over the expression on his face as he spoke, "But you are aware that you are not permitted to be in this part of Grayson, aren't you?"

"No, sir. I was not, and I am sorry for that," I responded, knowing all too well it was indeed off limits.

"Oh well, I suppose no one shall be the wiser. What... What might I do for the four of you on this fine day?"

"We're in the market for a tree, one we can decorate for the Solace of Imperium," said Miles.

Serra seemed impressed with Miles's mention of their yearly holiday.

"Yes, and we were hoping you could help us find one that would be perfect to put up in the boy's gathering room," said Aria.

"A tree?" asked Mr. Hordo, still looking a bit bewildered. "I suppose I could help with that."

Mr. Hordo stood and stretched the cramp in his lower back,

peering around his cluttered room. With narrowing eyes, he moved to the side of the fireplace and retrieved an old wooden handled axe, holding it firmly in his grasp.

"Well? Shall we?" he asked.

By the time the students of Grayson returned, we had managed to find the perfect, manicured shrub with the help of Mr. Hordo. The tall shrub that had once stood proudly just outside the main hall entrance was a beacon that the Solace of Imperium was upon us. Surrounded by gifts to be given to our classmates from the four of us, our humble shrub, now decorated in strands of icicle tinsel that Aria made by hand, had officially been promoted to the rank of a Christmas tree.

Bolliver and Gwillian were eager to learn what they had gotten—shaking their packages every opportunity they had, trying to guess the contents. The other boys and girls were quick to get into the spirit of the holidays and put the presents they had received from their parents alongside the others. It was beginning to feel a lot like Christmas, with warmth, cheer, excitement, and love all around. The way I hoped everyone back on Earth would feel.

The rest of the room was decorated with the ornaments and garlands we couldn't fit on the tree. There was a bright shining star hovering over the center of the room, compliments of Avantha. It added a welcoming touch and a sense of warmth. I now had a sense of excitement that we were about to celebrate an Alyssum tradition—a holiday I still had no idea what it was truly about.

"Just one more day!" said Serra enthusiastically as she made herself at home on our common room couch. "Then, we can open gifts and celebrate at the dance."

"Dance? No one ever said anything about a dance?" said Miles, nearly choking on a Pentwist that he had been sucking on all morning—trying to extract the chocolate like filling from the center. "I can't dance."

"Just stand there then, Red. Not sure anyone would dance with you anyway."

"How about you, Coop? Can *you* dance?" asked Miles, pointing his candy Pentwist drenched in saliva at me.

"Not, sure... I guess I never tried before."

I tried to remember the last time I had been sent off to an event that required me to be able to dance. But I had never been to one, not even at one of my many schools.

Aria finally made her appearance and joined Serra, Miles, and I comfortably sprawled out on the couch. Aria wasn't empty handed. She was holding a small, flat, wrapped gift. Before I could ask who it was for—Aria handed it to me.

"Merry Christmas, Coop," said Aria cheerfully.

It was a reminder that I hadn't given Aria the gift I had wrapped for her either. I reached down between the cushions and revealed that I hadn't forgotten my friend during the holidays. It was a crudely wrapped small box with a gift inside that I really hoped she would like.

"Merry Christmas and a Happy Solace of Imperium to you," I responded.

Aria looked it over, examining the poor job I did with the

wrapping. She never said anything, and put both the gifts under our tree.

"How about you, Aria? Can you dance?" asked Miles.

"What? Why?" asked Aria, hesitantly.

"Can you dance? There's a dance tomorrow night, and we are all going, I guess," said Miles with very little zest.

Aria stood motionless. It had obviously taken her by surprise. One corner of her mouth began to curl upward. But the smile was forced, and I knew this wasn't something she was looking forward to.

Serra was watching Aria's reaction, and quickly jumped into the conversation to avoid any potential chance Aria would back out.

"You don't have to dance—it's a celebration. You can just eat and hang out. It'll be fun, trust me," said Serra.

"If you say so," said Aria, apparently still unsure of the whole dance part of the invitation.

The boy's gathering room slowly emptied as the night skies began to fill with tiny bright stars. Had it not been for the mere fact it was unbearably cold outside, I would say it was the perfect evening. The kind of night you would spend laying on the lush grassy lawns gazing up in astonishment—and dreaming of a better tomorrow.

Instead, I lay awake in my bed, listening to Miles as he snored. He had already plunged into a world of dreams—hopefully, the kind of dreams you wished you never awoke from. The heavy breathing didn't shake the walls, as was the case with Mr.

Hordo, but it kept me from falling asleep as quickly as I would have preferred.

My eyes were heavy. The wheezing from my red headed roommate was beginning to fall into an abyss. Everything around me began to echo into silence—

—The next thing I knew, I was standing at the doors of a massive towering cathedral. The walls were much like they were at Grayson Academy—smooth stone being held together by rows of polished black and gold metal, surrounded by lush green landscape and surreal flying birds—that sang loudly in the open air. Looking upward, the sheer face of the palace extended high into the blue skies above. It was spectacular to see. It was Imperium.

Without notice, the doors began to slowly open… Revealing inside a great hall. The towering ceilings of crystal and stone were reflecting on the glass-like marbling ground beneath my feet. Up ahead, beyond the rows of the glistening pewter columns, and statues of powerful men, I could see two lone figures, shrouded in the shadows.

Whispers once again filled my head, drawing me further into the unknown. The two figures began to walk away. I tightly closed my eyes and balled my fists. The vein in my forehead pulsed and became engorged, I was trying to make sense of the voices—

"Cooooper," the voices whispered softly in my ear. It was a man and a woman's voice.

"Mom?" I asked as I popped open my eyes, expecting

to see the phantom figure standing by my side—hoping it was my mother, leaning in with her lips pressed to my ear.

I was still alone.

The figures turned and glided away at the end of the great hall—disappearing into utter blackness.

I sprinted toward the last place they stood, reaching out and shouting, "Mom? Dad? Wait!"

It was no use; my legs were weighted—and every step I took became more labored. I kept pushing forward, but it was a feeble attempt—I could go no further.

"Coooooper," the long whisper echoed. There was no way to tell where the voices were coming from. I was surrounded by their biddings.

"Join us," the soft voices continued.

The whispers ceased, and the air became uncomfortably warm as the wind within the empty great hall began to swirl all around. Gently at first, but that soon changed, and it was violently whipping all about. Burning red dust began to strike my cheeks, forcing me to cover my eyes. It was happening again, just like the first day I Folded to the City of Elise with Mr. Penrose.

Through shielded sight, I could see I was no longer in the great halls of Imperium. I was back to the deserted land of weathered and broken towering cloaked statues. Each side of the canyon was covered with jagged rocks and falling boulders.

It was familiar. It was just like the dreams that haunted me years ago.

I couldn't feel my legs. I looked down to see I was being swallowed by the red blistering sand. I struggled to free myself—doing everything I could to escape its stronghold before I became entombed by the scorching earth.

It was pointless—I was trapped.

"Join us—" the voices called out one last time.

The shallow air was being sucked from my lungs—I struggled to catch my breath. Suddenly, a hand grabbed hold of my shoulder, gripping me tightly. I let out a gut-wrenching scream in a last attempt to summon the strength needed to save myself from certain death.

I sat upright in the sanctuary of my own bed—drenched with sweat and sucking in air. I was no longer trapped in my nightmare. Miles was standing at the foot of my bed, looming over me with worry in his eyes. Of course, he wasn't alone. Along with a few other second-year students was Bolliver—watching me intensely. Bolliver had to be behind these voices—I just knew he was.

"You okay, Coop?" asked Miles, concerned. "You were screaming, and I think you woke up the whole school."

"Sorry, Miles—I must've had a bad dream is all," I told him, without taking my eyes off of Bolliver.

"What were you dreaming about?" Bolliver asked curiously.

He already knew. I know he did—but I wasn't going to let him have the satisfaction of tormenting me in both the waking hours and in my sleep.

"It was nothing. I don't remember."

CHAPTER EIGHTEEN

SOLACE OF IMPERIUM

The following morning, my head pounded and my heart raced. All throughout the night, I only slept for a minute or two, trying to rid my mind of that vivid nightmare. For hours, I suffered in silence. It seemed as though the sun took an eternity to rise, only to highlight the dreary gray skies. When the time finally came, I had realized that today was the Solace of Imperium. A day meant to be celebrated on Alyssum.

"Cooper! It's Christmas or Solace of whatever," shouted Miles excitedly from his bed. "Let's go see what we got."

I rubbed my eyes and looked around. I needed to put that dream behind me and make the best of the day. Opening gifts was the only true way I could think of to do just that.

"Race you to the tree!" I told Miles, leaping out of bed.

We both arrived in front of our traditionally decorated Christmas tree at the same time, winded and in awe. Something was different, and I was taken by surprise. Someone had added to the gifts we all placed under the tree.

Miles had already reached in and grabbed a present with his name scribbled on a tag dangling from a ribbon wrapped tightly around the package.

"What do you think it is?" asked Miles, shaking it vigorously in his little hands.

"Don't open it yet. Let's wait for Serra and Aria to come, and we can open them all together," I told Miles as I stared at a particular gift under the tree with my name printed on its tag. A gift that wasn't there the night before.

"They need to hurry!"

It didn't take long, and before Miles could finish sorting through the presents, Serra and Aria made their way into our gathering room. Still dressed in their pajamas with discombobulated bed hair, they stood in amazement.

"Wow! Look at all of these presents," said Aria, as she plopped down in front of the tree. "Where did they all come from?"

"I have no idea, but I can't wait to open mine!" Serra exclaimed as she took a seat next to Aria.

"What's all the noise about? Some of us are trying to sleep, you know," said Bolliver groggily, as he and Gwillian came walking in from their rooms. They stopped and looked around.

"Holy smokes!" said Gwillian, scratching his belly through his pajama top.

When it came to Bolliver, I had hoped he would find black coal wrapped under the tree just for him. It would be a fitting gift for someone that has had it out for me since I had arrived. I may not have known this for a fact, but my intuition was normally right when it came to kids such as he, or even Theodore.

"Here, Cooper, this one is for you," Aria said, handing me the square-shaped gift I had been eyeing since I came into the room. "Hmm, doesn't say who it is from... Open it."

I examined it for several seconds, trying to find a clue that told me who had given it to me. Maybe I was a bit untrusting and somewhat skeptical of something gifted from one that chose not to reveal their identity. At the same time, I hadn't really had many holidays in my life where I received anything from anyone.

Still somewhat unsure, I looked at Bolliver to see if he had taken any interest in the gift I held in my hands—he hadn't. Bolliver was more interested in the gloves he had been given and paid me no mind. Maybe it wasn't something gift wrapped by Bolliver that was meant to kill me after all.

I began to peel back the wrapping. Slowly and carefully at first, but the excitement took over, and I ripped it open quickly.

It was just a box. A dark mahogany box with seamlessly carved designs all over it and a small metal latch sealing it closed.

"I know what that is," said Serra, somewhat intrigued.

"Okay, are you going to share with the rest of us what it is then?" asked Miles.

"It's a permutation box—I haven't actually seen one before, but I am sure that's what it is."

"What's a permutation box?" I asked her, still examining it in my hands.

"They say you can put things inside of them that aren't what they appear, and once it is in there, it will reveal it's true identity," said Serra, taking it from my hands. "It's some powerful Guild stuff. Truthfully, I didn't really think they existed, and it was just a story made up by old people."

Serra lifted the latch and opened the box. Inside was a folded piece of paper resting on the bottom. The smell emitting from within reminded me of an old jewelry box, opened for the first time in a long while. I reached over and removed the note.

"What's it say, Cooper?" asked Gwillian, holding a new pair of uniform socks Serra, Aria, Miles, and I had given him.

We all looked at the folded piece of paper:

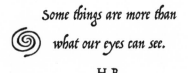

Some things are more than what our eyes can see.

H.B.

"What does that mean and who is H.B.?" asked Miles, enjoying a new bag of Alcoyi Breath Poppers.

"Who knows," I responded.

Like most things here at Grayson, the message was shrouded in mystery. No clear reason for why I received this, or even from whom. Unfortunately, I had become accustomed to not getting any answers to my questions, so I didn't think too much of it. Besides that, more gifts needed to be unwrapped.

Aria walked over to me, holding the gift that I had wrapped just for her. She reached out with her free hand and gave me mine.

"Now open this one," said Aria, with a shy smile.

Together we unwrapped our gifts to one another. I was careful not to damage its contents since it was flat and fragile. To my pleasant surprise, it was a framed photo of Aria, Miles, and me during our time together at St. Mary's, taken by Ms. Elsattera shortly after Miles had arrived. It was a sight to see how the three of us had already grown since we first met. It was a gift I would cherish for the rest of my life—as I would my friends.

I looked over to Aria as her eyes widened. From within a small box, she removed the Dezma charm that I had worn for as long as I could remember. She clenched it to her chest.

"Is it really for me?" she asked.

"Yes, of course. You seemed to like it, so I thought I would give it to you since I don't wear it anymore," I responded.

Aria quickly lifted it up and slid it over her dark, black, curly hair. It was a fitting gift. A lifeless object I had believed in some strange way brought me comfort—now given to a friend that has done the same.

The morning had been a success. We accomplished everything we had hoped to do. Together, we had managed to make the day special for the rest of the second-year students we shared space with inside the walls of Grayson. Both boys and girls had sat around, sharing with one another the things they had received, laughing, smiling, and enjoying one another's company. Whether it was candy only found here on this remarkable place known as Alyssum or something that could be worn throughout the year—no matter what they received, they were happy, and that was the best part.

But the day wasn't over I thought to myself, *we still had to face our greatest fears.* At least in my eyes. The fear of a school dance, inaugurating the Solace of Imperium.

"Hurry up, Cooper—we're going to be late," said Miles nervously, as he used his sweaty palms to smooth down his formal wear that had been laid out by Avantha.

"I didn't think you wanted to go," I said to Miles, staring at my reflection in the mirror. I was fitted in a long-tailed suit jacket with no collar and a white button-down shirt. It was an identical outfit to that which Miles was wearing.

"Ya, but there's going to be plenty of food there, and I'm starving."

"Are you two about ready?" Serra asked as she barged in—pushing Miles aside. "We're going to be late, and I hate being late, you know. They always stare at you when you walk in late, and I really don't like it when people stare."

Serra was dressed in a long, blue gown that sparkled in the light. The shimmering fabric reached down just below her knees and flared out as if it were in constant motion. An elegant dress you would expect to be complemented by a pair of glass slippers. Not with Serra. Instead, she had on pink sneakers—matching the color of her hair.

"You seem to hate a lot of things, Serra," Miles said, rolling his eyes.

"Just hurry up, bozo."

"He's waiting on me, sorry," I said to Serra. "This suit is itchy. Where's Aria?"

On cue, Aria walked in. She was dressed similar to Serra, but instead of a blue dress, hers was as green as her eyes. To me, Aria looked graceful. The necklace I had given her was draped just above her collar bone, adding a touch of elegance to her attire. I was speechless.

"Why are you staring at me? Do I look ridiculous?"

"Nah, you look okay, I guess," said Miles.

"Great, now can we please get going?" asked Serra impatiently.

Serra didn't give us a chance to respond. She headed out the door into the gathering room. Like most of the boys my age, I didn't express to Aria how great she looked and simply followed the pink-haired girl outside our bedroom.

We made our way to the Grand Ballroom of Grayson Academy. It wasn't an area we normally spent time in and for good reason. It wasn't used for anything really except for special events such as this. With floors that appeared wet to the touch, the room had been decorated in gold ribbons and green garland, spiraling down from the huge columns alongside the massive room. Music bounced all around—but the remarkable sight was the shooting stars erupting into a million particles high above our heads on the extravagant ceiling. The room felt alive.

All of the Pedagogues were chaperoning the dance. The two who stood out from the rest were Mr. Bonabos, twitching his leg to the rhythm of the music, and Ms. Pedigree, who seemed to be clapping her hands slowly together—completely out of rhythm.

Some of the older boys and girls were dancing to the melodies—while others stood opposite one another on the sidelines of the ballroom. At the end of the room was a table full of the largest feast I had ever seen, foods foreign to me but appealing at the same time. Miles wasted no time and made his way to the table.

"Hey Serra, I think Nactis is staring at you," said Miles, holding a plate full of exotic foods.

Nactis Hallwell was a fourth-year sandy haired student, who was often observed following the Bollcrees around the school grounds. He was unusually tall for his age, skinny, and seemed to fit in quite well with the wannabe Absolutes.

The hair on my arm stood up, and a chill ran down my back as I realized I was being watched closely by those Nactis stood with. Mr. Versarius and his most prized student Balthasar Parcells, were glaring at me.

"Gross," said Serra, turning her back to Nactis, from across the room.

"Ever get the feeling we aren't really welcomed by everyone here?" Miles asked, looking over at the group of seventh years wearing their standard crimson red robes.

Miles must have had the same gut feeling I had. It was the way we were being looked at—a glare that would make anyone feel unwanted. But it was more than an unwelcome feeling—there was a great sense of danger as well.

"Don't mind them, Coop. They hate everyone. They really think they are better than the rest of us and think they should be worshiped for being Bollcrees," said Serra, filling her glass full of Willow Whickle.

"I wish they'd stop staring at me."

"Well, they give me the creeps," added Aria, "but I say forget them—and let's have some fun!"

Aria took my hand and pulled me into the middle of the dance floor. She had far better dance etiquette than I did. Aria was a natural when it came to dancing. I, on the other hand, just looked awkward. It didn't matter. I was only focused on my best friends, forgetting about all the others who may have been watching and judging my lack of mobility.

Even Miles left the feast and joined in the middle of the ballroom floor. He began dancing with a third-year student, Penelope Twindore. Penelope—a fair-skinned girl with blonde hair and braces—was nearly as clumsy as I when it came to moving to the music. Once or twice, Miles would grimace, as Penelope stepped on his feet with her thick platform shoes.

The music suddenly stopped, and Chancellor Adimus took the stage. He was dressed the same as always in a wool three-piece suit and a long black overcoat. Chancellor Adimus lifted his hand, and silenced the room. Everyone was paying close attention, everyone except Mr. Versarius and his clones, who were whispering amongst themselves.

"Today, we celebrate the peace and kindness we were taught by the Imperium. Although it had been taken from us a millennium ago, we are to be reminded that we are to care for one another and pay tribute to those that were lost," said Chancellor Adimus somberly. "However, without bringing sorrow to an otherwise festive day, I want to express how proud I am of all of you for all you have accomplished thus far this year. As we enter into the new quartam, enjoy your evening and continue your quest to greatness."

As gracefully as he entered, Chancellor Adimus faded into the backdrop of the Grand Ballroom, leaving everyone with a message that we were to be better people. Care for one another and not to allow our differences to divide us. It seemed everyone had a sense of peace about themselves. Everyone, except for the Bollcrees who were no longer standing opposite of Serra, Aria, Miles, and I. They had found their way to us—expressions of hate filled them.

"Interesting choice of jewelry," Mr. Versarius told Aria, staring at the gift I had given her. "As though you possess the ability of the *Guild*."

"It's just a necklace," Aria said quietly.

"What's that? Speak up, girl! You dare to dismiss a symbol of our people as just a necklace?" said Mr. Versarius in a low growl.

"Awe, Crassus. I trust you and your fine students are enjoying the night?" said Mr. Hordo coming out from nowhere. Mr. Hordo was dressed in a brown, plaid, wrinkled suit. From his hair to his shoes, he was completely disheveled, except for the pendant pinned to his chest, a rustic looking charm of sorts that had a teardrop symbol in the center.

"I do say this is one of our finer Solace of Imperium's we've celebrated. Having new students and all. Allowing them to experience the peace it brings for the first time. Wouldn't you agree?" asked Mr. Hordo.

Mr. Versarius glared at Aria and her necklace, before turning his attention to Mr. Hordo. It was obvious he was not pleased with being interrupted by someone he likely felt was beneath him.

"We shall continue this discussion another time," said Mr. Versarius referring to Aria, as he looked at Mr. Hordo with a great sense of loathing.

Mr. Versarius swung his red cloaked robe around and swiftly headed out of the ballroom, with his Bollcrees lackies following.

"I remember when Crassus and I were Bollcrees together. You know we were fellow classmen here at Grayson—and sadly, he hasn't really changed since then. Still nasty as always," said Mr. Hordo, as he sipped from his cup of Willow Whickle.

"You were a Bollcrees?" I asked, slightly taken back by the new found discovery of his past.

"Oh, yes, I certainly was. I wanted to become part of the Absolute council at one time. Until I realized the truth," said Mr. Hordo. He stared motionlessly at me through his thick lensed glasses.

A look overcame him as though he had said something he may not have meant to say aloud.

"What truth was that?"

"Oh dear, I shouldn't have said that," said Mr. Hordo. "I shall be going now—you children have a wonderful night, and I shall see you again soon."

Mr. Hordo staggered away and began to make his exit from the Grand Ballroom.

"What was that all about?" Miles asked.

"I don't know—but I think Mr. Hordo knows more than we thought," I said, turning to Serra. "Did you know he used to be a Bollcrees, Serra? Serra?"

Serra was lost in thought, slowly shuffling away from the three of us—toward Mr. Hordo. "Nope—but now I know the answer to my riddle!"

CHAPTER NINETEEN

THE HEART OF THE SEA

We rushed out of Grayson's Grand Ballroom. The sound of music and laughter faded away as we ventured far into the dark corridors of Grayson. Aria, Miles, and I soon found ourselves following Serra into the restricted part of the school reserved for Pedagogues only. We were chasing after a kind-hearted and clumsy Pedagogue, deeper into a part of the school grounds without knowing exactly why—

But Serra walked with purpose. She had her reasons, and we followed without question. Anytime Mr. Hordo peeked over his shoulder, we ducked into a nook or cranny. At this point, it was feeling a bit reckless.

Shadows crept in from all around. It was so quiet. You could hear the sound of the air moving throughout the empty corridors.

"What are we doing, Serra," I asked nervously.

"Trust me, I know what I'm doing," said Serra, as she continued to chase the shadow of Mr. Hordo.

"You're going to get me expelled, and if you do, I'll never talk to you again," said Miles in a whisper, catching his breath as he tried to keep up.

"Sounds good to me," said Serra softly, as she put up her hand bringing us to halt.

Mr. Hordo reached the doorway of his study and entered, closing the door behind him. The four of us piled in behind Serra, waiting for her next move. Serra hesitantly knocked on his door. Standing out in the open to be caught by any Pedagogue roaming the halls made me feel increasingly uneasy.

It seemed like forever before the door swung open.

"Hello children—wait a moment, what are you doing here?" asked Mr. Hordo.

"May we come in and speak with you, sir?" Serra asked politely. "It's very important."

Mr. Hordo let out a rush of air stinking of Willow Whickle, while peering up and down the empty corridor outside of his study. I was certain he was about to lecture us on the rules of the Academy and send us on our way, but instead, he waved us inside.

"But of course, come in, come in," said Mr. Hordo, his eyes darting up and down the corridor one last time as we shuffled into his private study.

His room was warm and lit by the stone fireplace against his back wall, illuminating all of the great finds he had made over his tenure with Grayson Academy. It was only the second time I had seen his study and living quarters, but I was fascinated by its décor and felt as though it was the first time.

"Now, what has brought you here this time—might I remind you again that—that these halls are strictly off limits to students?" stuttered Mr. Hordo in an attempt to be stern.

"That's what I told her, Mr. Hordo, but she doesn't seem to listen to others," said Miles.

"Quiet Red," said Serra, giving Miles a dirty look.

Serra turned her attention back to Mr. Hordo, with a charming smile. "My father called you Seeminster when we first arrived at school. Is that your first name?"

"Well yes, yes it is, Serra. But students shouldn't refer to their Pedagogues by the proper name, you know. Chancellor Adimus would most definitely frown upon that," said Mr. Hordo adjusting his bottle lensed spectacles. "If I may be so inclined to inquire, why do you ask?"

"Mom and dad used to talk about a friend from school. They called him Sea, and they told me how they often explored with him on expeditions. Is that you—are you, Sea?" asked Serra.

"Yes, yes, that would be me. We went to Grayson together, your mother and father that is, and many of my classmates gave me the nickname Sea, but—but what has that got to do with coming to my study at such a late hour?"

"Your pendant on your chest? The one you wear over your heart—may I see it?" asked Serra.

That was it. She had figured out her riddle after all. The sea wasn't the ocean, but rather a person. I was shocked and excited at the same time. Serra would be the next one of us to solve the clue to her scavenger hunt.

Mr. Hordo placed his hand over the charm that was pinned

to his coat just over his heart and studied it for a moment.

"This old thing? Awe, yes, I imagine you would be interested in it. After all, I did discover it while digging with your parents, in fact, I can recall that very day. We were searching for the remnants of the elusive Goad."

Mr. Hordo turned his attention to Aria, Miles, and me. "That is what you would have called a winged dragoon back on Earth. Quite a remarkable creature. Longest neck you had ever seen and full of shimmering red and green scales. Now let me think. Oh yes If I remember correctly, we spent several days following evidence that led us to the perfect site to excavate. But I am sad to say, we never did find anything. Except for this charm... I found it fascinating and kept it."

"Dragons are real?" Miles asked eagerly.

"They are here, young man," said Mr. Hordo, with a wink.

Mr. Hordo removed the charm from his coat and looked it over for a moment.

"I suppose it's as much your family's as it is mine. I would never have found it if your father hadn't picked that exact location so many years ago..." Mr. Hordo was drifting off in thought. He snapped back. "Is that why you are here?"

"Sort of—well, you see—I think it's the object I need to find in order to solve the riddle to my scavenger hunt," said Serra, seemingly embarrassed she had gone to this extent to find it. "I am supposed to find a charm worn over the heart of the sea—"

"—Oh! Very clever, indeed. I do love the scavenger hunt," said Mr. Hordo excitedly, as he reached down and handed Serra the artifact he found so long ago.

Serra gingerly reached out, allowing Mr. Hordo to place the charm in the palm of her hand. Serra slightly jerked, waiting to hear three familiar chimes echoing about—notifying everyone she had completed her task. But there was nothing. No sounds, no bells, not even a whisper of any kind.

"Oh, dear," said Mr. Hordo filled with sorrow. "Apparently, this wasn't what you were looking for after all."

The five of us shared the same expression of disappointment. I truly believed she had figured it out. That was not the case, and without the three chimes, it was certain she had not finished with her scavenger hunt.

"I am sorry, Serra," said Mr. Hordo tenderly. "I know how disappointed you must feel at this very moment. I, too, could not solve mine in my second year… If it is merely a consolation, I want you to keep it. I believe your parents would want you to have it."

"Thank you, sir," said Serra gloomily. "I'm sure they would appreciate that."

The four of us eventually made our way back to the boy's gathering room—empty handed. The room was lifeless. It seemed everyone had gone to bed, exhausted from the celebration held a few short hours before. But none of us were ready to fall asleep quite yet.

I sat on the floor, pressing my back against the couch. The mahogany box I had received from an unknown giver sat atop some empty packages under the tree. I reached out and took it in my hand, and began fidgeting with it, while I searched for the right words to comfort my friend.

"I was sure that would have been what I was looking for," said Serra, finally breaking the silence. "Absolutely sure of it."

Serra sat behind me on the couch. Her head was down low—staring at the artifact Mr. Hordo had just passed on to her and her family. It was painful to watch a friend seem so down. It gave me a feeling of helplessness, knowing there was nothing I could do to make things better for her. All we could do was encourage her to go on.

"I guess you will have to keep looking," said Aria. "Maybe Miles is right—when we can go outside, we will check the seas for some sort of clue that will lead us to the right answer this time."

"Ya, don't give up. I am sure we can figure it out... Remember what Ms. Elsattera said—we need to do this together," said Miles. "Plus, it'll give us something to do since Coop hasn't figured his out either."

"Wonder what I am going to do with this thing?" I said, holding the empty box and trying to take Serra away from her thoughts, thoughts she seemed to be drowning in. I knew too well the feeling of falling short on seeking answers to so many questions. Maybe that is why I hadn't spent my free time searching for the item at the end of my riddle.

"You can use it as a keepsake box, Coop," said Aria sitting upright, looking down on me. "Start collecting things from around school and keep them there."

"Here, Coop," said Serra. "You can make this your first official keepsake."

With a flick of her thumb, the charm tumbled through the air—end over end. The tarnished pewter glistened as light bounced off the edges. It landed beside me, letting out a dull thud as it hit the floor. I picked it up. It was much heavier than I would have imagined.

"Thanks, Serra," I said. "I'll put it in here, and when you want it back, you know where to find it."

I gently laid my new keepsake inside the ornately decorated mahogany box that I had come to learn was supposedly a permutation box. As it rested at the bottom, I had sort of hoped it would suddenly change, and the answer would be revealed. But nothing happened. It was still the charm that Mr. Hordo had removed from his coat.

I closed the lid and latched it shut.

It was then I learned you must first *close the box* to activate the enchanted power it held. Blue light peered through the seams of the lid—beams of light exploded outward. Something began to happen. The box bounced around in my hands. I told myself to let go of this beguilded box. Let go before something dreadful happened to me or my friends. But, as I so often did, I ignored the voice in my head and firmly held on until the light dissipated, and the box settled once again.

Aria, Miles, and Serra stood up—now peering down on me, waiting for me to open the box and reveal what had materialized. I, too, needed to know what it was and carefully began to lift the lid.

The charm that I had just placed inside—was now gone. Replaced by a pewter antique skeleton key. It was no more than three inches long, with a single bit at the tip. The shank was gold and the bow shaped in the same teardrop design that was found on the charm.

"What just happened?" asked Miles in awe.

"I have no idea, but Serra, you need to be the one to remove it from the permutation box," I said, in case it was indeed what she had been searching for.

Serra cautiously stepped forward, kneeling down beside me. With her eyes full of passion, she paused for a moment, before reaching out her tiny hand. Gently, with the tips of her finger and thumb, she took hold of the skeleton key, lifting it into the air.

Just as we all had hoped, three chimes sounded—indicating Serra had solved the riddle to her very own scavenger hunt.

CHAPTER TWENTY

EMISSAR AUGTOR

The snow had melted and the last quartam had finally arrived. The hysteria of being cooped up inside the walls of Grayson Academy had started to diminish. Seeing that bright orb in the sky was a welcomed change from the last several months of brutally cold temperatures and the thick blanket of snow that covered the manicured landscape.

Bright and vibrant colors had returned to the shrubs and trees that surrounded our school. The campus grounds, full of stunning flowers seen nowhere else but here on Alyssum, had once again come to life. The air was filled with songs performed by the whimsical winged life grazing over the flowers that had recently bloomed—fragrant blossoms provided the nectar these tiny creatures of flight needed to replenish their swarms.

As we did every morning, Serra, Aria, Miles, and I sat in the dining hall, enjoying our favorite meal of the day—breakfast. Every so often, if you paid close enough attention, you could hear the three chimes of those who had discovered the answer to the riddles of their own scavenger hunt. This was generally followed by a round of applause and cheers from those who heard the announcement.

"How about today? We could just walk around until we figure it out," said Miles, staring up through the glass ceiling of the dining hall at the fresh blue skies.

"Figure what out?" I asked Miles, knowing all too well what he was talking about, especially because he had been reminding me about it every day since Serra found her antique key.

"Come on, Coop! You know what I mean," said Miles, shoveling in more sausages from his plate. "You are going to have to figure it out sooner or later."

"He's right, you know," added Aria uninvited. "The term is nearly over, and you haven't even tried once to solve your riddle yet."

"Ya, what's the holdup?" asked Serra, twiddling her pink pigtails. "You know we will help you if you want. You don't have any excuses for not getting this over with."

I was beginning to feel a great deal of peer pressure. My friends were becoming bothersome in trying to get me to begin my quest, but I had other things on my mind lately. Like finding anything that had to do with telling me where my parents were. A difficult task now that I learned I was temporarily banned from using Aurora.

Maybe they were right. Maybe finding the answer to my riddle would be far easier than finding those who abandoned me on Earth so many years ago.

"Fine," I said in defeat. "We can start looking if you really want to."

"We do!" shouted Aria.

"It's about time!" said Miles.

Maybe now that I agreed to begin my own adventure, I wouldn't be the focus of their attention any longer. We could just sit in peace and enjoy our breakfast. Besides, I never liked being the center of anyone's attention.

The four of us made our way from the dining hall into the busy corridors full of students of all shapes and sizes. We had no direction on where to go from here, but we were going to try and find a lead that would bring an end to the constant reminder I hadn't done what they all were able to do.

As we made our way through the sea of our classmates, I could feel the warmth of the sun beaming through the large arched windows onto my skin. Even if I ended up taking us on a wild goose chase, I knew we needed to go outside and try to make the best of our adventure while getting a breath of much needed fresh air. The others followed me outside—trusting I would lead them where we needed to go.

My enjoyment of getting outside was short lived. Once I passed the threshold of the grand wooden doorway, we ran into Bolliver and Gwillian.

"Hey guys, what are you up to?" asked Gwillian.

"We're going to figure out Cooper's riddle today," said Miles.

I quickly nudged Miles gently, trying to stop him from telling my archnemesis what we were up to, but it was too late. Miles had gotten the attention of Bolliver.

"We could help," said Bolliver, with a hint of enthusiasm in his voice.

"No, that's okay, we can do this," I said—somewhat rudely. More so than I should have been.

"Whatever," said Bolliver shrugging his shoulders. Together he and Gwillian walked off.

"That was rude," said Aria. "He was just trying to help."

"You really need to stop thinking Bolliver is out to get you somehow," said Serra, seemingly disappointed in my behavior. "He was only trying to help, and I think I would know if he was a monster disguised as a student by now."

"Oh, he's a monster alright, just wait—you'll see."

"I've known him his whole life, Cooper, and he's really not that bad," said Serra, catching up to me—preventing my escape from the two evildoers.

For a brief moment, I thought about calling out to Bolliver, as he made his way back inside. Inviting him and Gwillian to join us—but I stopped myself, keeping to my belief that something was wrong with him and that he was behind all of the near-death experiences I encountered.

"He'll get over it," I said.

Several months passed, and I was still no closer to solving this elusive riddle. No closer to hearing the chimes sound with excitement, putting a welcomed end to my scavenger hunt. Maybe karma had paid me a visit for my boorish attitude toward Bolliver when he asked to help in my quest. Because of it, it seemed as though I would never discover the meaning behind the clue given to me by an unseen force within the walls of Grayson.

The sun had set and the bright glow of the distant planets over the horizon came into view. I lay in bed, wondering what it was going to take to put this all behind me so I could concentrate on more important things. As I said before, I was doing extremely well in all of my studies, and I really didn't need any help with my Torts. It was beginning to feel like this game was more important to my friends, then it was to me.

Trying to slow my thoughts, I struggled to keep my eyes open. I was fading off into the realm of dreams. Dreams that once consisted of living a life beyond the walls of the St. Mary's Academy for Exceptional Youth or any orphanage for that matter. Now, they were dreams of living here on Alyssum and possessing the abilities of the Guild.

My eyes closed—tomorrow was another day.

What felt like just a few seconds later, I was startled awake at the sight of my red-headed friend leaning in, hovering above my head while I was trying to sleep. His eyes were wide, and a smile engulfed his entire face—revealing his less than pearly white teeth.

"Coop—," Miles softly spoke in my ear. "Coop, wake up."

"What is it, Miles?"

His grin grew, and he said to me, "I think I know what you have to do—,"

"—I do too, Miles," I said, rolling back over, covering myself with my blanket. "It's called sleep."

Miles yanked me back over and pulled the warmth of the blanket right off my small body.

"No, not that!"

Miles was looking a bit upset at the fact I didn't want to partake in this game of midnight hour mysteries. "The first! That's the answer. Just like my clue, it's the first! Get it?"

"No, I don't—now let me sleep," I said, trying to gain control over the blanket Miles had stolen from me.

"Come on, Coop—for someone that doesn't need any extra points toward their Torts, you sure are dumb."

I wasn't bothered at all about that comment. It was just Miles being Miles. But I had to admit it, no matter how badly I would rather go back to sleep and ignore this interruption, Miles seemed to have something important to say. Important enough to wake me from my slumber.

I rolled back over and sat up.

"Fine, what?"

"Never mind," said Miles, sounding cranky, as he got up off my bed and walked to his. "You obviously aren't interested in what I have to say."

"Sure I am," I said, trying to sound eager to learn more. "What did you find out?"

Miles sat quietly on his bed and pouted. I knew it would be just a matter of time until he got over the fact I dismissed him at first. As I had expected, it didn't take long at all before Miles leapt from his bed and ran over back to me.

"In my riddle, I had to find the first to be hung," said Miles, with a look on his face like he expected me to understand. But I was drawing a blank.

"Yours is the *first* who came. Like mine. Mine was Emmisar

Augtor, who was the first of the Chancellors in Grayson and the first to be hung. Maybe, just maybe, it's Augtor your riddle is referring to as well," continued Miles as he leaned back, folding his arms with a grand smirk. "Brilliant, right?"

Maybe I was just exhausted, and my brain hadn't fully begun to function properly at this late hour, but in some ways, Miles made sense. Besides, time and time again, we reminded ourselves what Ms. Elsattera told us. *"We needed to work together."*

"You know, Miles—you may have something there," I said, nodding my head and rubbing my chin in thought. "Let's find out tomorrow."

"Tomorrow!?" shouted Miles so loudly it should have awakened the entire boy's corridor. "This can't wait until tomorrow! Let's get the girls and go now!"

"Shhhhh, okay" I said, pressing my hand over Miles' mouth.

Miles and I, dressed in our pajamas with slippers covering our feet, made our way to the girl's gathering room. Every squeak of the doors made me feel that we'd surely be caught sneaking in to let Serra and Aria know what Miles had come up with. Thankfully, the solid floors didn't give way beneath the weight of our steps, and we were able to make it to Aria and Serra's room without being noticed.

"Aria," I whispered in her ear. "Wake up."

Aria opened one eye, and even with just the one, I could see a fiery glare.

"What do you want, Coop?" asked Aria coldly.

Miles responded first. "Sorry, but Cooper insisted that we wake you and Serra up to tell you that I think I figured out the riddle to his scavenger hunt—"

"—Really?" I asked Miles, but he ignored me.

"So?" said Aria.

"So? So, we got to go see if I am right," said Miles, as he pulled off Aria's blankets.

Miles then walked over to Serra, who was still sound asleep and yanked off her covers. "So, get up, and let's go!"

"Miles! What is wrong with you?" asked Serra, covering herself up from the cold breeze.

Aria slammed her palms down on her mattress, obviously upset at the fact we disturbed her from her rest. Without any further complaint, she got up off her bed and slid her feet into her slippers and huffed, "Apparently, Miles figured out Cooper's scavenger hunt, and it can't wait until morning."

Serra rolled off her bed, thumping onto the floor—trying to crawl herself back into her blanket that now lay in a heap on the ground below her bed. She stood back up, with her blanket wrapped around like a winter shawl. She shuffled groggily to their bedroom door, letting out a moan.

"Well? What are you guys waiting for, then?" asked Serra.

The hallways of Grayson Academy were eerily silent. Not a single soul was awake at this hour—leaving Serra, Aria, Miles, and me alone and free to move throughout the school, undetected. It seemed to be becoming a regular occurrence that we were spending time in these corridors—in complete darkness amongst the shadows, seeking answers to the questions no one else was willing to provide.

"Over here," said Miles, as he swiftly made his way into the

Hallway of Pedagogues. "This has got to work."

The four of us stood side by side in front of the large portrait of Emissar Augtor. The original Chancellor of Grayson Academy—frozen in time and superficially staring at the young Graysonians standing in front of him. Graysonians who were out of bed at such a late hour, praying that Miles' hunch was right.

Looking up at the imposing figure made of fine brush strokes, I realized that the portrait of Chancellor Emissar Augtor did seem unfinished. Something in his immortal painting was missing.

I stepped forward and rallied a voice from deep within to speak his name, "Emissar Augtor."

As Miles had predicted—three loud chimes sounded, and I had just solved the riddle to my scavenger hunt.

"Way to go, Coop!" said Miles excitedly. "You did it!"

Technically it was finally over—but it wasn't. I had no time to celebrate. As I stared at the old portrait on the wall, a book slowly began to appear in the empty hand of Chancellor Emissar Augtor. Hand written symbols were scribed on the cover of the old leather-bound book, now visible for all of us to see.

"What does it say?" Aria asked.

"I don't know," Serra responded, peering closer to read the words etched on the old book. "It's a really old language."

"Seek the truth within," I said, shocked at the words that had just left my lips.

"How did you know?" asked Miles awestruck.

"Ya Coop, how could you know what it says? I couldn't even read that," said Serra.

Serra had a point. How could I read what was written on the old leather book cover? But I did. The words were as simple as any other book I have seen since I learned to read.

"I don't know, but I want to find that book," I said under my breath. "I think it will tell me where my parents are."

"How do you figure that, Coop?" asked Serra.

"I just got a weird feeling about it," I said as I turned to them. "Maybe there's more to what Ms. Elsattera meant when she said we needed to work together and share our clues."

"Like what?" Aria asked.

"Maybe she was actually saying that everything we find from our clues would connect somehow, and together they can help me find my parents and that book."

"Geez, that's kind of far out there, don't you think?" responded Miles.

Miles may have been right, but it didn't matter to me how far-fetched the idea was. My stomach started to turn. All of these clues must mean more than just solving some scavenger hunt.

"I believe it," said Serra. "Considering all the really strange things that have been happening to you. Not to mention the fact you were able to read that old book—why not?"

Finally! Someone else was seeing what I had been since Miles led me to this corridor. This wasn't all a coincidence. There was a reason we had been given the riddles we were given… Ms. Elsattera and her speech… All of this had a meaning—and it was right in front of us.

"We need to find this room," I said, pointing to the old study that Emissar Augtor was painted in. "That book could be there."

"Sorry, but I doubt that room even exists anymore. At least I've never seen it," said Serra, dulling the mood.

"I have," said Aria with a slight grin. "It's on my map. In someplace called the Forgotten Corridor."

"I bet we need your key to get in, Serra," I said excitedly.

We stood quietly for a minute. I waited for one of us to realize that this was all just another grand fantasy we conjured up in our overactive imaginations, an idea from within the minds of eleven-year-old children making something out of nothing. But no one said it. None of us truly felt that way.

"Then there you have it," said Miles, rubbing his hands together.

"What do we have, Red?" asked Serra.

Miles had an intense look about him. Through his red hair, I could almost see the wheels spinning from a small furry rodent gasping for air as its tiny legs ran faster and faster in his head. Then, as his eyes narrowed, and his lips curled into a devilish grin, he looked over to the three of us who were readily awaiting his answer.

"We've got ourselves a real treasure hunt now!"

THE FORGOTTEN CORRIDOR

Miles was absolutely right—we did have ourselves a treasure hunt. I needed to find that book. Every inch of my being was telling me that is where I was going to find the answer to what happened to my parents. All we needed to do was find the forgotten corridor that would lead us to the study of Emissar Augtor.

Serra, Aria, Miles, and I made our way back to the boy's gathering room—after the girls recovered the items they collected during their scavenger hunt. The four of us decided that we didn't need any sleep. Our adrenaline was in full effect, and none of us were tired any longer. Tonight, we were going to finish this once and for all.

"Do you have your map, Aria?" I asked.

"How do you plan on finding his study from Aria's map?" Serra asked, joining me on the cold surface of the common room floor. "Even if it's on the map, that part of the school probably doesn't even exist anymore."

"I'm working on that," I said woefully. Serra had a point. That part of my plan hadn't been fully thought out yet.

"I got it!" said Aria excitedly. "Cooper, go get your Wuicken."

"I've got it on me," I responded, as I reached into my pajama bottom pocket and pulled out my Wuicken.

"You carry that around with you all the time, Coop?" asked Miles, a bit sarcastically. "Teacher's Pet, huh?"

I ignored his remark. It may have been a bit odd that I carried this object around with me even when classes were not in session—but I had my reasons. And the mere fact Aria needed it at that very moment proved it wasn't a bad thing I kept it close by.

"Give it here," Aria said, as she opened the map of the school. As the map appeared, Aria paused for a moment. "What's the red dot on here? It's in this room…"

Aria was referring to the red dot that tracked her location beacon, which we gave her for her birthday. I began to blush at the fact Aria now knew I kept an eye on her whereabouts from time to time.

"It's you," said Serra with a giggle, as she was pointing at Aria's pocket. "It's your location."

"Why—," Aria began to respond. "—Never mind, we will talk about a little thing called privacy later, Coop."

I lowered my head, slightly embarrassed that Aria learned that I had been watching her, even though it was me who she willed her beacon chip to. But I hadn't watched her to *intrude* upon her privacy, more so to see she was safe, and she wasn't lost or worse, being picked on by any of her fellow unguilded classmates.

The color in my face returned to normal as Aria removed the map from within her pocket and laid it on the floor. Right in the center of the map, a room had been drawn, and written across the middle of it read, *Emissar Augtor*.

Aria laid the Wuicken map over the old parchment. The old academy was dwarfed in size compared to the new. "There," said Aria, pointing. "Augtor's study used to be right here, in the forgotten corridor."

Aria found the study. However, it was not accessible through any of the current corridors within Grayson. It appeared as though there were stairs that led to his study, and those stairs were not directly attached to any hallway we had seen before. It would require us to be able to walk through walls in order to access them, a power none of us possessed.

"How do you plan on getting to those stairs?" asked Miles, scratching his red head. "I don't have a sledgehammer, and even if we did, I am pretty sure someone would hear us."

"We will figure it out when we get there," I said, picking up the map and Wuicken from the ground. "Let's go."

The four of us moved with haste, following the map to the hall that once held the passageway to the first Chancellor's study. As we journeyed deeper and deeper into parts unknown, my eyes began playing tricks on me—bringing to life every shadow that slithered across the walls. I was overcome with a sense of being followed. I was convinced it wasn't a trick of my mind. Something or someone was close behind.

"Does anyone else get the feeling we're not alone?" I asked, looking over my shoulder into the darkness.

"I didn't want to say anything, but I am sensing there is someone here too—I can't quite tell who it is. I just sense a great deal of anger," said Serra, looking back in the same direction I was looking. Serra may have possessed the Art of Eulalian, but it was still in the infant stage, and she hadn't fully honed her skill quite yet.

"Hold on—I think it is supposed to be right about there," said Aria, pointing to a wall of solid stone and metal. "Now what?"

"Hey Coop, can you use some of that super mojo you learned and open it?" asked Miles.

Crude as his description was—he may be right. Over the past term, Ms. Pedigree instructed the class to transform objects with this spectacular ability, objects that were much smaller than the stacked stone wall standing between us and the truth.

Could I transform this wall, I thought to myself. Maybe with enough strength, I could pull off what truthfully would be a miracle, considering I had never done anything remotely comparable.

"I can try," I responded with a tremble.

Squeezing my eyes shut, I reached out and placed my palm on the cold, smooth wall, willing the impenetrable wall to move out of my way.

Clenching my teeth—I gave it everything my tiny body had.

Suddenly, an intense feeling surged through me—the same feeling I had in the Nemus Garden. My hand began to vibrate. It was working. Something was happening. I opened my eyes and could see the walls were moving, spreading apart, and creating a doorway to a murky stairwell.

"You did it, Coop!" shouted Aria.

"That was amazing!" said Miles, patting me on my back.

"I had no doubt you could do it. After all, Ms. Pedigree does think you're the best student she ever had," said Serra mockingly.

"Stop it, Serra. I'm sure you could've done that too."

"I doubt it. Honestly, that's some pretty powerful stuff you did there, Coop. I'm not even sure a seventh year could have pulled that off."

The four of us peered into the black abyss, unable to see beyond the first few steps that were illuminated by the dim light from the distant planets. I went first, brushing aside the cobwebs that had formed over the many years since the entranceway was sealed.

My heart pounded faster. The feeling that we were not alone was intensifying. I looked over to Serra, to see if she too felt the ominous presence. The fear in her eyes was enough to tell me she did. It didn't matter. We were so close to our destination. I needed to put my own feeling of dread behind me and move on.

"I can't see a thing," said Aria as we bumped into one another, stumbling through the darkness. "Can't you do something, Serra?"

"Use your Wuicken, Coop," said Serra.

Why didn't I think of that? I reached into my pocket and opened the tablet, holding it out in front of me like an old kerosene lantern. It wasn't much, but it provided enough artificial lighting to reveal two or three feet ahead of us.

The cold stone walls, engulfed in cobwebs, were lined with doors on every side. Somewhere in the maze of old studies and classrooms was the one door we sought. It didn't take long before my makeshift flashlight rested on a large wooden door with a template pierced to the frame that read:

EMISSAR AUGTOR

"I found it," I said, turning to my friends. They all looked relieved that our journey into this chamber of terror had come to an end.

I reached out and grabbed the tarnished brass door knob and turned. It was locked.

"Serra, your key," I said quickly.

Serra reached into her pocket and pulled out the pewter antique key. She carefully handed it to me, as the key shook between her fingertips.

I tried to give her a comforting smile as I took it from her grasp, but my smile was disingenuous. I was feeling the same peril she seemed to have been. I turned and slowly slid the key into the hole below the brass knob. A moment of doubt overcame me, as I turned the key. A thought raced through my head, *the key wouldn't work and this was all for nothing.*

A loud click echoed throughout the blacked-out hallway. It worked—the door unlocked for the first time in a century.

The wooden slab crept open, letting out a bone-chilling shriek as the metal hinges were grinding against one another. Our shadows entered first into this dank room. The odor of rot nearly overwhelmed me—challenging me to go no further.

"What are you waiting for?" whispered Miles into my ear, as he was pressed against me. "Go ahead. We're right behind you."

"I can feel that," I said to Miles, nudging him back.

The four of us stepped into Emissar Augtor's study in unison. Shuffling our feet, in no hurry to see what awaited us beyond the wooden door frame. I nearly jumped out of my skin as a soft yellow light began to flicker overhead.

"It's just an automated sensor," whispered Serra, clinging onto Aria's arm.

"Why aren't those in the hallway—we could have used those in the hallway," said Miles.

The room was full of old furniture, protected in a thick coating of dust. Wall to wall bookshelves were a reminder that the previous occupant was a scholar of sorts, one who would have been filled with centuries of knowledge obtained from the leather-wrapped books still neatly placed on the wooden shelves.

On the far wall, ahead of us four curious onlookers, was a large fireplace framed by smooth rocks, much like the one we found in Mr. Hordo's study. A small round table supported by rough grain wooden legs sat directly in front of the fireplace. Next to it was an old oversized chair covered in torn fabrics.

The greatest find and what caught my attention next—was the lone, leather-bound book gently nestled on top of the rough surface of the table. A look of hope filled my wide blue eyes.

"We found it!" I said, "The book from the painting."

It was mesmerizing and covered in dust. I ran my hand across the cover, brushing away the soot, revealing the words that I had seen in the Hallway of Pedagogues. In an ancient language written in cursive were the words, *Seek the truth within.*

A thousand thoughts immediately crammed into my mind. Had I finally discovered the meaning of my existence? Somehow, were the answers to everything I needed to know inside these pages made from parchment and ink? Had the truth been written for me? I couldn't move. I was terrified to open it.

"Open it," said Serra. "See what's in there."

"Ya, Coop," said Miles. "We didn't come all this way to this creepy room for nothing, you know. Open it."

"Hey, give him a second, would ya?" Aria said with authority. "He'll open it when he's ready… just give him a minute." Aria could tell I was nervous. Maybe it was the sweat forming over my brow, or the quiver in my lips, but she was kind with her words when she spoke, "Just take your time, Coop."

It was just what I needed to hear. Knowing I was surrounded by my best friends put me at ease. I placed my hand on the cracking leather cover, prepared to see firsthand what words spoke to the truth. As I slid my thumb against the pages, I slowly began to turn the first page—

And suddenly, the room was full of screaming whispers, louder than I ever heard before.

"*Cooooper,*" they screeched out with dread. "*Coooooper!*"

TO SEEK THE TRUTH

Those deafening whispers had returned—ruthlessly pounding against my eardrums. I slammed the book closed and spun around. The doorway was filled with a black mist emerging where Serra, Aria, Miles, and I had just entered. Red and black sparks began to bounce in midair. Someone was Folding—but how? Folding was not permitted on school grounds. My eyes were filled with fear. Who or what was about to make an appearance?

There was only one thing to do—

"Run!" I shouted as I grabbed the book off the table, sprinting toward the doorway that was being choked by a dark cloud.

But before we could make it, my friends were flung through the air. They were pinned high against the bookshelves of Emissar Augtor's study as books fell to the ground, stirring up dust throughout the air.

"I can't move!" shouted Miles.

"I—I can't either," said Aria in distress.

I stood helpless and alone. Serra, Aria, and Miles were trapped—and unable to move. Something was trying to prevent the four of us from leaving that room. But who, and why hadn't I been cursed to their fate?

"Behind you!" cried Serra, looking past me, unable to point in the direction of whatever it was she was seeing. "Look out!"

A feeling of panic overcame me as I slowly turned back around—forming in midair was a cloaked figure. Draped in a velvet red robe, with a hood shielding its identity, someone now stood before me. It had to be Bolliver. He had come to finish what he had started ever since I arrived here at Grayson Academy.

"I know it's you, Bolliver!" I screeched in his direction. "Show yourself!"

The figure glided toward me, and the murmuring continued to resonate in my head. Several different voices, trapped in the waves of whispers, were crashing into my ears from all directions.

"Bolliver? You dare compare us to that child?" the voices growled. The cloaked figure came to a rest mere inches from me, as its gangling fingers reached out and pulled back the hood.

It was Balthasar Parcells—with eyes blacker than tar.

How could I have been so wrong?

"What do you want, Balthasar?" I asked, taking a step back.

"They want you, Cooper B.," said Balthasar emotionlessly. "And that book!"

"Run, Cooper!" bawled Serra in fear. "Get out of here!"

I clutched the leather-wrapped book of truths tightly against my chest. I hadn't come this far to let someone like Balthasar take it from me now. I turned to look for another way out. But I couldn't abandon my friends.

I twisted around and faced the vengeance of Balthasar head-on.

"Come with us, and you shall learn the truth you seek," declared the voices in a heavy whisper. "Everything you ever wanted to know will be revealed to you. Join us."

"Never!" I yelled.

Balthasar waved his hand in front of himself, dispersing the air all around. I was lifted from my feet and flung effortlessly across the room—crashing into a desk. My nose smashed into the corner of the wooden legs that supported the lectern once used by the old Pedagogue found in the painting.

Protecting the book, I tightly grasped in my hands, didn't allow me to protect my face. The sense of warmth filled my nostrils, and blood started to trickle down into my mouth.

"Don't be foolish, boy," said the voices. "You can't ignore your fate. You are destined to stand by our side."

I picked myself up off the floor, wiping away the blood with my sleeve.

"We are the ones that will show you the truth—we will show you your true power—we can reunite you with your parents if you join us now!" the voices continued to demand.

For a brief moment, I considered their offer and my body filled with a dark hope. No one gave me any answers to the questions I asked. These voices, whoever they were, were willing to. It may be the only chance I would have to finally discover who

I am and maybe be reunited with those I lost ten years ago.

"He's lying to you!" hollered Aria.

I could hear the pain in her voice, "Don't… don't listen to them."

"Silence, girl!" screamed Balthasar as he motioned his hand in her direction. Aria's mouth snapped shut, and she let out an awful shrill.

"Leave her alone!" I pleaded.

Balthasar's attention turned back to me, releasing Aria from the unseen hold he had on her. When suddenly, and without warning, an intense warmth covered my body, and the room erupted in light. Huge flames began prancing in the fireplace as a fire roared to life.

I stared into the flickering flames. Deep within my soul, I knew whatever was written within those pages could not fall in the hands of Balthasar. I turned around to the suffering of Aria, Serra, and Miles hovering above Balthasar. I wished there was a way to prevent that evil being from getting ahold of the only truth I wanted—finding the answers I sought somewhere in that book.

I was full of conflict. Give the book to Balthasar or suffer the unimaginable torture he brought down upon us. The answer was simple. I couldn't hand over the book, and I couldn't keep it.

A heavy weight sunk onto my shoulders and my chest tightened. I was prepared to suffer—I was prepared for all of us to suffer.

"Sorry," I said softly as I looked with regret into the eyes of my dear friend.

Aria smiled, and I knew that she understood what I must do. I spun around with all my might, and without another thought, I tossed the book into the burning inferno.

The old book and the truth within, burst into a brilliant white ball of light and disappeared into thin air.

"Nooooooo!" shouted Balthasar. His blackened eyes narrowed and pierced my skull. "What have you done?"

Balthasar rose higher off the ground. His robe began to swell all around him. His emotionless expression was now filled with hate.

This was the end.

"Now—you shall die," the voices called out from all around, bouncing about the small space we occupied.

Immediately, I could feel the muscles throughout my body begin to squeeze. Beyond the flesh and blood, my bones were being crushed—I gasped, fighting for air. My feet left the rough stone floor beneath me. Rising higher into the air, I let out a scream.

I was about to bear witness to the punishment I would be given for refusing to bend to the will of this seventh-year Bollcrees. About to discover my unknown fate, passed down to me for destroying the one thing the two of us wanted, when an unexpected feeling began to overwhelm me.

I no longer felt the pain brought on by the one who wished me great harm.

From deep within, I could feel an energy pulsing through my veins, searching for a way out. And without notice, that energy exploded from the very fabric within my consciousness. But this time, I didn't close my eyes.

I watched as Balthasar was hit with a bright sphere of white light that had originated from somewhere within me. From where, I did not know. I only knew I did not summon it, nor did I have control over it. It had a life of its own, its own objective.

The wave of light collided into him violently. Balthasar plummeted back into the hallway. His body crashed into the wall just beyond the door. The rippling effect of the energy I had propelled at him was followed by a black mist, escaping from within my assailant.

Lying lifeless on the cold surface, Balthasar's eyes began to return to his normal piercing green.

I didn't have a chance to give it a second thought, as I collapsed back onto solid ground. I looked up and could see that the mist was charging toward me. The loud whispers gave chase, as the black cloud was heading right for the very spot I stood— screaming in my direction. I braced for the collision. The heat of fire and hatred tore through my body.

As hard as I tried, I was too terrified to scream, and then it was gone. Gone as quickly as it appeared.

At that very moment, Serra, Aria, and Miles were released. They fell down and landed on a pile of books that had spilled out when they were pushed against the bookshelf.

"What did you do?" asked Miles. "That was so cool!"

"Cool? We almost died, Red," said Serra, as she stood up.

I walked over to Aria and helped her up onto her slipper covered feet. Aria reached out and wiped a small trickle of blood from my nose.

"Thank you, Coop," said Aria softly.

"Anytime, but I am not sure what it was I did exactly," I said perplexed. "I thought for sure we were all going to die."

"That's really comforting," said Miles with a smirk.

"Well, whatever you did, you saved us all," said Serra, with a look of bewilderment.

"The book!" I shouted, swinging around to the fireplace that was calm once again. It was as if it was never lit to begin with. I looked inside the empty nook. "It's gone... Now what?"

"Can we discuss this somewhere else? Like before creepy kid over there wakes up?" asked Miles, motioning to the Bollcree slumped on the ground outside of Emissar Augtor's study.

"Great idea, Miles."

When we emerged from within the dark stairwell, we were met by the morning sun rising above the horizon just beyond the school grounds. It was now morning.

The four of us made our way through the forgotten corridor, walking in silence. Only sharing in a sincere look from time to time, still trying to make sense of what we had just been through. Up ahead, a lone figure stood at the end of the hallway—it was Chancellor Adimus.

"Yep, we're in trouble now," said Miles, under his breath.

"Good morning, children," said Chancellor Adimus, as we approached him. "It looks as though you have had quite the night."

Chancellor Adimus was looking directly at me. Not directly

into my eyes of course, but rather at my nose. I slowly wiped away the last of the blood that found its way through my nostrils.

"Might I have a word with you, Cooper B.?" asked Chancellor Adimus. "I am sure you three could use something to eat."

Aria was hesitant to leave my side, but I simply smiled at her letting her know I would be fine. Aria forced herself to return the gesture with a sorrowful smile. Then she wrapped her arms around me and hugged me tightly. I had never felt this kind of genuine affection from anyone that I could remember. It was a feeling I would never forget.

Aria let go of me and walked off with both Serra and Miles as I slowly approached Chancellor Adimus. Awaiting my punishment for being out at such a late hour.

"I trust you found what you were looking for?" inquired Chancellor Adimus, as he gestured for me to follow him down the corridor reserved for Pedagogues.

"Not exactly, sir. I thought I had, but I lost it," I said, keeping my eyes fixed on each of my steps.

Chancellor Adimus stopped and placed his hand on my shoulder.

"Just because you do not have it in your immediate possession does not mean it is truly lost. In fact, the book of Emissar Augtor is now safely placed thanks to you and your brave friends," he said.

He knew? But how? I looked up into his eyes, curious as to what he actually understood about the book.

"How—"

"—you would be surprised to learn that nothing really gets

past me here at Grayson Academy, Cooper," he said to me with an endearing smile. "I make it a point to know what all of my students are up to, especially those that should be sound asleep in their beds. But that's a tale for another time."

Now that the Chancellor and I were alone, I figured this was as good a time as any to ask what was in the old book. Deep down inside, I knew he would never tell me, but it was worth a try.

"Can you tell me what is in it?" I asked, hopeful.

"Hmm…," said Chancellor Adimus, appearing to be in deep thought. "I really don't know, to tell you the truth. No one has ever actually read the book. A book thought to be lost in time. Some say it is full of rambling words conceived by a mad man. Others believe it holds the key to the answers so many before you have been seeking."

It was more riddles, and I was no closer to finding the truth now as I was before the book exploded into thin air. I felt a sense of loss. My chin rested on my chest—I ruined the only chance I had.

"Regardless," began Chancellor Adimus, as he took his hand and gently lifted my chin. "It was the purity of your thoughts that protected that in which you so desperately wanted. You were willing to sacrifice those that mean so much to you, in order to prevent those who seek to use that very knowledge against us. Powerful knowledge that is contained in those words written so long ago.

"Grayson gave you a choice, and you chose to follow your heart. Because of that, we owe you and your friends a great deal of gratitude for what you have done here today. But it saddens me to say, no one can know. With the exception of your friends, of course."

Of course, we weren't allowed to talk about this—and even if we were, what would we say? So far, the only thing I knew for sure was that a crazed Bollcrees tried to kill me and my friends. Then it hit me. I almost forgot about Balthasar Parcells lying unconscious in the hallway outside Emissar Augtor's study. He was the one who tried to steal the book for himself. The one I believed was Bolliver all along.

"Balthasar—why did he want the book?" I asked.

"I am afraid Balthasar was not himself. He allowed his mind to be vulnerable to dark influences," said Chancellor Adimus. "Darkness that seeks an absent mind."

"Influenced by who?" I asked.

The Chancellor turned his attention to the door we had been standing in front of for several minutes and spoke softly, "Let's save that for another time and another conversation, shall we? In the meantime, there is someone who wishes to speak with you."

As the door swung open, I found myself in the study of my Pedagogue, Ms. Pedigree. She looked tired, but she managed to greet me with the same smile I could still remember from the first day I met her in Cooper, Maine.

The space behind me lit up and Chancellor Adimus was gone.

"Oh dear, Cooper. You look a mess," said Ms. Pedigree, as she ran her hand soothingly across my cheek. "What have you children gotten yourselves into?"

"We're fine, ma'am. Nothing we aren't used to, I suppose," I said, trying to minimize our close encounter with death.

I sat down in the chair, as Ms. Pedigree looked through my eyes, lost in thought. For a moment, I was going to ask her if she could shed some truth on the book of Emissar Augtor, but I knew there was no hope. She was ready to tell me anything, or she just didn't want me to know.

Ms. Pedigree took in a deep breath of air and clasped her hands together. "The term is coming to an end—but I am afraid your troubles have just started, Cooper B.," she said, with sorrow. "No matter how hard I've tried to protect you over the years, it seems it has been for nothing."

Ms. Pedigree made her way around her desk and took a seat in her chair—adjusting the cat-eye shaped glasses that slid down her long narrow nose.

"All those years I tried so hard—and when I brought you together with Aria and Miles, I truly believed they would keep you grounded there at St. Mary's Academy for Exceptional Youth, and exceptional you are." Her eyes began to fill with tears, "I knew you needed friends—we all do. I am proud to say I personally handpicked those two children knowing they would help you reach your full potential."

"I was the reason they were sent to St. Mary's?" I asked.

"But of course you were, my dear boy. They needed someone like you as much as you needed them. Even Serra. I am sorry to say it wasn't a mere coincidence your paths crossed with hers. I believe there were influences beyond my control that made that happen," said Ms. Pedigree, thoughtfully. "That is why you must keep your true friends close. They can protect you when we aren't able to."

My head was throbbing. I was confused by all of this information she was giving me. Maybe this is why they've kept so much from me. Maybe I wasn't able to comprehend all they had to tell me.

"Protect me from what?" I asked bewildered.

Ms. Pedigree leaned back in her chair, and spun around, avoiding eye contact with me. As she sat motionless, staring out at the amber red and burnt orange skies beyond her window, I could hear her draw in a deep breath and slowly let it out.

"I'm afraid I can no longer keep you a secret from those who would not wish to see you succeed in your destiny. I am afraid they have now discovered who you are," said Ms. Pedigree, through the tears she tried to hide from me.

"Who am I?"

Ms. Pedigree slowly turned, gently wiping a tear from under her glasses. What she said next would change my life forever…

"You are the Vestige, Cooper B."

FAREWELL FOR NOW

Reuniting with my three best friends in the Grand Gallery, we passed through the massive wooden doors located at the main entrance of Grayson Academy and ventured outside into the blinding light of the early morning hours. The school grounds were coming to life with students of all ages awaiting their final Torts scores to arrive on their Wuickens. Scores that promised the lucky majority a promotion the following school year, taking all of us one step closer to graduating this magnificent school.

Amongst the crowd were the Bollcrees watching our every move. Chancellor Adimus had made it clear that no one should ever be the wiser to the events that transpired in the forgotten corridor of Chancellor Augtor's private study, but I felt a brisk chill on the nape of my neck—sensing that they knew. *Why wouldn't they?* It was one of their Absolute lackeys that had tried to kill us. But he was confined to an area of the infirmary where visitors were not permitted. Unless, of course, they were all part of it, and he was just the unfortunate one to be caught. I had to dismiss those thoughts. I needed a break from all of the plots against me that I had formed in my restless mind.

Aria, Miles, Serra, and I journeyed to a long, paved pathway that led into the wooded area surrounding Grayson Academy. The four of us should have been exhausted and fast asleep in the comforts of our own beds, but we were wide awake. The adrenaline from our early morning adventure still pulsed through our veins. For a short while, we walked in silence. I am sure their minds were swirling just as mine was, thinking about our brush with death. An experience reserved for adults, not children our age.

Aria slowed her pace, standing under the vibrant colored canopy of the treetops, breaking the silence we shared.

"What does that mean exactly, Coop? Being a Vestige and all?"

I didn't know how to answer her. The mystery surrounding the words uttered by Ms. Pedigree was lost on me, and neither she nor Chancellor Adimus had explained any of it or its meaning. Just as they had in the past several months, they left me wondering who I was and where I truly belonged.

"It means he's super powerful! He can do anything—that's what!" blurted out Miles. "That's how Aurora explained it."

"How can I be what Aurora described? I've just learned how to use one ability. Isn't there like *seven* levels of the Guild?"

"Yes, but that doesn't mean you don't possess them all. Maybe you're a late bloomer?" responded Serra. "Besides, it takes a while to develop your abilities, and you just found out you possess the Guild."

I had spent most of my childhood wearing the Dezma charm, preventing me from discovering these spectacular gifts. But that didn't mean I could actually do everything the Guild had to offer. No matter how long my newfound abilities had been suppressed.

"Dunno, I just want to be a kid for now and find my parents."

It was time to clear my mind and find what was really important to me. Who were my parents, and where were they? Being the Vestige didn't mean anything to me. All that mattered to me now, was finding the answer to why my parents had left me on Earth and if they were still alive.

"How do you suppose we do that?" asked Miles. "Wasn't the answer inside that book? Since you blew it up and all, how else are you going to find them?"

"We don't know if it's actually gone," said Serra.

"It burst into flames. No matter what Chancellor Adimus said, I'm pretty sure it's gone. And along with it, the whereabouts of my parents."

Depression was nestling deep into the core of my soul. There didn't seem to be any way I would be able to *seek the truth* without that book. Everything we had done was for nothing. I was better off back on Earth before I learned of my fate as it was told to me by Ms. Pedigree.

Luckily for my mental well-being, the Wuicken tucked into my pocket, let out a warning. I had received a message. But I wasn't the only one. The same warning echoed throughout the campus, followed with cheers that could be heard off in the distance. Our Torts scores had been published.

Across the school grounds, Wuickens lit up with some wonderful news we had all been eagerly waiting for…

TORTS 126

Congratulations, my young Graysonian. You have
Qualified for advancement into next semester.

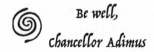 *Be well,*
Chancellor Adimus

The message from Chancellor Adimus, as generic as it most likely was, gave me a great sense of accomplishment and pushed away the sorrow that was filling my bones. I smiled for the first time in many days and, by the expression on Miles' face, he felt a sense of triumph as well.

"Sixty-Seven! Wait? Does that mean I passed? It says I am moving on, so that must be an amazing score, right?" asked Miles, still beaming with pride.

"Sure it does, Red. Looks like you'll be moving on to your third year after the first-quartam break. What did you get, Aria?"

Aria lifted her shoulders, not sure what to make of the score since this was her first Torts. "Says 144, is that good?"

"That's considered a perfect score! Way to go, overachiever," said Serra, laughing as she lightly punched Aria in the shoulder.

It looked as though we would all be back together again next year. A year that I hoped would be much easier than this one.

A few days later, it was time for everyone to head home for their yearly break, including Serra. She had packed all of the belongings that her father had sent to her after we had made our unexpected trip on the first day we arrived at Grayson. Serra was ready to go home to her family and try to put behind her the chilling adventures we all shared in our first year. But that didn't hold true for me. I wasn't going anywhere.

I was informed I would have to stay behind on campus as "it would not be advisable for me to wander too far from the grounds," while they continued to investigate who was behind the attack in Emissar Augtor's study. To me, the answer was simple, but Balthasar was maintaining his innocence and told Chancellor Adimus he had no memory of those events, or even being in the forgotten corridor. Nonetheless, he was sent home and asked never to return.

Aria and Miles were invited to spend the break with the Penroses. I was excited for them both. Mr. and Mrs. Penrose would surely make them feel at home. Unlike the other foster homes they stayed at in the past, there, they would be made to feel as though they belonged.

As excited, I was for them, I was also a bit jealous. Aria and Miles would be surrounded by loving and caring parents. Not their own parents, but they would never be treated as though they were simply guests. However, they deserved to be happy and I would try to get along without them for a few months. Especially since, Avantha was kind enough to provide me with some information on things to do around Grayson during summer.

"Hey Coop! Whatcha doing?" asked Aria as she barged into the desolate boy's common room along with Serra and Miles.

"Reading about Grayson Island. Did you know there was a small village on the other side of the island? I am going to have to check that out while you guys are away."

"Sorry Cooper, you're not allowed to go there alone," said Serra slightly saddened.

That's just my luck. I had found something that could keep my mind occupied while my friends were away enjoying their summer break. Only to be denied such small pleasures. It never failed. My life was destined to be full of sorrow and mysteries I would never solve.

"Ya, Coop. You can't go there alone. That's why Miles and I are going to stay behind and go with you!"

"Best news ever, right?" asked Miles.

I was shocked. Why would they be giving up an opportunity to stay in a warm household with a family like the Penroses? It's what we all had dreamt about while living behind the musky walls of St. Mary's Academy for Exceptional Youth.

I stared for a moment at Miles and Aria. There was no sense of regret in their guiltless eyes. No signs they had made this decision in an act of charity. Being the ones responsible for keeping the lonely orphan company, even though they would rather be someplace else.

"I am sorry Coop. I wish I could stay too, but Mom and Dad won't let me. I will come back early, though, I promise!" said Serra.

"That's okay, I understand. But why? Why would you two stay here when you could stay with Serra?"

"Cause we're a family, Coop. Where you go, we go," said Aria with such sincerity in her soft voice. "Besides that, someone's gotta protect you."

"Yup, and we need to talk about how we're going to put our plan together," Miles added.

"What plan is that?"

"How we're going to find a way to sneak out of this place and go to Imperium to find your parents," said Aria.

I should have known all along that they would never have abandoned me. Maybe deep down inside, I did know. After all, in a year's time, I had come to find two remarkable orphans and one quirky pink haired alien girl, who were now friends. Friends like I had never known. And Aria had put it all in perspective. Not only were they my best friends—they were my family. The very family I always dreamt of having.

THE END OF BOOK ONE

⑨ About the Author ⑨

Michael Shane Leighton is the proud author of the Cooper B. book series. *Cooper B. & The Scavenger Hunt* is book one in a six-book series and his debut novel for young readers. Michael was raised in Southern California but has made North Central Illinois home with his beautiful wife Kerry Lynn and their five very energetic children. Michael's passions are reading, laughing, helping others, but most importantly, spending quality time with his family. Michael has not only authored this series but has become a fan of the characters that breathe life onto the pages. "They remind me so much of my own children." He has sincerely enjoyed the writing experience of this truly imaginative series and is looking forward to more adventures with Cooper B. and the rest of the whimsical cast in the very near future.

◉ About the Illustrator ◉

Luana de Souza Sinclair was born in historically enriched country of Peru, and now lives in Spain. Luana studied art at the U-TAD in Madrid, Spain, where she graduated with a Masters in Fine Arts in 3D Animation. However, she has been painting her whole life and began teaching herself at a very young age. She loves poetry, mysteries, and fantasy books, and when it came to illustrating *Cooper B. and the Scavenger Hunt*, Luana felt as though she knew the characters so well. Luana is currently a Visual Development Artist for animation but looks forward to continuing to illustrate books for many years to come. *Cooper B. & The Scavenger Hunt* is her debut into designing artwork for books focused toward upper middle grade and young YA audiences.

Made in the USA
Las Vegas, NV
25 November 2020